The USSR vs the USA: Phase Two

Brusilov shrugged. "They are Americans, Comrade."

"Quasi-Americans. They live where the Americans died."

"And are descended from them."

"Perhaps I am descended from a Tatar tribesman. Does that mean I am one?"

"Comrade, the son of a cat is a cat, the son of a Russian is a Russian, and the son of an American is an American. I grant you, as a nation they have had their hats pulled down over their eyes, and they have been chucked under their chins with sledgehammers. As a nation they are crippled, just as we are perhaps not quite so vigorous as we once were. But we are both still the same people. I say this not to be argumentative, but because I have spoken with them, and fought with them.

"They are not English, French, Canadian, Chinese, or anything else but Americans. They do certain things because it is the historical policy of Americans to do them. The Americans unload forty tons of bombs on you, then they offer your children chewing gum and make you a loan . . ."

THE STEEL, THE MIST, AND THE BLAZING SUN

CHRISTOPHER ANVIL

ACE SCIENCE FICTION BOOKS
NEW YORK

THE STEEL, THE MIST, AND THE BLAZING SUN

An Ace Science Fiction Book / published by arrangement with
Baronet Publishing Company, Inc.

PRINTING HISTORY
Ace Original / July 1980
Second printing / November 1983

ISBN: 0-441-78571-9

Ace Science Fiction Books are published by The Berkley Publishing Group,
200 Madison Avenue, New York, New York 10016.
PRINTED IN THE UNITED STATES OF AMERICA

I. The Inheritors

1.

The sky was dark, the snow deep, and the wind bitterly cold as the little file of men on snowshoes awkwardly made their way forward. Each clutched with thick mittens the rope that kept him from losing the others when the whirling snow was all there was to see. The leader, at the head of the file, glanced frequently back over his shoulder at the studious-looking man who came next in line, and who looked often at a small gray box he carried in his left hand. This box was attached by a smooth, thick, black cord to a pack on his back, from which projected a shiny antenna. He now called out sharply and, at the head of the file, the leader reached inside his thick fur coat, took out a whistle, and blew a long shrill blast.

The file came to a halt. The men began to help each other unload their packs. The leader, after an intent glance all around, conferred with the man next in line, who gave a final look at the little gray box, and helplessly spread his hands. As the wind died down, both men glanced uneasily around, as if they might be overheard, and lowered their voices.

"I may be a scientist, Comrade," said the studious-looking man, "but still I can't be sure. The astronomers are the ones who predict the timing, and they leave themselves a good margin for error."

"I don't want to get too close too soon," said the leader. "Are we at least sure that's the spot, up ahead?"

"What is 'sure'? We carry out the calculations as best we know how, analyze the data, rely on the surviving geodetic satellites to help us fix position accurately, and try to correct any erroneous assumptions that creep into our calculations. Nevertheless, we calculate according to assumptions that may or may not prove valid in any given case. I think that's the spot. There is no way I can know."

"The last one of these little expeditions," said the leader shortly, "didn't come back. That was how it was discovered that their predicted intensity was wrong."

"Well, I am responsible for the present intensity prediction, and I am here to take the consequences."

The leader blinked, then grinned, and clapped the scientist on the shoulder. "It will give me great pleasure to see you go, too, if your damned calculations are wrong. But at least you are here to listen to my complaints. Would that these higher-ups of ours were a little less remote."

"It is best not to speak of such things."

"And I hope the Americans, at least, got well paid back for this."

"Shh. It wasn't as you think. In any case, they did. But we cannot talk of such matters."

"Who is to hear, in this place?" Nevertheless, the leader glanced around uneasily. After a silence, he said, "Can't you give me some idea when it will start?"

"In all probability, it *will* start, that is all I can say. We are given a time-band that is supposed to represent an extreme limit of possibility. But. . . . Look! The snow!"

Ahead of them, the snowfield grew brighter, reflecting a new glow of the clouds overhead. The leader put his whistle to his lips, and blew a succession of short blasts.

Before them, the reflected glow strengthened. The snow shone with a white light. The glow became a glare. Then the snow ahead was one dazzling blaze of blinding light.

At that moment, the leader, turning to check that his men had their instruments in use, chanced to see the expression on the face of the scientist.

Afterward, what the leader remembered most clearly was that expression. He had seen it somewhere before, knew it from the past, and it connected with strong emotions somewhere beneath the surface of his memories. But at first he could not recall where or when he had seen it.

It was only later, back in the barracks, that he remembered. Lying awake in the darkness, in the early morning chill, he could see again his brother's face, long ago, back in the time after the famine and the migration, when a wandering drifter had broken into his parents' cabin while his father was away in the woods. He had smilingly insulted his mother, and with easy slaps knocked the two small children out of his way. He had helped himself comfortably from the table, cuffed their mother when she tried to gather the crying children to her, and then, grinning, had suddenly caught her by the arm.

At that moment, the door with the freshly broken latch had come open behind the intruder. Gun in hand, their father stepped in.

It had been then, and in the moments following, that he had seen the grim exultant expression on his brother's face, and hadn't thought of it since, until, with that merciless blaze pounding down from the sky, he had seen the same expression again, on the face of the scientist.

"Why?" he asked himself, lying in the darkness. What was there about that terrible light and heat and glare that was like the father returning home as the family was in desperate need?

Lying motionless in the dark, he recalled the bits of information that were all he had managed to wring from the scientist:

The Americans had been paid back; but don't talk of it; and it wasn't as you think.

Frowning, he lay in the darkness thinking it over, and for the first time he wondered, what had it been like on the other side of all that had happened? He lay for a time recalling the contradictory accounts of the Americans that were all that he had heard. It was little enough to go on, and, always, it was wisest to say nothing, best to ask no questions, most prudent to offer no comment, as the scientist had warned him.

Thinking of it, he again fell asleep, and his mother was there, comforting him, and his father's deep voice was in the background, reassuring and steady, and everything was all right, and he was sound asleep, no longer thinking about the Americans, and the war, and what had happened back there in the confusion of the past.

2.

Thousands of miles away, Calder still lay, the service rifle beneath his hands, turned toward the entrance from the tunnel that led to the old abandoned mine shaft. From the place where he lay, the location of the massive steel door that closed the mineshaft end of the tunnel was easy to see. The odds on anyone coming in through that door were almost nil, but the general had insisted that one place where the Reds excelled was in the gathering of intelligence, and he would take no chance on the assumption that they didn't know what was concealed here.

Calder's assignment had been to guard this entrance, and he lay now in almost the same position he had chosen when that sudden premonition of trouble had struck him, just after he had come down and relieved Minetti, who had complained that this was a damned hard floor, either to stand on, sit on, or lie on, and they should have made it out of wood instead of this damned concrete. Concrete was bad for the arches, gave people rheumatism, and aggravated other unmentionable complaints that Minetti described in full and enthusiastic detail, and then, grinning, he had said, "Enjoy yourself, kid," and started back down the corridor. And nothing had seemed to change here, nothing had seemed to change at all, deep inside the mountain, until the grating noise had sounded at the massive steel door, and the vibration had traveled up the corridor, and the bright steady light had come in through the ring of new holes in the door, and then at last the big section had been tilted out, and now the men came in through the opening, neither in Russian uniforms nor in the American uniforms worn by Calder and Minetti. These men, in their strange gray uniforms, advanced warily up the corridor, led by a tall man with a full white beard, who, frowning, knelt beside Calder as the brilliant white lanterns shone down, felt carefully at Calder's wrist and throat, looked up wonderingly, slowly straightened, and turned to the man with him.

"This is the uniform of the Old O'Cracys themselves. But this body shows no wounds. And it is not decomposed. Yet the air in here is breathable. This air should support life, including the life of the organisms of decay. Look up the corridor— there lies another soldier of the O'Cracys. What killed these two men? And why is there no decomposition?"

A look of intense speculation crossed his face. "Could the Old Soviets have attacked this place to kill the defenders without destroying what they defended?"

He turned to an officer whose branch of service was indicated by a small silver disc at the lapel of his uniform jacket.

"Send to Arakal over the flasher our time of entry through that door, and two sentences: 'O'Cracy installation. Seems intact.' Sign it 'Colputt'. Use the code book, and query every half-hour until we have confirmation."

He glanced intently up the corridor, took the pad held out to him, and initialed the message.

The communications officer went quickly back down the corridor toward the mine shaft that led up to the outside.

Colputt led the way past the two bodies into the silent interconnecting corridors.

II. The Chiefs

1.

Arakal, King of the Wesdem O'Cracys, was in the Plot Room, bent over a model of the territory that once had been the eastern United States. The contoured surface showed rivers, lakes, and oceans in blue; forests in shades of green; and stretches of cultivated land in brown; with light gray for mountaintops, and pale yellow for large towns and cities. The carefully detailed surface was mostly green, with little yellow anywhere. Arakal was now examining a branching narrow black line with tiny crossbars which threaded its way from the northern border southward.

"The southern end of the iron road—Where is it now?"

Beside him, Buffon, the white-haired chief of the Special Operations Staff, said, "Still at Thomasville, sir. Before they go down into the Peninsula, they want to look over the ground."

"Swamp?"

"Yes, and a certain amount of lingering radioactivity."

Arakal nodded, and straightened. Absently, he adjusted the belt and shoulder strap that held his sword, and his left hand felt warily for the twin-headed, sharp-beaked bird that long had adorned the sword hilt. His groping fingers felt a new hilt designed to fit his hand as the weapon's blade fit the need to cut or pierce.

Arakal was reminded of other improvements since the last campaign against the Russ. He glanced at the model, noting the more numerous blue markers that represented the country's militia, and the large tan markers, bearing Roman numerals from I to IX, that stood for the reinforced divisions of his army, concentrated now in the nest of bays, rivers, and inlets that was the former Russ Maryland-Delaware Colony.

Arakal noted improvements, and also something that remained the same—the overlapping dull gray disks along the model's western edge, that blotted out the blue and green and brown as if the land there had been transformed into the hammered face of the moon.

Just then, a sergeant stepped over, carrying a slip of paper.

"Pardon, sir. New positions for the fleet."

Not far out on the dark-blue surface that represented the ocean, the sergeant moved tiny markers closer, along with a small symbol in white and blue and red—the Old Flag that now flew again from the Slagged Lands of the West to the Atlantic, from the Florida Peninsula to Kebeck and New Brunswick in the north.

As the sergeant left, Arakal glanced again at the gray western borders.

"Any news from our expeditions?"

"Not yet, sir," said Buffon. "But settlers trickle in who haven't been able to find a way through."

"Any recently?"

"A hunter, yesterday. His party gave up five or six weeks ago. Last week they made it out to the iron road. While the rest went on south, he came in to collect the bounty for their records."

"Where did they try to get through?"

"West of the Ohio Territory, where we'd heard rumors of a corridor just south of the lake. He said it was even worse there than further south."

"You talked to him yourself?"

"Yes, sir. He seemed reliable."

"Well— It makes sense. The old maps show good-sized cities there. Cities that size nearly always got plastered."

Buffon nodded regretfully.

Arakal considered the model, and shook his head.

"Sooner or later, the Russ will recover from our last fight. Meanwhile, they'll build a bigger fleet. Then they'll be back over here. Unless we can develop our strength, there's no reason why they shouldn't finish with us what they started with the Old O'Cracys."

"At least there are limits, sir. From questioning their men, it seems clear that while they have a good deal of Old Stuff from before the war, it doesn't include the kinds of usable long-range rocket-bombs that did all this damage."

"Even without them," said Arakal, "they have the wherewithal to either beat us, or keep us endlessly fighting off invasions. We can't rely on their making the mistakes they made the last time."

Buffon began to speak, hesitated, and glanced at the small symbols of ships that the sergeant had moved closer to the mainland. "Well, we'll know more soon enough, when Bullinger gets back."

Arakal nodded. He glanced around the Plot Room, noting roughly dressed engineers and road builders examining freshly prepared contour maps and, across the room, three of his generals bent intently over a large-scale model of the Maryland-Delaware Peninsula. Not far from where Arakal and Buffon stood, intent artisans in paint-spotted overalls were putting the finishing touches on a large model of Western Europe. Arakal thoughtfully considered this new model.

Buffon followed the direction of Arakal's gaze, and looked troubled. "Sir, we might forestall the Russ. But it would be very risky."

"If," said Arakal, "we can't open up a way to the West—"

"You're thinking that, as things stand, we don't have the potential strength the country had before the war?"

Arakal nodded bleakly. "If we can't get through to the West, we'll take things in a different order. But it would be better to recover first what the O'Cracys held on this continent."

Buffon hesitated, then frowning, began to speak. Then with a look of relief, he glanced around at the interrupting sharp rap of approaching heels. He looked up as a young lieutenant, the silver disc of Communications at his lapel, came hurrying across the room to Arakal.

"Sir, a message just in from Mr. Colputt."

"Good." Arakal reached for the folded paper.

2.

At the moment that the message was delivered to Arakal, far away around the curve of the Earth, the high official spoken of respectfully as "S-One" stood at his office window, looking into an enclosed courtyard. His face bore a look of deep contentment as he drank in the courtyard's blaze of red and yellow and violet. With a connoisseur's interest, he noted that certain shades of color, seen against dark-green leaves, looked almost fluorescent.

Smiling, he glanced up at the braced overhead structure of steel and glass, partly opened now in early summer, that gave the flowers a head start despite the temperatures that afflicted this part of the world.

His spirit refreshed, S-One turned away, sat down, and glanced at the thick bound stack of typed pages that lay open on the polished walnut surface of his desk. His chiseled features grew set, and his gray eyes acquired a remote considering look as he picked up the report.

His gaze rose to the opposite wall, with its map-like display of the North American continent, its center marked from the Great Lakes to the Gulf of Mexico in overlapping disks of dull gray, its west and east coast regions marked in scattered gray disks overlapped with green, blue, or brown.

Centered on the west coast region was a small symbol—a hammer and sickle within a white star on a blue disk.

S-One frowned at the flag, then opened his thick sheaf of papers, the edge darkened from much handling, to read:

". . . true insight into their motivations is problematical, as we have as yet no reliable source within the controlling group. We are forced to rely largely on electronic methods, which can be grossly misleading, because of:

1) Poor coverage.

2) Changes of plan. Sudden reversals by Arakal, Slagiron, Colputt, and other leading personages of the present quasi U. S. Government are common.

3) Secretiveness. The present quasi U. S. Government is, in its essentials, an absolute monarchy. In such a government, the true intention may be known only to the monarch.

The effect of such factors is to very seriously hamper our planning. . . ."

S-One shook his head in irritation. He put a hand on the edge of his desk, pulled out a slide inset with numbered pearl-colored push-buttons, and with the ease of long familiarity selected a button well up in the right-hand column.

Across the room, the display lit up to show nine small numbered markers, representing Arakal's army, clustered in the former Maryland-Delaware Colony. The locations of two of these markers differed slightly from their positions on Arakal's Plot. Off the shore, tiny symbols represented Arakal's ships, with no perceptible difference between their location on S-One's display or Arakal's Plot.

S-One glanced at his clock, shoved in the slide with its rows of buttons, and picked up the interoffice phone.

"General Brusilov is here?"

"Yes, sir. He arrived exactly on time."

"Send him in."

The door opened, and a broad bear of a man

came in, his expression wary, but his jaw out-thrust.

S-One came to his feet, stepped around the right side of his desk, and held out his hand.

General Brusilov, surprised, gripped the proffered hand.

S-One said gravely, "Please seat yourself, General. I appreciate your punctuality."

Brusilov spoke gruffly. "I believe in being on time, even for my own execution."

S-One sat down. "We are all, in one way or another, 'executed' eventually. In my job, I must sometimes accelerate the date of such executions. That is not so in your case. There are three reasons why your only punishment will be the loss of one day's pay."

Brusilov blinked in surprise.

"The first reason," said S-One, "is the testimony of the former Soviet plenipotentiary, Smirnov. Smirnov returned to us in a state of shock. He took the entire blame for the American disaster on himself. His testimony exonerates you completely.

"The second reason is that you came back to us voluntarily."

"The third reason is the statement of Smirnov that you were friends with the present U. S. leader, Arakal. Is this correct?"

Brusilov gazed briefly out at the flowers, then turned to look S-One in the eyes.

"Arakal, and his officers and men, were nearly always friendly. Not only to me, but to most of my officers and men. That is," Brusilov added drily, "between fights."

"After you had fought with them, they were still friendly?"

"On all occasions, except in our attack through New England toward Quebec Fortress. Brutal methods were used in that attack. The ill feeling was relieved only by blood."

"They were usually friendly. Yet they fought?"

"They fought like wildcats."

"But afterward, they were friendly?"

"Yes."

"Do you understand their reason?"

Brusilov hesitated, then shook his head.

"How can I be certain? Their reasons seem to me to be questions of temperament, of Arakal's calculation, and of historical policy."

S-One sat back, frowning. He picked up the thick report lying on his desk.

"Take a look at the size of this. Weigh it in your hand. This is an exhaustive strictly secret critique of the U. S. A. as we now see it. But is it right? Are we intellectualizing our opponent's whims or reflexes? You know them."

Brusilov thoughtfully weighed the report in his hand, shook his head, and passed it back to S-One.

S-One said, "Why do you suggest 'historical policy'?"

Brusilov shrugged. "They are Americans, Comrade."

" 'Quasi-Americans' in the words of that paper. That is, they live where the Americans died."

"And are descended from them."

"Perhaps I am descended from a Tatar tribesman. Does that mean I am one?"

Brusilov's right hand, resting on the arm of his

chair, lifted, palm out.

"There is a difference between a Frenchman and a Finn. The Poles are one thing, and the English another. The Americans are something else again."

"For the sake of argument, not to correct you, I say that the Americans *were* something else again."

Brusilov's voice was respectful, and his expression very serious.

"They were. And they are again."

"You regard this Arakal—this *King of the O'Cracys*—as an *American?*"

"He is an American, and so is his chief general, Slagiron, and so are all the rest. And it was the historical policy of the Americans, in their own view of things, to bind up the wounds of the suffering, attack tyranny, shoot pirates, twist the lion's tail, and spit in the eyes of those in authority. In a fight, the Americans, Comrade, love to spring a nasty trick on you, and then afterward they clap you on the back. There are no hard feelings, finally."

S-One gestured to the display on the wall behind Brusilov.

"The people you speak of sound like giants. Observe the gray region in the heartland of their country, after some specimen of which, perhaps, your friend Slagiron is named. The only real Americans, if there are any left, are on the *West* Coast. These East Coast people are tribesmen."

Brusilov looked at the map, and nodded absently. His voice was polite, but without hesitation.

"Comrade, the son of a cat is a cat, the son of a

Russian is a Russian, and the son of an American is an American. I grant you, as a nation they have had their hat pulled down over their eyes, and they have been chucked under the chin with a sledgehammer. They have also had their ribs smashed. They are crippled, as a nation, just as we are perhaps not quite so vigorous, as a nation, as we were once. But we are both still the same people. I say this not to be argumentative, but because I have spoken with them, and fought with them, and they are not English, French, Canadian, Chinese, or anything else, but Americans. Their ancestors may have been foolish. I do not say they are giants. I say simply that Arakal, Slagiron, and the others *are* Americans. And they do certain things because it is the historical policy of Americans to do these things. The Americans unload forty tons of bombs on you, then they offer your children chewing gum, and make you a loan. These are the Americans all over again. But there is, I admit, a difference."

"What is this difference, then?"

"Now they have the recent experience of a terrible near-total defeat. And, too, they have Arakal."

S-One frowned. "You say Arakal's *calculation* has to do with their attitude?"

"Yes."

"What does this king of the Americans—"

"That is an error."

S-One blinked. His face, which had been friendly, was suddenly expressionless.

Brusilov said, his voice courteous but somehow flat, "Arakal's title is 'king'. But it is not what we mean when we say 'king'. A better word might be 'chief', but that is not right, either. There is the word, 'boss'—the person who runs things, who decides how things are to be done. There is no trace of divine right in this title of 'king'. The office is elective.''

S-One glanced at the thick report, then at Brusilov.

"Elective?"

"He told me so, himself. Certain things they have had passed down to them from the survivors of our attack. Arakal is the boss, the chief—Where this word 'king' comes from, who knows? Their present civilization grew up in the ruins of their former civilization. They used what pieces they could find, and that word, perhaps, was all that was ready to hand at the time.''

"Then to call their government an absolute monarchy is an error?"

Brusilov thought a moment.

"Call it an elective absolute monarchy governing through a nonhereditary oligarchy. The closest thing I can think of is some form of republic; but I am not sure that is right, either. Frankly, I don't know what it is. But I know it works. I have seen it work.''

S-One exasperatedly looked at the report, then out into the garden, and rested his eyes on the glorious colors. After a moment, he turned back to Brusilov.

"How does Arakal calculate this policy of friendship?"

"It is calculation, I think, that shows him there is no gain in the pointless multiplication or intensification of enmities. With him we have, not festering enmity, but friendship interrupted by con-

flict. Friendship is what he appears to aim at, by
courteous behavior and strictly fair treatment. Of
course, friends may fight, because of opposing
beliefs or desires. He wants to recover the Land of
the O'Cracys'. We claimed control of all of it.
There is the basis for as much conflict as anyone
might wish."

S-One smiled at the expression, "the Land of
the O'Cracys."

Brusilov shook his head.

"Do not think that they are foolish because we
cannot correctly translate their tongue. The meaning of that expression, 'the Land of the O'Cracy' is
emotional: 'the powers, insight, and territory
which once were ours.' "

"World dominion?"

"Their idea is simply to free North America,
plus England and France."

"Not Germany?"

"They have lost the awareness that West Germany was an ally."

"You mentioned one other factor—temperament."

"That can be explained in a few words: They are
friendly."

S-One stared for a moment, then sat back,
frowning.

"So, what we are up against is a people heavily
armed, friendly, risen out out of nuclear disaster,
led by an elective absolute monarch ruling
through a nonhereditary oligarchy, and whose
policy is to courteously smash the opposition,
and then nurse the survivors back to health? How
do we contend with a thing like that? Is that, at
least, the total of it?"

Brusilov stolidly shook his head.

"That is true, as far as it goes. But there is still another factor."

S-One regarded Brusilov with no great warmth.

Brusilov said, a trace of stubbornness in his manner, "It is the temperament of Arakal and his people that they, in general, like us. As Arakal said, approving of our colonists, 'They are good workers.' I heard such comments, myself."

S-One spoke seriously, "I appreciate all such first-hand information. We have had little enough of it. Go ahead."

Brusilov said, "It is historical policy with the Americans to accept—even to invite—immigration. They did not attack our colonists, as nearly any other people would have done. Instead, they moved in by surprise, in force, with no bombardment, and explained in a friendly way that the land the colony was on belonged to the O'Cracy, but that our people could become O'Cracys, and keep everything they had, and the only difference would be that the colonists would no longer have to take orders from us. That block of colonists moved from our side to their side with scarcely a sign of complaint."

S-One said exasperatedly, "There is the language problem. How will they solve that?"

"There is much trade between Arakal's own people and our former colonists. They have a school system now, with many small schools. Perhaps they will teach English in the colonists' schools, who knows?"

"This will cause trouble."

"Comrade, there is a noticeable tendency, with Arakal, for things to not work out as you expect."

S-One nodded moodily.

"In any case, what we have, then, is an elective monarchy governing through a non-hereditary oligarchy. The monarch is tactically shrewd. Monarch and people are descended from the East Coast survivors who lived through our nuclear bombardment. They have certain characteristic past American traits, including friendliness and a readiness to accept deserving outsiders as new Americans. They also, while fighting our troops in their own territory, have succeeded in gaining several victories, including one very damaging success, which won them all that remained of our seagoing fleet." S-One looked at Brusilov. "Is that correct?"

Brusilov considered it.

"It is largely correct, as far as it goes, but it contains one element of serious error. There is a condescension toward Arakal and his men which is characteristic of all of us, until we have felt their blows. You say he is 'tactically shrewd'. The word 'tactically' denies him status in the spheres of strategy and high policy. That is an error. Arakal is, in my opinion, a great master of conflict, alike in policy, strategy, tactics, and perhaps also in personal combat. One element of his strength is our condescension. In my opinion, he is not our inferior, but very possibly our superior."

S-One looked at Brusilov without expression, and Brusilov looked back with a stubborn yet not disrespectful expression. Finally, S-One gave a grunt, and sat back.

"You are outspoken, General."

"Even unpleasant truths may be serviceable. Lies break under strain."

"Is it true, as Smirnov said, that you regard Arakal as 'a master in the realm of ideas'?"

"As a master of conflict even in the realm of ideas. Yes."

"Do you feel," said S-One, his voice even and smooth, "that our ideology is subject to overthrow by Arakal's superior understanding?"

Brusilov frowned. S-One sat absolutely still, studying the general intently. Finally Brusilov cleared his throat, and looked directly into S-One's eyes.

"I am a military man, Comrade, not a political expert. But I will give you the best answer I know how to give. First, your question seems to presuppose knowledge of a conversation between Arakal, me, and Arakal's chief general, Slagiron. If you have knowledge of that conversation, you will understand that my personal opinion of ideology is low. I fear its teeth—the power of enforcement of those who are devoted to it—but I have a low opinion of ideology itself. It seems to me that first one side, then another, embodies its beliefs in a set ideology, which gains or loses power, depending on the force at the disposal of its followers, and on the shrewdness with which that force is used. As Arakal said, 'Ideology counts. But usually when it counts, it does the counting with a sword.' Considering the force at our disposal, no, I don't think Arakal can overthrow our ideology."

"Does he *wish* to overthrow it?"

"He wants to recover the lands of the O'Cracys. I don't think he wants to overthrow our ideology."

S-One said, "Can we overthrow him?"

"I don't think so. He is too strong at home."

S-One leaned forward, his gaze focused intently on Brusilov.

"And what if Arakal comes over here?"

Brusilov nodded slowly, almost sadly, then suddenly he laughed. "Yes, if Arakal comes over here, we well might beat him."

"Why do you laugh?"

Brusilov shook his head. "Comrade, how do I explain? A boy might laugh at the thought of a red-hot rivet dropped down the neck of an octopus. It is the thought of two such contenders coming together."

S-One nodded, and settled back. He looked at Brusilov and smiled.

"Well, he is coming. I am sure of that. And it is, I think, the opportunity of a lifetime. Do you agree?"

Brusilov nodded, and now his expression was somber and foreboding.

III. The Planners

1.

The evening of Admiral Bullinger's return, Arakal and his chief lieutenants gathered in the Plot Room. Maps lined the walls, and the model of the East Coast of North America stood near the new model of the West Coast of Europe.

The admiral, short, clean-shaven, with two tufts of hair that stood straight up at the back of his head, put his finger on the new model where it showed a curving body of water that wound back between dominating hills on the big island Arakal and his men knew as "Old Brunswick."

"This," said Admiral Bullinger, "is Glasgow, where the biggest shipyards are located. There are other shipyards, all working overtime, where the Russ are starting to build their new fleet. These yards are all hard to approach. None appears defended now, except Cherbourg, which was their main Atlantic base. That is, none of the fortifications, which date from way back, seems to be actually armed. But they will be. And this shipbuilding program is something we can't match. Five years from now, the Russ could be back here with a new fleet, and another invasion army."

24

Arakal said, "You're sure these shipyards aren't armed *now*?"

Bullinger shook his head. "I'm morally certain, that's all. We entered every one of those ports except Cherbourg. I was careful not to risk the whole fleet at once, and we didn't open fire; still, the situation was pretty tense when we went in, flying the Old Flag. The local people went crazy. The Russ have dominated them all this time, and they could have ended the uproar quickly, by sinking us, *if* they'd been ready. Not a shot was fired."

There was a silence, then broad Slagiron, Arakal's chief general, spoke in a low growl.

"Yellowjackets don't make much trouble in the springtime."

Smith, speaking for the absent Colputt, nodded. "In the summer, when there are more in the nest, look out."

Slagiron's chief organizer, Casey, studied the curving waterway leading into Glasgow.

"Why wait till they arm these places?"

Arakal glanced at Admiral Bullinger.

"Suppose we wrecked every shipyard they're using. How long till they rebuilt them?"

"I think it could take them several years."

"And *then* they'd have them so fortified we couldn't touch them?"

"Yes."

"How many local people would we kill in the attack?"

Bullinger hesitated. "That, I can't say. I suppose we could warn them. But it would be risky. We don't know how much rolling artillery the Russ may have."

Casey said, "The right way to do it would be to

appear unexpectedly, hit with everything we've got, then either land or get out."

Arakal shook his head.

"Our aim isn't to turn everyone into allies of the Russ. Suppose you were over there, and our fleet sailed in without warning, and killed your brother and father in a surprise attack on a defenseless shipyard. Would you love us for it?"

Slagiron said drily, "War and love aren't exactly the same."

"It's easier to make enemies than friends."

Admiral Bullinger said, "Once the Russ get all these new ships afloat, it won't make much difference whether the Old Brunswickers love us or not. We'll have another Russ army at our throat."

"There's a question," said Arakal, "whether we'd be better off facing another Russ army in five years, or a Russ army plus the active hatred of Old Brunswick and Old Kebeck a few years later."

Slagiron thoughtfully massaged his jaw, and turned to look at the contour model of the East Coast of America. He glanced back at Arakal.

"It's true that, using a bloodless method I didn't think would work, we freed the Russ colonies, and they joined us willingly. But that was a special situation. And, as you remember, there was a bloodbath worse than sticking pigs when the Russ went for Keback Fortress the long way. It took killing to win that."

Arakal's voice was ironic. "That's true. We've had no trouble with enlistments from Maine since the Russ went through."

There was a silence as Casey, Slagiron, and Bullinger stared at the walls or ceiling, then nodded ruefully. Bullinger cleared his throat.

"All the same, we'll regret it when the Russ control the seas again."

Arakal nodded. "But you say the people went wild when you entered the harbors?"

"Yes. And the fishermen and coastwise traders we picked up were friendly, too. They all agreed that to get the Russ out of there is going to take an armed force of great power. I could follow most of their reasoning, but they didn't understand our actual situation. I had the impression they all thought we were comparable to the Russ in strength."

"Would you say that the people were ready to throw out the Russ?"

"Yes. If we'll do the main part of the work. They don't think they *can* do it."

"They wouldn't fight on the Russ side?"

"No."

Arakal walked slowly around the new contour model, looking at the harbors, studying the bays and inlets, and the outthrust peninsulas. He turned, briefly, to look back at the more familiar contour model of the East Coast of America. His gaze rested on the flat, gray, slightly glazed markings that formed the western border at the edge of the massive table. He turned back to Admiral Bullinger.

"Did you see any such damage across the ocean as there is here?"

"No, sir. But then, the damage would probably have been further inland, where they would have fought to stop the Russ coming from the east."

Arakal nodded, and again considered the new model. He looked up, to glance from one massive table to the other, and then to Buffon, standing

respectfully back from the little group around the
tables.

"These two models are to the same scale?"

"Yes, sir."

"Good." Arakal glanced at Bullinger. "You
didn't make any try at getting into this—
hmm—Mediterranean Sea?"

"No, sir. The entrance is fairly narrow, measured by the range of a coast defense gun, and our
information is that the Russ control both sides.
Incidentally, a chart of the Mediterranean that we
bought from a coastwise trader disagreed with the
charts on board the fleet when we captured it."

"Had this coastwise trader ever been there?"

"No, sir. It was just one of a set of charts he had
on board."

"How were your charts?"

"The ones we used were accurate."

Arakal looked the two models over, frowning.
"Despite the shipyards we've captured here, the
Russ have a greater capacity for building ships
over there?"

"Yes, sir," said Bullinger. "Much greater."

"And yet, so far as we know, the Russ were
using only the Maryland-Delaware Colony to
build warships before?"

"Yes, sir. The yards over there were used before, but as far as we can learn, they were used
only to build fishing vessels, freighters—things
like that."

"You didn't try to enter the—let's see—the
Baltic Sea—to the north?"

"No, sir. We stuck to the coasts of Old
Brunswick and Old Kebeck. That is, what they
call 'the U. K.' and 'France'."

"What we have here is a bigger puzzle than we had to start with. You saw no Russ ships?"

"No armed Russ ships."

Slagiron spoke, his voice a low growl.

"Except for the shipbuilding, everything seems about as we would have expected."

There was a murmur of agreement from Casey; but Smith, Colputt's assistant, was frowning. Arakal nodded to Smith.

"What do you think?"

"That's just it. Except for the shipbuilding. And, excuse me, what about their aircraft?"

Slagiron looked startled. "That's right." He glanced at Bullinger.

The Admiral shook his head. "Not a single iron bird."

Arakal said exasperatedly, "Why not build their warships at home?"

"These present yards they're using may be bigger," said Admiral Bullinger.

"Then why did they ever build ships over here? Thanks to that, we now have three new bombardment ships that should be finished late this summer, on which we can mount very powerful guns, and which will run on coal, not oil. Yet, when they lost these yards, what did they do? Start construction in other yards, again outside Russland. Why? Why, in the first place, build on this side of the ocean when they could have used the yards over there? There's something here we don't understand."

Admiral Bullinger nodded. "Unfortunately, I can't add anything more."

Arakal said, "How was the Fleet's oil usage?"

"It matched what the Russ volunteers had told

us. Counting the stocks in their colonies here, and
in two little tankers we captured, I'd say it could
last us from three to four years, assuming they
don't find some way to blow it up on us."

Arakal looked back at Smith.

"What would *you* say about the way they build
their ships?"

"They must," said Smith, "build them where
they do for reasons that make sense to *them*, at
least. But there must be something wrong in their
arrangements. It doesn't make sense to build
ships where they're vulnerable to attack. It must
be that, for some reason, conditions are even
worse elsewhere."

Slagiron said stubbornly, "All this is
guesswork. The *facts* are that if we let them use
those shipyards, wherever they're located, we
lose the only advantage we have."

"Yes," said Admiral Bullinger.

Arakal, examining the indentations in the
coastline, glanced at the Admiral, and rested a
forefinger on the port Bullinger had called "Cherbourg."

"You think this port, at the end of this peninsula, was their main base?"

"Their main Atlantic base, sir. In the Mediterranean, I suppose, they would have had another
main port."

"It's protected against the weather?"

"Yes, sir. For one thing, there's a tremendous
breakwater."

"Do they have oil storage there?"

"I think they'd be bound to. Our information is
that they do."

"You think the fortifications there *are* armed?"

"That was our information, and it seemed reasonable, since this was their main base."

Arakal glanced around, and Buffon said, "Scale, sir?"

At Arakal's nod, Buffon handed over a small folding measure. Arakal held one end on Cherbourg, and swung the other end successively to Le Havre, Bordeaux, Dover, and Portsmouth. As his men watched intently, Arakal carefully measured the sides and width of the narrower portion of the peninsula, at the end of which was Cherbourg. He glanced at Bullinger.

"Why would they make this their main port?"

"For three reasons, sir. First, as you see, it's in a central location. Second, it's apparently ice-free in winter. Third, it's on a peninsula, which they could seal off in the event of an uprising on the mainland."

Arakal nodded, and glanced at Buffon.

"Do we have a detailed map?"

"Yes, sir. But it's based on information from before the war. Just a moment."

As Buffon unrolled a large map of the peninsula, Arakal, Slagiron, and Casey bent over it. Arakal's gaze settled on the peninsula's eastern coast, and he glanced at Bullinger.

"Have you seen this coast here?"

"Yes, sir. Though we didn't get too close."

"Did you notice any fortifications or batteries?"

"No, sir. They may be there, but we didn't see them."

Arakal studied the map in silence.

"Buffon?"

"Sir?"

"What's the accurate range of those big guns

we're planning to mount on the bombardment ships?"

"The last test showed them still accurate at eighteen miles, sir. We won't really know until they're mounted, and the ships are afloat."

"And the total capacity of those Russ troop transports we captured?"

"Thirty-six thousand men, sir, with normal loading."

Arakal straightened.

"If we do nothing, the Russ will recover, and, sooner or later, we'll find ourselves right back where we started. We'll have gained time, but that won't be enough, because we don't know how to use that time to strengthen ourselves beyond Russ interference. We're hemmed in on the west by the slagged lands, and hobbled where we do have control, by the same thing. Everywhere we turn, there's another orange marker to show where the spotter teams have found some more 'lingering radioactivity'."

There was a murmur of agreement, and Arakal went on, "Now, for the time being, we have the power to strike back freely, whenever we choose. But a few years from now, that power expires, since the Russ are building a new fleet. We can gain more time, if we wreck the shipyards. But then we kill our own friends, and possibly turn them against us. Yet, now, these same people cheer us. Meanwhile, though we know the Russ are far stronger overall than we are, we have a clear suggestion, in the way they build ships, that there must be some weakness in their arrangements that they have to make allowance for. It seems to me there is only one thing to do."

Around him, their expressions varying from rapt attention to alert worry, Arakal's lieutenants watched as he put his forefinger on the contoured model's port of Cherbourg.

"Here we have the former main base of the Russ fleet, with guns and stores of fuel. And it is situated on a peninsula, which could be held against superior numbers. All along this east coast, there are beaches. If we land there, we either make it ashore without a fight, or else we're fighting Russ, not O'Cracys. And if enough Russ get drawn in there, how do they hold down the population at the same time? And what will the population do? There could be one flame of revolution, to throw the Russ back a thousand miles to their own territory. If not, we might still capture this peninsula, take their fortress port from behind, base our fleet in easy striking distance of their main captured ports and shipyards, cut their sea lanes between Old Brunswick and Old Kebeck, force the Russ in Old Kebeck to fight us in prepared positions, and rattle the Russ in Old Brunswick on their perch. From this base, fighting the Russ, who are the common enemy, we can call on the workers through all the territories of the Old O'Cracys to cut up the Russ from behind, blow up their iron roads, and lag and shift at all the work the Russ call on them to do."

"Yes," said Smith, Colputt's assistant.

Admiral Bullinger nodded his approval. "From our information, there could well be enough stored fuel in Cherbourg for a year's service."

Casey, his face twisted with concern, glanced at Slagiron.

Slagiron, jaw outthrust, growled, "And what if

half the men drown on the way ashore, and the rest get sunk in this damned swamp it shows on the map? Or if the Russ have machine guns set up at the edge of the beach? Where do you take cover on a beach? And why attack here, of all places? This is nothing less than the Russ citadel! Of all the choices on the whole continent, do we have to ram our heads into that? This is the very place they must be best prepared to defend!"

"Against an uprising," said Arakal. "But this is a landing from the sea! Why should they prepare against that when they had the only fleet in the world?"

"And what the devil," Slagiron went on, "do we know about landing over a beach? Did you ever try to run on sand? Isn't it enough that the Russ will probably have tanks by the dozens and cannon by the hundreds to slaughter us as we come in? How do we unload so much as a single one-pounder off a boat onto a beach? Why not, for the love of heaven, land, at least, in a port? There we could walk off onto a dock. Anyone who wants to swim ashore with forty pounds on his back, and a rifle in one hand, is welcome to it!"

Arakal, smiling, said, "What do I have generals for, except to help me work out these details? What you are talking about is why it will be hard. What I am talking about is why it is worthwhile. Do we want to do what the Russ expect? Or do we want to hit them where they don't expect it, and where, if they lose, they have to fight us with one foot in a hole? Look at the lay of the land. Do you see any other port so useful to us, that we could expect to hold against the Russ the way we could hold this one?"

"We have to take it first. And we don't know the first thing about landing on a beach."

"What do you think we're going to practice between now and the time we go over there? If we land in that port, and it *is* defended, then we lose not only ships, but also we wreck the port. If we land on this beach, right here, north of this small river, we are at the rear of the port, and we should also be inside the Russ defenses of the peninsula toward the mainland."

Slagiron bent beside Arakal, over the map.

"Yes, but— Let's see, here . . . I can foresee one sweet mess trying it. All right, if you want to do this, let's take time, and do it *right*. This year, hit those shipyards, so we end that for now. By next spring, we could have troops trained to go in over a beach, and we could have rafts, or *something*, to bring in the artillery. That way, we can try it, at least, the way it ought to be done."

"Yes," said Arakal, "if we can just get the Russ to go to sleep till then. By next year, when we're satisfied we know how to do it, the Russ could have guns defending every target we want to reach, their troops at a fever pitch, and half the continent hating us because of the stories and pictures of the unarmed people we slaughtered in attacks on defenseless ports. And who has the bigger productive power—us, or the Russ? Why should the passage of time favor us, once we get past the time when those bombardment ships come into our hands?"

Slagiron, his hand to his chin, eyes narrowed, glanced at Arakal. "You want to try it as soon as the new bombardment ships are ready?"

"We need to be *ready* to try it then."

Slagiron studied the model.

"If it works . . ."

Then he turned to Casey.

"We're going to need a beach to practice on, and we've got to find some way to float in the guns . . ."

2.

S-One shook his head, and put the report down carefully on his desk. His window was partly open on the inner court, and he could hear the rain pouring down on its glass roof. From somewhere came a gurgle of water flowing through gutters and downspouts, to be fed downward into the underground filter tanks and cisterns. The murmur of flowing water was usually a cheerful sound for S-One, but today it fit into a general gloom and sense of disappointment. S-One picked up the interoffice phone.

"Is General Brusilov here?"

"He is waiting, sir."

"Send him in."

The door opened, and Brusilov, big, bearlike, clear-eyed, came in, and nodded respectfully to S-One.

S-One said solicitously, "You look well, General. Sit down."

"Thank you," said Brusilov, a look of wariness crossing his face.

S-One said, "I am disappointed in your hero."

Brusilov looked blank. "Sir?"

"Arakal proposes to land his troops in Normandy."

Brusilov frowned in puzzlement.

"Yes," said S-One, settling back, and watching Brusilov alertly, "we now have information on Arakal's plans."

Brusilov's face cleared. "From the ships?"

S-One smiled. "He gained and lost when he captured those ships. It is a great loss to us in power, but a gain in information. What is sad is the mystery stripped away when your opponent reveals his imbecility in all its obscure convolutions."

"Arakal is not stupid."

"They are having practice landings now. Think of it. They plan to come ashore on the old Utah Beach, strike inland behind Cherbourg, and capture the narrow part of the peninsula. They will do this with no more than thirty-five thousand men."

"What is stupid about this?"

"We can sink his whole fleet in the bay, and slaughter his landing force. I am embarrassed for this Arakal. His general, Slagiron, sees the difficulties. Arakal will not be moved."

Brusilov leaned forward.

"Comrade, there is a difference between ignorance and stupidity. Arakal is profoundly ignorant of conditions here. Even, doubtless, he has been misled."

S-One smiled in satisfaction. "To the degree that we could misinform his Admiral Bullinger, Arakal has been misled."

"What do you propose to do?"

S-One shrugged.

"An elaborate deception plan has been prepared. It seems a shame to waste it on such a donkey."

"Comrade," said General Brusilov, his expression worried, "invariably Arakal is underestimated—I have done it myself—and invariably, a rude awakening follows. Whether it will be the same here, on our own ground, I do not know. But take no unnecessary chances. *Arakal does not always do as you expect.*"

S-One's eyes narrowed, and for a moment he studied Brusilov thoughtfully. Then he nodded.

"Very well. An excess of subtlety is always dangerous, and I was about to say that we should expect to destroy this fellow and his fleet in the bay and on the beach. And I think, still, it is what will happen. But, just in case, we will continue with the deception plan. Who knows? He might show flickers of sense even yet."

Brusilov said earnestly, "When he appears stupid, that is the time to take extra precautions."

"He appears extremely stupid now," said S-One with feeling.

Both men turned at the sound of a rap on the door.

S-One's second-in-command apologized for interrupting, and stepped in, frowning. S-One spoke half-jokingly, "What is it, S-Two? You do not look happy."

"Arakal, sir. A second coded message has arrived for him, from his chief scientist, Colputt."

S-One looked interested. "What is it about?"

"We don't know," said S-Two indignantly. "Arakal decodes the messages himself, and explains nothing to the others. And the others don't dare ask him, though amongst themselves they are consumed with curiosity. And now he has left by rail, and we have no way to know what is happening!"

IV. The Unknown and the Known

1.

Arakal followed white-bearded Colputt along the corridor, noting the number of interconnecting passages. They were now well beyond the end of the electrical cables that stretched down the mine shaft from the clearing, and were relying on Colputt's mantle lantern, which lit the corridors brightly as he led the way around a corner, and pushed open the door of a metal staircase that led them down and around, and down and around, seemingly endlessly, through a succession of landings blocked by heavy doors that must be shoved back, until they pushed open one last door, and the brilliant light of Colputt's lantern was swallowed up in an enormous room, its rough ceiling supported by massive pillars of uncut rock.

As Arakal peered into the gloom, he could see, beside the nearest of the pillars, a huge shadowy frame resting on coil springs. Within the frame was what appeared to be a metal box roughly the size of a large room.

"That's what you wanted me to see?"

"That's the lead-lined protective case around it."

As they walked forward, Arakal soon began to feel dwarfed by his surroundings. Only very slowly did the position of the pillar seem to change, while the frame, as he came closer, loomed higher and higher. It seemed a long time before he was at its base, looking up.

Colputt handed Arakal his lantern, glanced up at a raised metal ladder on the side of the frame, reached up, got hold of the lowest rung, swung himself up onto an awkwardly located platform to the side, knelt, and reached down. Arakal handed up the lantern, and Colputt stepped back on the ladder, and climbed carefully up. As he stepped off at the top, Arakal crouched, squinting up into the glare and the shadows, sprang up, and pulled himself rapidly onto the ladder. He climbed up in the sudden dimness as the lantern passed beyond the top edge of the frame.

As Arakal reached the top, Colputt held the lantern up high.

"Look at the size of this."

Arakal had the impression he was on the deck of a ship. The flat surface stretched into the shadows, with a straight dark line down its center, and strongly braced metal arms reaching out from the surface to either side, bearing massive counterweights.

"This top opens?"

"Down the center. Each side of the deck swings back and up—like opening gates."

Colputt lifted a hatch in the deck, and led the way down an enclosed ladder into a confined metal booth with a narrow door. They stepped out on a metal walk, several feet above a billowing gray cushion-like surface. Some fifteen feet away, reflecting the lantern light in a few bright points, was a low, wide, smoothly curving metallic form with a broad dome rising toward its center.

Arakal moved further along the walk, to find a better angle of vision. A second set of reflections, further away, shone back at him.

Arakal glanced at Colputt.

"Two of them?"

"Yes."

"What are they?"

"If I'm not mistaken, they are two samples of the Old O'Cracys' 'ground-effect machines'. If so, they can cross solid ground, quicksand, swamps, beaches, rivers, and even stretches of ocean. So long as it's fairly level, it's all the same to a ground-effect machine."

"They *fly*?"

"Not exactly. They ride above the surface on a cushion of air. They use the air the way a wagon uses wheels."

"What do they use for power?"

"I hardly dare say it," said Colputt, "but from a list we found in an office upstairs, I think these use a form of atomic engine. Incidentally, they aren't as big inside as they look. Only the center part seems usable."

"What was the list you found?"

"Fuel requirements. It listed amongst other things, 'platform couriers'. There were apparently eighteen 'platform couriers', plus two more for spares. We think these are the two spares. Beside each of these 'platform couriers' was a little number that referred to a note, 'See Nuclear Fuels Section'. The list was all we've found, so far."

"Are these in as good shape as everything else seems to be in here?"

"We don't know yet. If you care to go a little closer, I'll show you the problem."

They dropped from the walk, plunged through the cushioning material, and climbed out on the curving metal surface. Colputt stepped forward, and held the lantern so that the light shone through a transparent section of smooth upcurving dome. They leaned forward.

Inside was a sort of padded armchair before a wide curving covered panel. Everything they could see had a sleekly finished appearance, with no working machinery in sight. Arakal straightened, frowning, and looked around. The outside surface was smooth, with no visible joins or openings. Even the transparent window seemed of one piece with the metallic sections that adjoined it. Arakal ran his hand across the join, and felt only a smooth unvarying surface. He glanced at Colputt.

"I begin to see your problem."

Colputt nodded. "If there's a handle, hinge, latch, catch, or even so much as a pinhole here, anywhere, we haven't been able to find it."

"Could they have entered from underneath?"

"I suppose it's not impossible. But we've pushed underneath, and found no opening, and I don't see why they should have done it that way. And that is by no means all we don't see. The trouble is that our technology is nowhere near as advanced as theirs was. We'll just have to hope that somewhere in this collection of shafts and tunnels, we'll find something to help clear up the problems we can't work out on our own."

When they went back up to the surface, Arakal and Colputt found a quiet place amongst the oaks and evergreens, overlooking the new clearing where a rough shed had been built over the entrance for the mine shaft. Beside the shed, a massive steam-crawler ran the generator that supplied light and power to the crews working underground.

Arakal looked down into the clearing for a moment, then turned to Colputt.

"How long, do you suppose, before you'll be through here?"

"Well—first, we need a better way to ventilate the tunnels. Second, there are the questions raised by those dead but undecomposed bodies. Third, there are the ground-effect machines. Fourth, there's the problem of what this installation was, and how it fit in with the O'Cracys' plans. We may never find that out, and yet it could be important. Finally, there are your standing orders in case of a discovery like this, that we be very careful not to spread the news, since it might find its way to the Russ. That limits the people I can have here to a specially selected group."

"Nevertheless," said Arakal, "let's stick to it. I'm sure the Russ have ways of learning our arrangements that would surprise us."

"Well, then, there also are the details of the things in there. There are books, instruction manuals, tools, equipment, even several workshops, and a sizable laboratory." Colputt shook his head.

"There's no way to predict how long it might take."

Arakal nodded. "Don't rush the work. This is just what we've hoped to find. It wasn't wrecked in the war, or stripped afterward. Take your time, and do it right. By the way, Bullinger is back with the Fleet. I suppose Smith explained our plans to you?"

Colputt looked faintly guilty. "He offered to explain them. I was too busy."

"In that case, I'll explain them, myself. The main thing, though we don't know, is that there may be survivors of the Old Soviets' attack, somewhere to the west. If we could find a way, I would link up with them. We haven't been able to get through."

Colputt's gaze grew remote. "Some could have survived. Who knows? But is it so important?"

"It is to the survivors—and to us, if they have any of the Old O'Cracys' technology still in use."

"In time, we should get through."

" 'In time' may not be soon enough. If you study the old records, you find many centers of technology to the West. But it's three thousand miles from one coast to the other. The Russ are not a great deal further away from our West Coast than we are. While we are locked up on the East Coast, they could take over the west. They could, perhaps, even turn the remains of the 'Old O'Cracys' technology against us."

Colputt's eyes narrowed. "But since we can't get through—"

"Then we aim to cross the Atlantic, and free Old Brunswick, and, if possible Old Kebeck."

"What if the Russ are too strong?"

"It all depends on details." Briefly, Arakal described his plan, and Colputt, looking worried, said, "I am no general. But there is a serious risk from the Russ technology. In the first place, they may well have a spy network with transmitters planted in one of their former colonies. They could then get wind of your practice landings, and report them. Second, they may have ways to detect the approach of your ships. They could then shift their troops by the iron road, to meet you where you landed."

Arakal nodded. "It won't be easy. Now, what do you think of their building their war-ships, first over here, then where they are building them now? Why not build them at home? Why should they do it this way?"

"There are only two reasons I can think of."

"What?"

"Ice and enemies. If their home shipyards are iced in, they might prefer to build elsewhere. They might have preferred to build here, instead of across the ocean, because they could control their own colonists better than foreigners."

"Would their shipyards be iced in?"

"In winter, perhaps. I don't see any reason why it should be worse than before the war. There's certainly been no great climatic changes, or we'd have felt it here."

"The one certain thing is that they aren't stupid. They must have some reason."

Colputt nodded. "There has to be a reason. But it's hard to imagine what it could be."

2.

S-One looked up at the strongly reinforced barrier of glass and steel above the dim courtyard. It looked as if it had been heavily dusted with flour. He shook his head, turned, and sat down at his desk.

"No word of Arakal?"

"He is back with the ships. They had another practice landing, this time at night."

"How did it go?"

"A disaster."

S-One smiled, and sat back.

"What happened?"

"Confusion amongst the units. There was bad weather, some of the troops reached the wrong beach, the arrangements for getting artillery ashore didn't work—Slagiron and Casey had an argument with Arakal— Just about everything went wrong."

S-One leaned forward, smiling.

"What about the argument?"

S-Two smiled, leafed through a sheaf of papers, separated one section from the rest, and handed it to S-One. S-One sat back comfortably, and read:

Slagiron: "But it can't be done! And I'll be damned if I'll be responsible for landing men straight into the meat grinder!"

Arakal: "What about you, Casey?"

Casey: "After tonight, sir, I'll resign before I go on with this. We've got a hundred and fifty men missing, right now, just from the storm alone. We can't—"

Arakal: "Are you saying that I don't care about those men?"

Slagiron: "A devil of a lot of good it does them whether—"

Arakal: "I was speaking to Casey."

Casey: "I don't say you don't care, sir, but that doesn't help them a bit. They're missing, possibly dead."

Arakal: "I see I am subject to criticism because I stayed on the ship instead of leading that landing. Well, that wasn't my idea. I'm going on the next landing."

Slagiron: "That won't *help!* It isn't—"

Casey: "Then *you* might be killed! That water is vicious! And in the dark—"

Arakal: "I want the next practice landing scheduled for tonight. Officers only. There's no army on earth better than ours, and if they can't do this, it's because we're giving them the wrong orders. The only way to fix that is to find out what's wrong for ourselves."

Slagiron: "But, even if we finally learn how to do it on *this* beach—"

Arakal: "Do we have any better beach?"

Slagiron: "It can *still* be a disaster on another beach!"

Arakal: "When those bombardment ships are ready, *we've* got to be ready. If we put it off any longer, it will be too late. This is the only chance we may ever have!"

Slagiron: "Sir, there isn't any time limit. We don't *have* to go now!"

Arakal: "The Russ aren't fools. Bullinger's visit has warned them that their shipyards, ports, and seacoast are vulnerable. One thing we know the

Russ can do is make cannon. Another thing they
can do is to calculate, and bring force to bear on
obvious weak points. When we have beat them,
it's been by surprise, and because they underestimated us. If we try to outcalculate them, and
match force to force, they will win. We have to
surprise them. We have to be stronger than they
realize. We have to strike at a place they don't
expect us to hit. We can't count on time to favor
us, because time may be on their side. While we
argue, they build. We have to appear off that coast
before they think it's possible!"

Slagiron: "Buffon was saying—"

Arakal: "Buffon thinks we have land enough already. That we can develop what we have and
defy the world. If we could get through that barrier of radioactive slag, he might be right. But we
can't. So we don't know what's on the other side."

Casey: "In time, sir, the radioactivity should die
down, and then—"

Arakal: "That's part of the problem."

Casey: "How—"

Arakal: "When that happens, what will we find
on the other side? We are blocked from going
through. But the other side is open to the Russ,
coming from the West."

Slagiron: "You don't think they could be
colonizing—"

Arakal: "How do we know what they're doing?
It's easy for us to imagine that we are big, because
we can all remember when we had practically
nothing. But all we are is the half-alive head and
right arm of the O'Cracy, with the rest of the body
unconscious, dead, or smashed. Most of our
memory is gone—the Russ even correct us as to

what we call ourselves. We can't match the Russ until we recover the lands of the O'Cracy. And since we can't go West, we'll go east. But we have got to get there before the Russ expect us."

Slagiron: "About this practice landing tonight—"

Arakal: "I'm open to suggestions."

Slagiron: "Some of the officers who are going to end up going out are completely beat. It would be almost murder to put them through it again tonight."

Arakal: "Can you get together officer volunteers for one boat?"

Slagiron: "I'll volunteer myself. But it's going to be a worse mess than anything you can think of."

Casey: "I'll volunteer. But aside from possibly killing the lot of us—"

Arakal: "I am now murdering you personally?"

Casey: "I didn't say that."

Arakal: "I've explained my reasoning. But I am very close to the end of all explanations."

Slagiron: "Excuse me, sir. Casey—"

Casey: "To go out there tonight—"

Slagiron: "Casey! Who in hell do you think you are? Do you realize that for the last ten minutes you've been laying down conditions, questioning the judgement of your superiors, and generally inviting trouble? You think you're protecting the men, and you've done more complaining than any fifty of them, and half of that in the wrong tone of voice. Go out there and get the volunteers! No officers below the rank of colonel, except by special permission. And if you drown six hours from now, you can thank me you lived that long. *Not another word! Get out!* . . . The damned fool!"

Arakal: "How did you know?"

Slagiron: "I was there when Cotter said we had to give up. I remember how that went. He had almost exactly the same tone in his voice, and you told him almost the same thing—that you'd come to the end of explanations."

Arakal: "What's wrong with Casey?"

Slagiron: "His younger brother's missing. And, farcical as it may seem, Casey promised his mother he'd protect his brother."

Arakal: "It was my mistake not to be out there with the rest."

Slagiron: "Sir, you were worn out."

Arakal: "The water would have woken me up. But Casey had better come to an understanding with his mother, or get a guarantee from Almighty God for his brother. We can't make the training soft. And we can't be crying over a hundred and fifty men missing when the units are all mixed up. The wonder is we don't have a thousand missing."

Slagiron: "I think we ought to do this practice landing in daylight."

Arakal: "Good. Then we'll do it twice."

S-One lowered the papers, and glanced at his deputy.

"How did all this turn out? The officers in the boat?"

"They went out twice, sir, and got wrecked on the beach each time, the second time at night. They came back in an indescribable frame of mind. But it was very popular with the men."

"With—" S-One blinked. "What was that?"

"The men, sir. The ordinary soldiers were delighted."

"I see. And the losses? The men who were missing?"

"Most turned up the next day, sir. Some had got lost on the beach; others were still in the wrong units."

"There is an aspect to this that is difficult for me to grasp. What are the relations now between Arakal, Slagiron, and Casey?"

"Back to normal, sir. Casey apologized."

"I see. . . . Well, there is still one thing, at least."

"What is that, sir?"

"Arakal recognizes that they need surprise." S-One smiled. "Though he is blockheaded, he does recognize that. But—" S-One handed his deputy the papers "—they can't surprise us, whatever they do."

V. The Invasion

1.

Arakal clung with aching hands to the rail of the *Panther* as the bombardment ship wallowed through seas that dropped away like canyons, then heaved themselves up like mountains rising to the sky. Arakal's gut was sore, his head ached, and his senses swam. There was nothing stable in any direction. The ship, massively reinforced to sustain the shock of its big guns, shuddered to the crash of uncountable tons of sea water.

"Sir!" called a voice, and Arakal turned from the slanting walls of gray water, to see Admiral Bullinger clinging to the rail with one hand, his expression concerned.

Arakal managed to nod, and the Admiral leaned closer.

"We've found a spy device—built into the ship."

"A— *What*?"

"Spy device sir. A listening device."

Arakal's attention was abruptly riveted on Bullinger.

"Is it effective? Can they hear anything with it?"

Bullinger leaned closer in the wind.

"It's a long-talker, a radio, sir. We've traced the connections. It's possible the Russ have over-heard everything we've said on board since we captured the ships."

Arakal clung to the rail.

Bullinger, who had silently debated with him-self how to tell his chief this terrible news, saw in surprise a brief look of grim exaltation as Arakal leaned closer.

"It's in working order?"

"Yes, sir."

"They could use it at this distance?"

"Can't be certain. But they could have arrange-ments to relay it. There are still satellites up there."

"Where does it pick up conversations *from*?"

"Your cabin, mine, the bridge—it's apparently connected to every cabin we use."

"If they picked up the signal, they know our plans?"

"Yes. . . . If. There's still some hope, sir, that they didn't. But we don't know."

Arakal clung to the rail and watched the gray water climb up against the sky.

Bullinger said, "Shall we rip it out?"

"No. Leave it. You haven't disabled it?"

"No, sir."

"When was it found?"

"Late yesterday."

"In this storm?"

"Yes, sir."

"How?"

"There was a file case in the radio room, and it

wasn't properly secured. It fell over, and split the paneling. There was wiring behind the panel."

"Who saw it?"

"The radio officer. He got curious, traced it, realized what it was, and showed it to the ship's captain. The captain took me out into the storm and told me. We've been very careful with the damned thing. We haven't said a word aloud where *it* could overhear."

"Who knows about it now?"

"You, me, the captain, the radio officer, and the three radio ratings. They've been working all day and all last night to trace it."

Arakal looked briefly over the rail, down into a sickening chasm of spray and spume and huge moving surfaces of gray water.

Bullinger now saw with astonishment that Arakal was smiling. "Sir— What do we do?"

"Swear them all to secrecy. Cover up the damage. Hide it, that is, and say nothing. Could the Russ know we've found it?"

"Not unless they can recognize the sound of prybars in this storm. Should we warn the other ships?"

"No. But tell me at once if *they* report finding anything."

Bullinger nodded, waited for a favorable tilt of the ship, and let go the rail.

Arakal looked around at the sea where the sky should be, and his face paled. Sickeningly, the sea rose. The ship plunged. Arakal's insides churned.

But if he could just live through it, this storm was bound to end, sometime.

2.

S-One shook his head, careful to keep his bearing courteous. He reminded himself that in the formal hierarchy of the State, the man across the big table was his superior.

"No," said S-One, "I see no danger from this so-called invasion."

Across the table, his gaze intent, the tall, lean, faintly studious man formally identified in the table of organization as "G-One," for "Head of Government," and also as "P-One," for "Chairman of the Central Committee of the Party"—this individual looked intently into S-One's eyes, until S-One felt the impact like a bright light glaring directly onto the retinas of his eyes, to explode across the back of his brain. But S-One neither flinched nor looked away.

Across the table, S-One broke the contact, and glanced around at the others seated at the table. No one ventured an opinion. G-One said, "General Brusilov?"

"Sir?"

"What is your opinion?"

Brusilov did not hesitate.

"I think it represents a great danger, and a great opportunity."

"Why?"

"It is a danger, because Arakal is a master of conflict. It represents an opportunity, because, if we can make peace with the Americans—a real peace—we should be able to overcome some serious problems."

G-One frowned, and glanced at S-One.

"Your reply?"

"I repeat what I have already said. Neither Arakal, his army, nor his disastrous plan, represent any danger to us."

G-One glanced at Brusilov.

Brusilov, some strain evident in his voice, said, "I don't want to seem insubordinate—"

G-One nodded. "We are well aware, General, that our defeat in America, and the loss of our fleet and our colonies there, was no fault of yours. We know that the fault lay in one who, contrary to your warning, underestimated this same opponent our colleague here—" G-One glanced briefly across the table "—tells us is no danger to us now. This precedent requires some attention on our past. Let us hear your honest opinion."

Brusilov waited a moment, then spoke in a careful voice.

"I have, speaking of my own experience, found Arakal to be honest and steadfast in friendship, and totally unpredictable in war. He is without conceit, free of serious delusion, and profound in his understanding of conflict. His blows dislocate the mind, as well as overwhelming physical resistance. His army is not to be judged by its numbers alone. His spirit actuates this army."

S-One spoke sharply. "What is the meaning of this statement: 'His spirit actuates this army'?"

G-One's eyes glinted, but he glanced curiously at Brusilov.

Before Brusilov could speak, S-One went on:

"The General speaks as one mentally dominated by another."

Brusilov's voice was suddenly flat. "I am warning you of what I have experienced myself. I will say frankly that from the information you have given me, I, too, would think Arakal has no chance. But I have been asked for my opinion, and I will state it:

"Arakal is dangerous. So is his army. Don't laugh at him because he speaks of the Wesdem O'Cracy, and before his army appeals to God for aid. Don't smile when you measure him against his ancestors. A part of the risk is that it is so hard to take such seeming backwardness seriously."

"I smile at him," said S-One, "when I consider his plan. Of all the places in Western Europe where he might land, and do us damage, he selects the one spot where no popular enthusiasm can help him, where we can destroy him as if he were a nut in a nutcracker."

Across the table, G-One said thoughtfully, "What is your plan?"

S-One controlled his voice.

"In deference to the General's warning, I am holding in reserve a carefully worked out deception plan, in the event Arakal should actually set foot alive on the continent, and survive the first day, which I do not expect."

G-One nodded. "This is prudent."

S-One waited a moment, to be sure that his voice was level.

"If, however, things work out as now seems probable, Arakal and the larger part of his force should be too badly mauled in the landing attempt to cause us any serious trouble."

"What are the specifics?"

"Arakal intends to land by moonlight at the full tide on a beach southeast of Cherbourg, on the east coast of the Cherbourg Peninsula. This is the old World War II beach known as 'Utah'. The Americans successfully landed there in 1944. In World War II, however, they came from Britain. Arakal is coming all the way across the Atlantic in one bound. They have already passed through a severe storm. They will arrive weak and none too fit for combat."

Brusilov spoke politely but definitely.

"Excuse me, Comrade, but those troops are tough. And we know they are well trained. This is not the first storm they have experienced."

S-One waited a moment before speaking. His candid belief was that he was surrounded by a pack of fools. This belief might find its way into his voice and manner if he was not careful. He cleared his throat, and spoke politely.

"Have you ever been seasick, General?"

Brusilov said gruffly, "More than once."

"I think you are as tough as Arakal or his men. How combat-worthy did you feel after you had just been seasick?"

"I was as weak as a kitten."

There was a murmur, and a sense of relaxation around the table. Even G-One, across the table, looked relieved.

S-One said quietly, "Arakal's invasion force, which we estimate at not over thirty-five thousand men, should arrive off the old Utah Beach in time for him to put his men ashore somewhere around dead *low* tide—not high tide—since we managed to insinuate into Admiral Bullinger's possession faulty tide tables for the region. The Admiral, despite his rank, is inexperienced, and so are his men."

"So," said G-One, "the troops will arrive at low tide? What is the practical significance of this?"

"The beach is very flat. Their landing boats will run aground far out."

"Their walk inland will be longer?"

"Yes, and exposed to our fire all the way. We will allow the attack to proceed until Arakal is well committed. We will then open fire on the ships with our very powerful camouflaged guns. We will destroy the men by fire from machine-gun nests at the base of the cliffs. The fortifications of the peninsula were planned to stand a siege, and could be held with ten thousand men, such is the degree of automatic control. Actually, we have forty thousand men on hand, ready for anything."

"So, even if he should break through locally, you should still smash him in the end?"

"Even if there were no up-to-date fortifications, as is the case elsewhere, we should be able to smash him here. We can hit him when part of his men are ashore and part are still on the ships. The important thing is, we know where he is coming, and we are ready. It would be a different matter if we had to guess which place he would strike. We do not have to guess."

There was a murmur of approval, and, across the table, G-One nodded grudgingly, and glanced at Brusilov.

"General? What do you say of this?"

"So far, so good," said Brusilov. "But where is our main reserve?"

S-One barely held back a sarcastic reply. Before he could find an answer suitably polite, there was a rap, the door opened, and an apologetic voice spoke urgently from the doorway. S-One recognized his own deputy, and watched in astonishment as S-Two crossed the room rapidly toward him.

"Sir, excuse me! This won't wait!"

He thrust out a slim sheaf of papers, and S-One recognized the usual form of translated comments received by way of hidden electronic devices on the ships. Searching his deputy's face, he recognized an urgent look of warning.

S-One's calculation suddenly vanished. His voice came out harsh and cold. "This is a report of *what*? Speak up, S-Two."

His deputy's voice was low. "Of a meeting of Arakal and his generals on board the bombardment ship *Panther*. On page four, sir—"

S-One spoke sharply. "Don't try to spare me. Speak up! What's wrong?"

"Arakal, sir! The attack is not going in against the Cherbourg Peninsula, after all!"

S-One felt as if the earth moved under him. The blood roared in his ears.

"What? *Where*, then?"

"Le Havre, sir."

S-One swore, heard the uproar around the table, and then Brusilov's voice, patient but grimly persistent:

"Where is our main reserve in France?"

S-One drew a deep breath. "Metz."

"Then it can't help us. He'll get ashore. What do we have between Le Havre and Paris?"

S-One thought carefully.

"Nothing."

Brusilov nodded moodily.

"We have just been outmaneuvered."

S-One's deputy was still right there, his expression still urgent.

Across the table, G-One spoke drily.

"Is there more?"

S-One looked back at his deputy. His voice was harsh, strained, and he made no attempt to conceal it.

"Tell us frankly. There is no way to break news like this gently."

"Sir, Arakal gave instructions that, and I quote: 'the signals for the uprising should be sent'. We already have word of coded signals that, so far, have not been possible to interpret."

Across the table, G-One held his hand palm-out for quiet. His eyes were unreadable as he looked at S-One.

S-One turned to his deputy, and held up the sheaf of papers.

"You have read this? Or did someone else summarize it to you?"

"Both. After the summary, while the information was being verified, I read it."

"What explanation did Arakal give, that he had changed the landing site?"

"That, in war, misdirection is the key to victory; that it would be suicide to attack the main Soviet base in Western Europe when that base was warned in advance of the attack; and that, since the plans and preparations had been made in the vicinity of our former colonies, we were certain to have been warned of the practice landings, and the target; and so we would be waiting in the peninsula. This fact, that we had been misled, would clear the road to Paris, and the seizure of Paris would in turn strike a heavy blow to our prestige. The uprisings would maintain the split in our forces, which, united, would doubtless be more numerous than theirs. Beyond that, he said, it was impossible to predict, since everything depended on particulars. But with the fleet, with a mobile army, operating in a country where the transportation system could be cut, on signal, by the guerrillas . . ."

"The guerrillas?"

"I believe he said, 'the local patriots', but the real meaning was guerrillas. In such a situation, with part of our troops locked up in Normandy, and another force trapped in Britain, there would be bound to be opportunities."

There was a silence. Across the table, G-One turned to Marshal of the Armed Forces Vasilevsky, who had said nothing so far, and even now sat dourly staring at the far wall, his clasped hands resting on the table top.

"Well, Marshal?" said G-One.

Vasilevsky turned his head to look at G-One. It was as if he aimed a gun. His voice was a rumble, as of artillery in the distance.

"You want me now to make war on a map?"

G-One grappled with the comment, and, without a word, turned to Brusilov.

Vasilevsky went on. "The next thing, we soil our pants with fear of this American. He is still on his ship, isn't he? Let everyone stand to his guns where he is, and start the reserves from Metz toward Paris in the morning. If he lands at Le Havre, so be it. Let's see how much artillery he brought with him."

Brusilov said at once, "I agree."

G-One exhaled, and glanced quizzically across the table.

S-One, hearing the Marshal's rough voice, felt

the pressure fall away. Brusilov, too, he noted, had not panicked. Good. But an uprising in Europe would make far more than military problems. He shook his head.

"We can undoubtedly beat *Arakal*, just as a large cup of water can extinguish a match. The trouble is, the cup of water cannot necessarily extinguish the blaze that the match may cause when it is dropped into a pile of dry wood."

Vasilevsky grunted. "The French are not happy with us, eh? Well, I'm not sure the Germans are, either. Or the Dutch, or the Italians."

"That's the point."

Vasilevsky was silent a moment, then he shrugged. His voice was stolid, fatalistic.

"I have given my advice."

Across the table, G-One said, "If the Marshal's advice does not appeal to you, S-One, what do you suggest?"

S-One saw the wedge driven between himself and the Marshal, but ignored it. He turned to his deputy.

"What is Arakal's immediate plan?"

"Some of his ships will drop anchor off the Normandy peninsula. The rest will continue toward Le Havre. A few boats will set out toward the Normandy beaches, and make sounds to deceive us. Tomorrow, his fleet will enter Le Havre, and the troops will entrain for Paris."

"When, tomorrow?"

"He was evidently illustrating what he said with a detailed map, or a blackboard. We assume there was a diagram showing the relationship of the different parts of the attack, and the times. There was a good deal of confusion at first, and the analysis of the conversation is not yet complete. We have the expression 'at dawn' repeated several times, but we do not know with certainty what it refers to.''

S-One looked across the table, and saw from the bland expression of his superior that this reverse was not without its incidental benefits from the viewpoint of G-One, the Head of Government.

S-One spoke with a humility much more real than the restraint he had imitated before.

"I believe," said S-One, "that it is still possible to forestall Arakal militarily, thanks to the reports of this conference of his. If not, we will at once activate the deception plan. The aim of the deception plan is to deflect the force of any popular uprising. If the deception plan should fail—which does not seem possible to me—but if it should, then we must seek a military solution. In preparation for that, our military forces have already been drawn back to mutually supporting positions. This is the reason why our Reserve France is back at Metz."

Marshal Vasilevsky spoke up.

"Where is our Benelux Reserve?"

"Liege."

"And the Forward Reserve Germany?"

"Trier."

"Where is our Main Reserve Germany?"

"Muhlhausen."

The Marshal nodded.

S-One continued, "I will have to give the orders at once if we are to lose no time. My intention is to move the troops in the Cherbourg Peninsula by rail to Rouen. Depending on the speed of Arakal's movements, we may be able to forestall him at Le

Havre. At the very least, we can block his way to Paris."

G-One looked questioningly at Marshal Vasilevsky.

The Marshal grunted. "Who can say? We may get beat. On the other hand, while he tries to fool us, maybe we can catch him with half his men still on their boats. At least, we will find out what there is to this guerrilla business."

G-One looked surprised.

"You approve?"

"I am not in charge. I neither approve nor disapprove. It is not what I would do. I have already told you what I would do. But it may work. These things are not decided on a map, but on the ground."

G-One said, "General Brusilov?"

"I would use Marshal Vasilevsky's plan. But I am not familiar with all the factors, and this present plan may work."

G-One nodded, and turned to S-One.

"Very well. Proceed. The matter is entirely in your hands."

S-One came to his feet, bowed, and left the room.

VI. Blows in the Dark

1.

The sea moved in long slow swells, beneath a moonlit fog that hid the beaches, the bluffs, the other boats, and the ships that were the source of the heavy rumble of anchor chains heard far out in the bay.

Through the fog, like fuzzy images of beetles crawling across a surface of dark and slightly rippled satin, came long, low, open boats, the men laboring steadily at the oars, the officers crouched tensely at the bows, peering into the fog.

Wrapped in a cloak, one hand gripping the boat's wet gunnel, the other cupping a large watch whose luminous dial showed two minutes before 3:00 A.M., Arakal spoke in a low voice to the trumpeter crouched close behind him.

"We should be almost there. Stay right with me. And when we get out, keep that flag case up out of the water."

"Yes, sir."

Arakal snapped the inner cover shut over the watch face, pressed shut the outer cover that fitted down onto the hopefully waterproof gasket, slid the watch into its oilskin pouch, and methodically checked its fastenings. He counted silently as he checked watch, sword belt, map case, canteen, bandage box, cartridge box, and the bulky leather case for his long-seeing glasses. He eased his sword's fastenings around, and gathered up the edges of his cloak, as either sword or cloak could trip him getting out of the boat. Then he waited, and he continued to silently count:

. . . ninety-nine . . . one hundred . . . one hundred and one . . .

There was a clash of oars, and the helmsman's voice, low and patient, guided the oarsmen back into unison.

Arakal mentally rehearsed what to do when the boat hit the sand. As he thought over the possible complications and their answers, he was still silently counting:

. . . two hundred sixty-one . . . two hundred sixty-two . . . two hundred sixty-three . . .

Behind him, the huddled trumpeter shifted the flag case uneasily.

Arakal peered ahead, to see through the fog the glimmer of open water still in front of them.

The rhythmic splash and pull of the oars continued. Absently, he counted:

. . . three hundred and six . . . three hundred and seven . . . three hundred and eight . . .

Still, ahead, he could occasionally glimpse the water.

The rhythmic splash, and the gurgle of water past the boat, went on.

Tired from the storm, with the drifting fog around him, Arakal's eyes went almost shut.

There was a hiss of the hull scraping over sand.

The boat slowed. The helmsman growled, "Stow—"

Arakal was suddenly wide awake. "Not yet. There's water in front of us. We've hit a bar."

The men fitted their oars back between the pegs. There was a scrape and thump as the helmsman unshipped the rudder. Again, he gave his low chant. With a faint grinding sound, the boat slid unevenly forward.

Arakal peered around in the fog as they glided ahead once again, and again time stretched out.

Where was the beach?

2.

S-One tensely watched the display.

By now, at last, the laden troop trains were finally passing through Rouen. Position indicators for the ships showed a swerve in course, as the bulk of Arakal's Fleet swung past Normandy, and approached Le Havre. Left behind, several ships still lingered off the east coast of the Normandy peninsula. Reports from a small scout force left at the old Utah Beach told of the sounds of anchor chains, of faint rumblings and thuddings, even of the sounds of oars—but nothing whatever had yet appeared on the beach.

The wall opposite S-One's desk now showed a detailed representation of Normandy, the Bay of the Seine, and the railroad lines connecting Cherbourg to Rouen, and Rouen to Le Havre. On the display, blue lights in the bay showed the approach of Arakal's fleet to Le Havre, while on land short bright-red bars moved steadily along a black line, representing S-One's troop trains, which soon would be approaching Le Havre. The display suggested a close race, which should soon be decided, one way or another.

S-One felt the throb of a more rapid pulse, and a faint sense of shortness of breath.

Brusilov, across the desk, sat with his chair turned, watched the lighted wall, and said nothing.

Methodically, S-One thought over his dispositions. Le Havre, for all practical purposes, was defenseless. But he had over forty thousand men on the way, and by dawn the first troops should be close to the port. Surely they would be in time to smash Arakal's beachhead. But even in the event of military failure, the deception teams were already warned and ready, and could act in Normandy, Le Havre, or elsewhere. If, somehow, Arakal should see through the deception plan, then S-One would hand the whole situation over to Marshal Vasilevsky, who had already tacitly approved the location of the troops.

Testing the connections of these arrangements, S-One found no flaw. Yet, as time passed, it was becoming increasingly hard for him to breathe.

Across the desk, Brusilov's head turned, as from the east a line of light passed slowly across the map, leaving it lighter. The glowing markers on the map darkened by contrast. The change represented the coming of daylight in France.

S-One stared at the display.

There was an urgent rap on the door.

S-One called, "Come in!" and the door opened, to admit his deputy.

"Sir," cried S-Two, "we have reports that Arakal has landed. *In Normandy!*"

3.

Arakal, and the other men from the first boats to reach shore, had climbed to a kind of shelving terrace partway up the slope above the beach. By some miracle, they had all reached the same beach, and Arakal was now crouched with Slagiron under the hastily erected tent. They had a map spread out before them, and a small portable lamp trailed a thread of smoke as it cast its flickering shadows over the map. Around them, the tent slatted in a rising wind, and Slagiron, one big forefinger on the map, shook his head.

"Nothing matches."

Arakal noted the small blue Xs that marked the positions of the ships anchored off the coast. He slid a marker along the edge of the scale, clamped it at his estimate of the distance the small boats should have traveled, considering the time that had passed, held the pin at the end of the scale to nearest blue X, and swung the scale around.

"The tide must still have been going out. So, we were coming in against the tide. And, on top of that, there must be a current out there."

"Bullinger claimed to have accurate tide tables."

"They must have been like those maps of the Mediterranean he told us about. We're going to have to bring the bulk of the men ashore at dead low tide."

"Ashore. But where?"

Arakal lifted an edge of the map to get the flickering light more directly on it.

"Look. Back of this other beach, over here, where it isn't so steep. The distances match, if we make allowance for a current."

Slagiron swore under his breath. "This puts us
on the wrong side of the river. On top of that,
there's the marsh, and we're on the wrong side of
it, too."

"But everything fits. That second bar we hit
would have been about here. And we finally
landed here. And now, we should be—" He put
his finger on the map, back of the beach"—here."

Slagiron peered at the map. "We can't reach
Cherbourg from here. And we could get bottled
up in this hole."

"But at least," said Arakal, "we're on *land*."

"There is that," said Slagiron with feeling. "All
right. Do we try to get to the right beach? Or do we
use this one?"

"If we try to get to the right beach from here,
we'll have a mess like that fourth practice landing. There won't be any unit not mixed up with
some other unit. Just keep them coming in. And
give your account to Bullinger on paper, so if their
spy system still works, we don't tell the Russ
about this."

4.

S-One gripped the arms of his chair, looked
back at the display, then at his deputy.

"Normandy?"

"Yes, sir."

S-One glanced up.

Off Le Havre, on the display, the ships were
now swinging away, moving further out into the
bay. And now a blue marker had appeared on the
Normandy coast.

For the second time in two days, S-One felt the

world step aside, to go on without him. He kept his voice calm, as he turned to his deputy.

"Activate the deception plan."

S-Two said, a trace of anguish in his voice, "Sir, the scout team on the spot reports that the coast defense system is still undamaged. There has been no bombardment or actual penetration of the defenses."

"And?"

"We can open fire on Arakal's ships, turn the troops around in Le Havre and start them back toward Normandy."

"That will take time. How many of the enemy are already ashore?"

This time, S-Two's voice was clearly anguished: "We don't know."

"A hundred? Five thousand? Twenty thousand?"

"We can't be sure! There may have been more deception. I would guess between three and twelve thousand. But we don't *know*."

"And how many men do we still have in the Citadel?"

"Very few, sir. But until there is heavy damage, the guns can be worked by automatic control. It is a very efficient system, designed and built before the war."

S-One hesitated, and glanced at the display. Suddenly he sat straight.

"But that is not Utah Beach!"

"No, sir. They completely avoided Utah Beach."

S-One sat very still.

"In short, we have received from them nothing but misleading information?"

S-Two nodded.

S-One glanced briefly at Brusilov, who sat stolidly, saying nothing.

S-One looked back at his deputy.

"What they have done is nothing less than to use our electronic information system to lead us around by the nose." He glanced at Brusilov. "What would you do, General?"

"Roughly as your deputy suggests."

"How do you think it would work out?"

Brusilov considered the map, and shrugged.

"Who can say? No matter what we do, it could turn into an ugly mess before it's over."

S-One considered it, narrow-eyed. He turned to his deputy.

"Order the last of our troops out of the citadel. Reroute the units at Le Havre to Metz. Activate the deception plan, at once."

S-Two stiffened, gave a slight bow, and hurried out.

S-One looked at Brusilov.

"As a purely military solution, I suppose my deputy's idea has its merits. But I see now that we have to aim at more than military victory. Arakal has acted on a different level entirely." S-One paused, frowning, then looked at Brusilov curiously. "This is what you meant, when you spoke of Arakal's blows 'dislocating the mind'?"

Brusilov nodded. "This is a sample of it. And if you will excuse me for giving too much advice, I think the situation is now so dangerous that it would be better at once to hand over command to the Marshal. In my experience, the riskiest way to fight Arakal is with subtlety. In a plain straightforward fight, we can wrestle him to a standstill. He is tough, but so are we, and our weapons are better. But when the bright ideas begin to flow, look out. He has the edge, there."

S-One nodded. "I can well believe it, General. And if it were a question of a fight, I would do exactly as you suggest. But I have discarded that idea. I am not planning to fight Arakal."

Brusilov blinked. He glanced at the display. Then he looked again at S-One.

"Arakal is ashore in France, with the world's only battle fleet, and thirty-five thousand men at his back, and France by your own reckoning is a tinder box awaiting the match. *And you are not going to fight him?*"

S-One smiled. "That is correct, General."

"Then, if I may ask, Comrade, what *are* you going to do?"

"The deception plan, that I spoke of, is already in action."

VII. The Welcoming Party

1.

Arakal, by his own estimate, had four thousand men ashore, a number of machine guns, half-a-dozen small rocket launchers, and two one-pounder cannon. The sea, so calm last night, was now rough; the tide had come in, and a triple line of bright-yellow marker buoys bobbed on the churning waters of the bay. Each buoy was held by a long slender cord, its far end attached to some artillery piece that now rested on the bottom, where its raft had overturned. From his height above the beach, Arakal could look to north or south along the shore, and see the painted snouts of Russ big guns looking out to sea from turrets disguised to match the surrounding rock of the bluffs.

In both directions, Arakal could make out little groups of his men looking up at the guns, wondering perhaps how quickly the sand and rock they had fed into the snouts of the guns could be cleared out from inside if enemy gunners were in there. So far, nothing had happened. But Arakal had word of more Russ guns, these still out of his reach to north and south, but probably well able to smash ships landing troops here.

Slagiron had gone out to Bullinger, the troops already ashore were moving inland rapidly, the weather was still getting worse, fewer and fewer reinforcements were reaching the beach, and Arakal, looking down at the surf, at the sand and pebbles below, at the men staggering ashore from an overturned boat, and seeing in his mind the map and what was further inland, groped for the next unpleasant surprise.

Just then, a strongly built sergeant ran down a path from behind a clump of small trees bending in the wind. He raised his hand in a quick salute.

"Sir, we've found a way into one of the turrets!"

"Good! Where?"

"Just above here. It's a kind of vent shaft or escape hatch, planted around with brush. A steel ladder runs part way down the shaft. At the bottom of the ladder, there's a room cut in the cliff. From there, you can fire the gun."

"Any sign of the Russ?"

"No, sir. The place was empty."

"Let's get a look at this."

2.

S-Two bowed very slightly. "The deception plan is activated, sir."

S-One sighed in relief. "Good."

3.

Arakal squirmed feet-first under the upraised rock, found the ladder, eased down into the vertical shaft, and then, from below him, the sergeant called, "The gear-wheel, sir! Watch out, or you'll get caught in it."

Arakal freed his sword from the ladder rungs,

twisted sidewise, and pulled his cloak loose from the geared mechanism that raised the rock at the top of the shaft. He paused to consider this mechanism, which was free of rust, and freshly greased. Then he made his way down the ladder, to step carefully off the last rung into a sort of wide recessed archway, where the sergeant pushed open a heavy door, and then Arakal found himself amongst several of his men, in a dimly lit room perhaps forty feet across.

To the right, at the far end of the room was the gun. The breech, the massive wheeled mounting, and the tracks for the wheels, took up most of that end of the room.

To the left, in the middle of the rear wall, was an open door into what appeared to be a kind of large dumbwaiter. Several low massive tables stood nearby, and a low, heavy, wheeled cart.

Directly across from Arakal, on the opposite wall, was a detailed map of the shorefront, and, above the map, several dark grilled openings. From the high ceiling, two shiny brass tubes reached down, bearing near the lower end of each, a pair of outthrust handgrips and a set of eyepieces. Through one of these, a frowning corporal with five campaign stripes was now looking, his hands tense on the grips. Beside each of the tubes padded headsets hung down on thick black wires.

Arakal glanced across the room at the gun, to see another dangling headset, its cord hanging from an overhead bar that appeared to pivot in unison with the traverse of the gun.

Arakal's glance met the gaze of one of his soldiers, standing to the side of the gun, with a look of baffled curiosity.

Arakal took hold of the free set of handgrips, and pulled down. The shiny tube with its eyepieces slid easily down, and suddenly he was looking out at two separate views of a ship riding at anchor on a rough gray sea. He twisted the handgrips, and the images separated further. He twisted in the opposite direction, and the images merged. With a sense of shock, he recognized one of his bombardment ships, a faint slender cross superimposed on its center. As he moved the grips, changing numerals came into view below the view of the ship. With each turn of the tube or twist of the grips, came a low heavy rumble from across the room.

He tore his gaze from the eyepieces.

Across the room, the gun was now more elevated than when he had first seen it. The bar holding the upper end of the dangling headphones had swung slightly to the left.

Outside the room, in the shaft, the ladder rattled.

Near the gun, a soldier cleared his throat.

"Sir, this gun follows every move you make with that tube."

Carefully, Arakal turned the handles until he saw nothing but an unfocused view of a large-numbered buoy floating in otherwise empty water. He stepped over to the gun, examined the mechanism intently, then straightened, frowning.

At the other tube, the corporal said soberly, "This scope also controls that gun, sir. But the scope you used overrode it. There's a red button on the handle of each of these scopes."

Arakal nodded. "Don't touch it, or we could get a nasty shock. The barrel is plugged with pebbles and dirt."

"It looks as if one man could aim and fire this thing."

Arakal nodded. As he looked around, it also appeared to him that a part of the gun that he hadn't understood was an automatic loading mechanism.

From the doorway leading to the shaft, a voice called out, "Sir, we've got a funny kind of prisoner up there. You might want to see him."

Arakal went up the ladder, crawled out at the top, and found two men and a bemused corporal standing beside a slight dark figure with a large moustache, face smeared with charcoal, wearing a camouflage suit, leather boots, and a narrow red-white-and-blue armband.

The corporal said, "Listen to him a minute, sir."

Arakal nodded to the slight mustached figure, to be rewarded by a quick grin displaying a mouthful of stained teeth. The figure spoke briefly and rapidly, in French. After a moment's uncertainty, Arakal pieced together what he had said:

"Moi, je suis Pierrot. J'ai detruit les russes."

Arakal took a hard look at the slight figure. The two sentences rang in Arakal's head. "I am Pierrot. I have destroyed the Russ." Arakal thought of the gun, and of his bombardment ship in its sights. With an effort, he framed in French the question, "How did you do that?"

"It was very simple," came the answer, and, listening intently, Arakal followed as the words poured out. "Follow me and I will reveal to you the means. I am Pierrot. It is I who command the Striking Force for Independence. The Russ here are no more. You will join me in the march on Paris."

Arakal glanced around.

His men were streaming up the path from the beach, and heading inland. Dark clouds were rushing past low overhead. The trees swayed in the wind.

Arakal spoke slowly as he groped for the words:

"When you say the Russ are destroyed *here*, do you mean on this beach?"

Pierrot made a wide sweep of the hand.

"Throughout the Normandy Citadel."

"And Cherbourg?"

"Cherbourg is mine."

"You say you have destroyed all the Russ in this peninsula?"

"It is as true as that I stand before you."

Arakal strained to get the slight figure into focus.

"You *personally* destroyed them?"

Pierrot looked startled.

"Personally? But no. I am the brain of the Striking Force for Independence. I am the spirit which controls the Striking Force for Independence. The Striking Force for Independence, is, as it were, my body, and in that sense, yes, I destroyed the Russ personally. But not with my own hands. No. And those of them who are not destroyed physically are destroyed militarily. They are in desperate flight, the Russ. It is I, Pierrot, who tell you this. Throughout the Normandy Citadel, from Cherbourg to Saint Lo, from the Bay of the Seine to the Bay of Biscay, the Russ are dead or in flight."

Arakal glanced from Pierrot to the corporal, at whose collar was the small blue diamond-shaped emblem signifying that he could speak the tongue of the Kebeckers.

"Do you understand this?"

"Yes, sir. That is, I understand the words."

"You don't believe him?"

"Not the way he tells it."

"Why?"

The corporal smiled, man-to-man. "Just look at him, sir. I'll believe he's beat the Russ when I see a mouse chase a panther up a tree."

Arakal turned intently to Pierrot.

"Do you have means of transportation?"

"Everything the Russ have not fled in belongs to me. Have you need of transportation for your troops?"

"Yes."

"I, Pierrot, can provide it."

"Good. And you say you can prove the Russ are beaten here?"

"Follow me and I will show you."

"How far?"

"Down this ladder and down a hallway."

"That ladder goes down to a room, not a hallway."

"It goes down to a room and then to a hallway. I know the Russ fortifications here as I know my own hand. I saw to it that the Russ could not fire upon our allies as you approached. It is I, Pierrot,

who have struck the sword from the hand of the
Russ in their Normandy Citadel."

"Show me."

The corporal said earnestly, "Let a few of us go
along, sir. Don't trust yourself to this hero."

Arakal nodded. He glanced around, to see a
colonel crouched with a captain at the head of the
path from the beach, frowning over a map. It was,
if anything, even darker than it had been. Not far
away, thunder rumbled, as a patter of rain swept
along through the trees. Arakal turned back, to see
that the corporal had already got half-a-dozen
men together.

Arakal turned to Pierrot. "Lead the way."

Pierrot inclined his head, slid under the inclined cover, and swung easily onto the ladder.
Arakal followed, then the corporal and his men.
Below Arakal, Pierrot stepped off the ladder, and
pushed into the room.

Arakal and the rest filed in.

Pierrot reached out, took hold of the ladder,
lifted, and pulled down. The ladder ran down
with a clicking noise, to come to a sudden stop.
Pierrot stepped onto the ladder and climbed
quickly down.

Arakal followed. Pierrot stepped off, and
pushed open a heavy sliding door that led into a
wide dimly lighted corridor, which ran in a long
gradual zigzag past another door like the one they
had just stepped through.

"These doors to the right," said Pierrot, "each
lead up to a shaft coming down from a gun. Each
gun had a commander and a crew of five. The gun
could be aimed, fired, and reloaded by power,

under the control of one man. Or, if the power should be lost during an attack, the guns could be worked by hand. Both methods were practiced on a regular schedule. All this fortification was planned in advance, before the occupation that followed the Russ attack on America, and the American abandonment of Europe. When, several months ago, your fleet stood well off the shore, and examined this coast, these guns were registered on a few of your ships. But whoever commanded the ships was wary, stayed well out, and the Russ did not fire. That silent confrontation was our notice that once again America was interested in Europe, and if Europe wished to free herself, Europe must prepare to help the Americans when they returned. We have kept a watch ever since, especially along this coast. Last night, when your ships anchored in the bay, the Russ sentinels were overpowered, and our plan was put in action throughout the Citadel."

To their left were double doors, and Pierrot pushed them open.

"The mess hall for this unit of coast artillery is just down this hall."

Arakal glanced back.

Behind him, his men looked suspiciously around, their guns at the ready.

Pierrot shoved open a second set of double doors, and gave a sort of solemn bow, his expression grave.

Arakal stopped abruptly. Ahead was a large room, where at tables and on benches, green-uniformed men sprawled unmoving. The smell of vomit was overpowering. As Arakal slowly turned his head, he saw men outstretched on the floor, men who had fallen over backwards from benches and lay partly on the floor. Here and there others had dropped to the floor while carrying trays. The eyes of most of the men were open, and their expressions fixed.

Pierrot said, "Underground, here, there is protection against nearly everything—except a poisoned air supply. We considered poisoning the food, but that involves too many uncertainties. This was quick."

Arakal stepped aside, to let his men come in.

Pierrot said quietly, "Other situations in other places required other measures. Most of the Russ fled. You may, since we are nearby, care to see one more point of interest down here—the obstacle store room."

He led the way back down the hall, took out a set of keys, and opened a wide sliding door. He led the way along a corridor that seemed to run straight back into the cliff. He slid open another door.

Arakal looked into a chamber that extended back for possibly a hundred feet, and that appeared to be forty feet or so deep, vertically.

This chamber extended to the right, buttressed at intervals by thick pillars. From the ceiling dangled large hooks on chains that hung down from traveling hoists. The room was packed with stacked pyramids of welded iron, some painted a dark red, others the color of wet sand. The sharp points and edges glittered like oiled blades.

Pierrot said, "There are enough obstacles packed in these storerooms to block this whole sector of beach. These devices would force you to come at high tide and risk having the bottoms of

your landing boats ripped out, or else to come at
low tide and cross a wide flat beach on foot under
fire." He pointed to sliding doors in the back wall
of the chamber. "Back there they have elevators,
to carry these obstacles up to the loading point.
From there, they go down on tracked transporters
to the beach. They also had mines with multiple
trip-wires to plant amongst the obstacles."

Arakal said carefully, "Did they also have aircraft?"

"Aircraft? No. It is rumored that they had a
helicopter stored here somewhere. We have never
seen it."

Arakal cast a last look at the stacked obstacles,
and stepped back.

Pierrot said, "Now, you need transport?"

"We do. The sooner we can get ashore in Cherbourg, the better."

The next few hours passed in a blur, compounded of thunder and lightning, pouring rain,
countermanded orders, missing units, and bad
tempers—to end finally with the men who had
started inland from the beach settled instead on
flatcars moving through a tunnel lighted at intervals, dropping deeper and deeper, then crawling
upward to settle finally into a steady run at some
twenty to twenty-five miles an hour, with a cool
wind in their faces, and an occasional glowing
white light that appeared out of the darkness,
showed them a brief glimpse of a white concrete
pillar and curved brackets supporting conduits of
varied sizes, and then passed and faded swiftly to
a dot behind them, while, far ahead, another dim
white glow appeared.

At last, a brighter glow appeared ahead, the repeated click of the wheels on the tracks came at more and more widely spaced intervals, and then a long lighted platform pulled into view as the track leveled out. The train moved past this platform slowly, passed through a dimly lighted place where the tunnel widened, and swung around to the right where the light reflected from a dizzying pattern of tracks, and then again they were moving at twenty-five miles an hour down a tunnel lit at intervals, and then a second lighted platform pulled into view. The train of flatcars slowed and stopped.

Pierrot let go the lever in the lead flatcar, swung off a low stool, and waved to the beaming camouflage-suited men who appeared on the platform, carrying rifles and submachine guns. Here and there amongst the rapid exchange of comments that passed, Arakal caught a word or two. Then Pierrot turned to him, and spoke a little more slowly:

"This is East Fort, near St. Pierre Eglise. From here, you can contact your ships by radio. They will have to enter Cherbourg Harbor, and it would be prudent to send our pilots to bring the ships in. I trust you have interpreters?"

"Yes, we have interpreters."

"Then we must waste no time. The sooner we are on the track of the Russ, the less chance that they might recover and give serious resistance."

That same afternoon, Arakal stood on a dock in the brilliant sunlight that had followed the storm, as the main body of his troops marched in to the cheers of a crowd wild with enthusiasm.

VIII. The Tiger in the Trap

1.

S-One rose slowly behind his desk as G-One entered, then found himself waiting, as if to see whether armed troops might follow the Head of Government.

G-One smiled ironically, "The execution squad? Not yet, at any rate."

"You must admit, this is unusual."

"My motives were of the most common. I wished to find some place to talk undisturbed. And largely unobserved."

"Everything you say here will be recorded."

"I am not unaware of the fact. But the records are in whose custody?"

"To tell the truth, I don't know."

"You astound me. If I had your job, that is one of the first things I would find out."

"Then you would not have my job. One of the first things we learn is complete trust in the organization."

"Even after you are the head of it?"

"Those who judge our trust are capable judges of character. If we did not truly trust, we would be unlikely to be considered for the job."

"And if I ask you to find out?"

"You are the head of government. I will certainly obey."

"You don't say 'comply with your request'? You say 'obey'?"

S-One shrugged. "You have the authority. If you impressed me as incompetent, or dangerous to the security of the state, then my thoughts might follow a different track. But I have problems enough to do my job without seeking to obstruct you in the performance of yours."

"Shall we, then, come to the point at once?"

"And why not?"

"Very well. The military are uneasy about the situation that has come about."

S-One nodded.

"From a military viewpoint, we have a disaster on our hands."

"That bad?"

"From a military viewpoint, yes."

"And from a political viewpoint?"

"It should soon be equally bad."

G-One looked at him soberly.

"Frankness is often a great virtue. But it cannot stand alone."

"I am not attempting to cover failure. I said 'disaster', not 'failure'."

"I have to admit, to me they are certainly very close to synonymous."

"In my position, I must look beyond disaster."

"You assert a primacy of your position?"

S-One shook his head.

"I take it for granted that there can be no conflict of authority between you and me. It is a very simple situation. If you dislike me, you can remove me. But I must do my job to the best of my ability. Any explanation you want, within the limits of what is permissible, you will have."

G-One's frown had grown longer as S-One spoke.

"Comrade, what is this now if it is not a conflict of authority? You say that you will obey what I suggest within the limits of what is agreeable. This is a conflict of authority."

"Then my meaning is not clear. I am saying, you can remove me at any time. But while I am in charge, I have no choice except to do my duty to the best of my ability."

"While you are here, you will do as you choose?"

"Let me make an example. The house is on fire. You send for the firemen. The head fireman is directing the pumps and hoses when you say to him, 'I have greater authority than you. I order you to direct the stream of water not where you are directing it, but over there, where my judgement tells me that you should be directing it.' What do you expect him to do?"

"You tell me."

"If he is competent he will say, 'Either let me do my job or replace me.' He will not obey you, because he has been trained for the job, and is therefore more competent in it than you, not having had the training, may realize."

"Then you assert an expert knowledge that I cannot appreciate."

"What I am asserting is that I have reasons for my actions, even if those reasons are not yet evident."

"And these reasons are based on expertise?"

"Yes."

"Could a military man understand your reasoning?"

"It would depend on the military man. It would, however, run counter to his training."

"I repeat that the military are profoundly uneasy."

"I am not surprised. We have had already a military disaster—our ousting from France."

G-One stared at him. "I was not aware that we had been driven out as yet."

S-One smiled. "We are on the run. Next will follow the political disaster. France will rise up. Next, Arakal will attack us more deeply, as the nations of Europe rise against us."

"I will have to tell you that this plan, assuming that it is your plan, does not fill me with confidence."

"You doubtless wonder," said S-One, "how we can prosper from being overthrown."

"Yes." G-One was watching him alertly.

"The answer," said S-One, "is that, of course, none of these things will happen. The head of the firefighters must sometimes permit the fire to run on its way, in a direction which does no damage, in order to protect that which is truly valuable."

"That sounds very good. What is your actual plan?"

"If I should reveal it to you, would you tell the military?"

"That is a question of my own discretion."

"In that case, I must respectfully decline to explain. Because the military, by their actions, might nullify the effect of the plan."

"In that case," said G-One, his face darkening,

"I will regretfully have to point out to you that it is my responsibility to see that the state survives this invasion. A state cannot have two heads. You will either tell me the nature of your plan, or I will have no choice except to relieve you of authority."

S-One nodded. His voice was calm, unconcerned. "Certainly you have that authority."

G-One blinked.

S-One looked out at the garden and smiled. "Isn't it beautiful? Such floods of color."

G-One did not move.

S-One said, "What you have said is very true: 'A state cannot have two heads.' But it *can* have a head, a heart, a liver, a spinal cord— There is no conflict in such different and separate organs which complement and reinforce each other. Just so, the state can have a number of organs, which may function on different levels. I have said that you can remove me, and you can. I will offer no resistance. But let me point out what you doubtless already know. I *could* resist."

"I am aware of it."

"Yes," said S-One. "Power in a state always resides somewhere, and it does not always reside in the obvious place. You, for instance, possess the formal authority, according to the table of organization of the state. I defer to that authority. It is largely in that deference that the true power of your position resides. If you set me aside, as you can, you must then deal with another head of my department. You may set him aside—" S-One looked directly into G-One's eyes, and smiled "—if you wish. But there are circumstances in which your wish might not be truly effective.

However, if you agree to say nothing to the military, I will at once explain the deception plan to you. Believe me when I say that I have no desire to take over the formal authority of your office. There can be no such competition between us. The head must always delegate certain functions because of a simple lack of time, if nothing else. Now, do you agree to say nothing to the military?"

2.

Arakal, who detested wild celebrations, was able to see the victory party coming even before Pierrot, who had been insisting on pursuit of the Russ, suddenly announced that "the people demand a celebration."

By dint of heaping praise on Pierrot, several mayors, Slagiron, Casey and his own three dumbfounded corps commanders, and after giving a brief speech in halting French on "la liberation de la belle France," Arakal was able to make himself progressively less conspicuous; he pretended a trip to the men's room, found a side door unattended, slipped out, crossed the alley to a small white-painted hotel, and went up the steep narrow stairs to his room on the fourth floor. The guard outside the door snapped to attention—he was one of Arakal's men—and Arakal looked at him thoughtfully.

"Would you like to go to that party?"

"Well—yes, sir, I would. But—"

Arakal wrote rapidly on a small pad, tore off the paper, and wrote again on the sheet beneath.

"This first note releases you from guard duty this evening. The second is for General Slagiron.

You'll find him at the head table, surrounded by
Old Kebeck mayors in civilian clothes, and guerrillas in camouflage suits."

The guard looked thoughtful.

"Thank you, sir. But I'll be back after I give this
to General Slagiron."

Arakal, putting his key in the lock, looked up in
surprise.

"You can stay."

"I'm not too crazy about these guerrillas. And
I'd lock that door, if I were you, sir, till General
Slagiron gets here."

The guard was gone before Arakal could make
any reply. He stepped into the room, turned the
key in the lock, and paced the floor until a knock
sounded, and Slagiron's deep voice broke in on
his thoughts.

Arakal opened the door. Slagiron, one hand to
his head, smelling powerfully of wine, stepped
in.

"Thanks for getting me out of there. My God!
What if we should have to fight tomorrow?"

"According to Pierrot, the Russ are on the run."

Slagiron shut the door, and through the crack of
the closing door Arakal could see the guard take
his place outside.

"Pierrot," growled Slagiron. He glanced at
Arakal. "I'll have to give you credit for the way the
landing worked out. I thought we'd have a fight."

"Pierrot hasn't explained why we haven't?"

Slagiron thrust out his lower lip, and put his
right hand on his chest. "I am Pierrot. It is I,
Pierrot, who have enabled you, our allies, to come
ashore unharmed. It is I, Pierrot, whom the Russ
fear as a nightmare.' About that time, he got going

faster than the translator, so I don't know the details."

Arakal soberly described the big guns set into the rock face, the sighting and aiming arrangements, the obstacle storeroom, and the mess hall with its unmoving occupants.

Slagiron listened soberly.

"We seem to owe him something. But yet—"

Arakal said exasperatedly, "Do you believe his story?"

"No."

"Then what did happen?"

Slagiron said, as if trying the words to test their sound, "You tricked the Russ out of here. The rest is pure fakery."

Arakal said, "How do we account for those dead bodies?"

"Prisoners of the Russ put to death to fool us."

"They were in Russ uniform."

"More trickery."

Arakal shook his head. "It's getting too elaborate. It begins to suggest an organization as big as their army. And where's the gain?"

Slagiron thought it over and shrugged.

"Maybe Pierrot is real. But he seems fake to me."

"Where's Bullinger?"

"The last I knew, well out in the bay. He was planning to keep the bulk of the ships out of Cherbourg Harbor until he had a clearer picture."

Arakal nodded. "The catch in all this is, we're relying on someone else. If it works, all right. But—" Arakal glanced toward the door. "Our guard, out there, doesn't like the guerrillas. Since Pierrot showed up, I've had a corporal, two

sergeants, and a private, warn me offhand to keep
an eye on him, or let them stand between me and
him, or let them go along, just in case."

"He's helped us."

"Yes."

Slagiron massaged his chin. "Suppose this is a
trick? How the devil does it work? And what can
he do to gain by it?"

"*If* the Fleet had come into the harbor, conceivably
he might have captured it."

"Knowing Bullinger, that, at least, isn't likely."

"Suppose there's something they're holding
back?"

"But what?"

"I don't understand why the Russ used iron
birds against us at home but don't seem to have
them over here."

"Of all the Old Stuff from before the war, what
is there that's trickier to use or harder to maintain?
Beside that, they eat fuel like starving rats in a
grain bin. The Russ would get more value here out
of iron roads, the same as we do at home."

Arakal thought it over, then shook his head.
"There's still something out of focus."

Slagiron said, "It's been too easy. We expected a
fight. Instead, we've had the whole thing tossed in
our lap, and we don't believe it. We're sure there's
a catch somewhere. Meanwhile, we're full of at
least four different kinds of wine. It may all seem
different tomorrow."

3.

The next day, Arakal's men found themselves
up early, many still asleep on their feet, as Pierrot

warned through bullhorns in the hands of shouting translators, "We must pursue the Russ! Never, never must we give them a chance to make a stand! All France is aflame! The Russ bases throughout all Europe are under attack! Now is our chance! We must pursue them!"

Meanwhile, Arakal, stung by the experiences of the day before, had been the first up, and had delivered his message to rudely awakened generals and colonels: Each unit must be kept together. Each must be fit for combat anytime. No unnecessary reliance must be placed on the guerrillas. This picnic could end any time, possibly in some form of ambush or betrayal. But until that happened, the guerrillas must be treated with strict courtesy.

Out in the harbor, supply ships had been unloading all night, and now the admiral's flag was flying from the bombardment ship, *Panther*, whose huge guns were exciting the admiration of an enthusiastic throng. As the unloading went on, Arakal insisted to Pierrot that the supplies must go with the troops. During the delay caused by the loading of supplies, Arakal boarded a launch sent in by Admiral Bullinger, and went out to the flagship, where now the men were drilling at the guns, which swung slowly around, aimed out to sea, and fired a salvo whose crash rattled the harbor.

Arakal, smiling, met the admiral in a cabin with a bare stripped look that told of ripped-out listening devices. Bullinger was uneasy.

"I brought *Panther* in here as soon as I could. I thought you might want something visible as a token of strength."

"I'm also happy with the supplies. I don't care to depend on somebody else for food and ammunition."

"If you pursue very far, you're bound to depend on them, at least for food."

"The longer we can put that off, the better. Have you any word from Colputt?"

"A signal for you, sir. As you asked, I decoded it myself. Just a moment."

Bullinger stepped outside, and came back with a sealed envelope. Arakal pulled out the slip of paper to read: "Both platforms work. Power supply as we thought. We are sending for *Alligator*, which is just finished. Will be there as soon as possible, but can't predict time. —Colputt."

Arakal thoughtfully considered the message. *Alligator* would be their new vehicle-carrying ship.

From back toward the stern of the *Panther* came a heavy crash, a shock felt through the deckplates underfoot as well as heard.

Bullinger said mildly, "The crews need drill at the guns. And there's no harm letting it be known that we have teeth."

Arakal nodded, and folded Colputt's message into his pocket.

"When do you think *Alligator* will be ready to make the trip across?"

"Impossible to predict. We haven't made a ship of that design before. It might do anything."

"We still have this question of supplies. You remember, at the start, we considered various possibilities. If the landing failed. If we had a half-success. If we had a success in landing, but got stopped at Cherbourg. If we had full success. If the populace then rose up and threw out the Russ. But what we actually have here didn't occur to us."

Bullinger nodded.

"Yes, sir. I remember."

"We are obviously going to need to be supplied now. Can you do it?"

"I have the arrangements set up. That was taken care of before we started. It's something I can cancel, but that otherwise will take place as arranged. But what happens in Cherbourg? Will they, perhaps, eat up the supplies themselves? Or throw them in the sea? Or sell them for what the traffic will bear? I can bring the supplies to the dock. There it ends."

"I'll make arrangements for them to be sent on."

"If these guerrillas control delivery, they've got their hand at your throat."

Arakal nodded, and Bullinger growled, "It would have been a lot more convenient for us if we had fought the Russ for this place and it was ours. This business is a mess."

Bullinger's remark occurred to Arakal in the launch. It occurred to him again as he climbed onto the dock to find Slagiron waiting, and, behind Slagiron, Arakal's three corps commanders, all in evident ill humor, and two of the three apparently in none too robust health.

Arakal nodded to Slagiron, returned the salute of his officers, and said at once, "Who has an outfit we can trust to unload supplies and ship them to us by the iron road?"

Burckhardt, the burly commander of I Corps, queasily eyed the slosh of water against a nearby pier, and said nothing.

Beside Burckhardt, Simons, the well-built, pugnacious, and often profane commander of II Corps kept his mouth shut.

Arakal looked at Cesti, the slender and thoughtful III Corps commander. Cesti's right eye was half-closed, and his head was oddly tilted toward his half-closed eye. His face, like Burckhardt's, was unusually pale. Cesti met Arakal's gaze dully; other than that, he made no response.

Slagiron looked around at the corps commanders, gave a grunt, glanced at Arakal, and said, "I'd say the Beaver or Groundmole Divisions could do it, sir."

Simons, his three divisions named respectively, "Lightningbolt," "King Snake," and "Panther," nodded agreeably.

Burckhardt said, "If we get into a spot where—" He swallowed and paused a moment before going on "—where we have to dig in, we'll miss the First Division."

Arakal nodded thoughtfully. The First Division, the "Groundmoles," had yet to be thrown out of any place they had decided to hold.

Cesti said fretfully, "We may have to cross rivers."

Cesti's Beavers specialized in river crossings.

Arakal glanced at Slagiron, who, eyes slitted, gnawed briefly on his lip. "That's true. In that case, I'd say the King Snakes could do it."

Simons stared at Slagiron as if Slagiron had slapped him. He turned to Arakal.

"Sir, Second Corps is the shock troops of the Army."

"That's true," said Arakal. "But the Russ are

supposed to be already on the run. And I think the King Snakes could handle this better than anyone else. If they controlled the trains, as well as the loading, it would be better yet."

Slagiron nodded. "But can we convince Pierrot?"

"We can find out."

Simons turned back to Slagiron. "Damn it, sir, we're supposed to be here to *fight*. Without the Fifth Division, I'm cut almost to half-strength."

"Two-thirds strength," corrected Slagiron.

"There's only sixteen to seventeen percent difference between half-strength and two-thirds strength. On top of that, the artillery synchro units are with the King Snakes."

Slagiron frowned. "Nevertheless—"

"And," said Simons, "if there should be a stab in the back, the Russ may end up with those units."

Arakal and Slagiron glanced at each other.

Arakal said, "Let those units stay with the Second Corps."

"Good," said Simons. "And, since it shouldn't take much to do this job, maybe we should leave a battalion on this end to handle it."

Arakal looked at Simons' expression of obedient helpfulness. Since each of Arakal's divisions were composed of three regiments, and each regiment counted three battalions, what Simons was suggesting was that roughly *one-ninth* of the King Snake Division be left to do the job.

Arakal shook his head. "If our supplies should get cut off, it would be like slitting the throat of the whole army. We have to have a strong force here to prevent that. We can't fight the Russ while we're worried about what's going on behind our backs."

Simons looked stubbornly unconvinced, but held his peace.

Arakal glanced at Slagiron.

"Where's Pierrot?"

"I've been trying to find him. He disappeared after that early-morning harangue."

"In that case, let's get hold of the mayor. He shouldn't be any more hung over than anyone else around here."

"I don't know about that. I saw him put down almost half a bottle of that rotgut in one long pull."

Burckhardt, as Slagiron mentioned the Mayor's half-bottle, glanced desperately around. He stumbled over to the side of the pier, and bent over the edge. Cesti went in a hurry to the other side of the pier.

Slagiron shook his head. "Five days of seasickness, and then a damned drinking party. Let's hunt up the mayor."

The mayor, just outside his office, showed himself delighted that Arakal planned to leave troops in the city. He spoke enthusiastically in his own tongue:

"But that is magnificent! And would it be possible to leave someone to protect the guns?"

"Guns?" said Arakal, as Slagiron looked on with the elaborately unconcerned expression of one who understands nothing that is being said.

"The fixed artillery of the Russ," said the mayor, "in the fortifications around the city, and commanding the harbor. If bad elements should get control of them—"

"No one has control of those guns?"

"The Pierrot had suggested that I put my constabulary in charge. In the flush of enthusiasm, I agreed. But this is not practical. They are too few in number, and who, then, will do *their* work?"

"You are agreeable that my men control the defenses?"

"But, of course! That is understood. These fortifications are in the Military Zone. They are outside the jurisdiction of any civil authority in Normandy. It is natural that you control them, until they are one day turned over to the central government in Paris." He looked shrewdly at Arakal, and said, "I realize it is an extra care. But if *I* had ships which were to enter that harbor—"

Arakal bowed.

"We will do everything we can, regardless of the difficulties."

On the way back, Slagiron listened in astonishment. "This changes the whole picture."

"Let's hope Cesti and Burckhardt are still alive."

Back on the pier, the two generals, sick and miserable, listened dully.

"We could," said Burckhardt, "end up split into fragments."

Cesti was frowning. "On the other hand, this gives us a foothold. The wonder is Pierrot hasn't taken over."

"He wants to chase the Russ," said Burckhardt, "and that's the way to use your strength. What good do the men do back here?"

Slagiron glanced questioningly at Arakal.

Arakal said, "Just suppose that we're entangled with the Russ, and for some reason our supplies don't get through. Pierrot and his men melt into the scenery. They speak the language and know the country. What do we do?"

Slagiron glanced at Burckhardt, who said, "We fall back to the coast."

"With no established base here," said Arakal, "how can Bullinger even stay on this side of the ocean? Worse yet, suppose anyone but us takes over the guns?"

"Yes," said Burckhardt, frowning, "But we'll miss every man we leave here, once we're up against the Russ."

Arakal nodded. "That's undoubtedly true." He glanced out at the *Panther*, riding on the sparkling waters of the habor. He thought back on the coast defense gun, moving as he moved the aiming device.

"Well," said Arakal, "we can't hope to equal the strength of the Russ on their own side of the water. But we have a fleet, and we should soon have a base." He glanced at Burckhardt.

"We're going to need your Groundmoles with us, when we attack the Russ. And I think we'll need your Third Division. Together with Simon's Fourth, they'll keep the Russ on the run if anyone can. But pull your Second Division out of the loading plan. We're going to need them here."

"But, sir— My God! We can't—"

Slagiron said quietly, "You have your orders, General."

Burckhardt swallowed, shut his eyes, and swallowed again.

Slagiron took a fresh look at Burckhardt, and seemed surprised to find him still standing there. Slagiron's dark brows came together.

Arakal had turned to Cesti.

"Your Seventh Division is already loaded?"

"Yes, sir," said Cesti, nervously. "Well, it's loading."

Arakal, frowning, considered that Cesti's Seventh Division was nicknamed the "Nutcracker," for its stubbornness at blasting opposition loose from tough positions. The Seventh had more and heavier artillery than any other division except Cesti's Ninth, known as the "Sledgehammer Division" for the size and power of its guns.

Arakal was vaguely aware of Slagiron speaking to someone, somewhere, but the words didn't reach him. He was balancing whether to leave behind the Seventh Division or the Ninth Division.

Cesti, through some feat of telepathy, said urgently, "Sir, I think the Russ were more wary of the Ninth than of any other unit."

"What I'm thinking of is the Russ tanks," said Arakal.

"Yes, sir," said Cesti, looking relieved.

"But," said Arakal, "the Seventh can also take care of tanks, especially since Colputt got those explosive rockets worked out. And if there is anything that can get bogged down, in bad weather, it's the Ninth Division."

"Yes, sir," said Cesti, "but—"

"And it was raining yesterday," said Arakal.

"Sir," said Cesti, "our information is that the Russ are particularly strong over here in artillery."

"We're getting into that part of the year where we can expect bad weather. And there's one other reason to leave the Ninth here. They're artillery-men. We need artillerymen to handle these guns; if anything should go wrong with the power load-ing and aiming arrangements, we have no one else so well equipped to work out what to do. Moreover, if the Russ armor should attack and break through the defenses, we've got no other unit so well equipped to stop them."

Cesti nodded moodily. "I'll pull them out of the loading pattern, sir."

"The only question," said Arakal, "is whether that's enough." He turned to Slagiron, to find him, jaw outthrust, eyes narrowed, just returning the salute of a pale and shaken Burckhardt. Arakal glanced back at Cesti, returned Cesti's salute, and turned back to Slagiron, who was running a handkerchief around the inside of his collar, his eyes still narrowed.

Arakal shook his head.

"Sir?" said Slagiron.

"I'm tempted to leave Burckhardt's Third Divi-sion here, too. It would put more teeth in the defense, if we needed it."

Slagiron's jaws clamped with a look of grim pleasure, but then he shook his head.

"I don't think we'd better do it. We've got each of these divisions overstrength, for us. There are three more men in each squad, and we used to have nine-man squads. When we take one divi-sion out of each corps, that reduces our strength by a third, which brings us back not much below the strength, in men, that we had to begin with. We have one-third fewer formations, but each formation we have is one-third stronger. So if we stop there, it's not so bad as it seems."

Arakal nodded. "The overall effect is as if we had detached one division, instead of three. Well, it should keep anyone from overrunning the defenses here on the spur of the moment."

Slagiron smiled. "It should do that, all right. And it leaves us enough strength to do something with. But, of course, Burckhardt is right about one thing."

Arakal nodded. "We'll miss every man we leave behind."

IX. The Judo Master

1.

S-One turned from the brilliant colors of the enclosed court to his deputy, who said respectfully, "Sir, news of the enemy's latest dispositions." He laid the sheaf of papers on S-One's desk.

S-One glanced from the papers to the display on the opposite wall. He sat back, frowning. The fortified narrow part of the Normandy peninsula was now colored blue. Blue oblongs were moving toward Paris along the narrow lines that represented railroad tracks. Along distant extensions of these railroad tracks, red oblongs were drawing back toward the northeastern part of France.

"Hm," said S-One. "I have to admit, S-Two, that this barbarian has a nasty habit of changing his mind. When did he decide to occupy the Citadel?"

S-Two looked embarrassed. "We don't have any word on that yet, sir. The last we knew, he regarded the Citadel as definitely in Pierrot's province."

"What this means, of course, is that the Americans now have a solid foothold here. How are we

going to dislodge them from those fortifications?
They can be supplied by their Fleet, from outside.
Where is Arakal himself?"

"With the trains, sir."

"We are sure of that?"

"Yes, sir."

"That is something, at least. You realize, we
will have to make a stand somewhere in France."

"Yes, sir."

"Are we prepared?"

"Yes, sir. There is no problem in that."

"Good. Now, you perhaps are aware of a certain
disagreement between myself and the Head of
Government?"

"Yes, sir."

"I must, of course, accept his decision. But it
would be unfortunate if his decision caused any
rupture in our deception plan. It would be a help
to me, and, I think, a service to the state, if unex-
pected actions on his part could be avoided, or at
least moderated by foreknowledge."

"Certainly, sir. Our latest information is of a
meeting between the Head of Government and
Marshal Vasilevsky, General Kolbukhin, and
General Brusilov. The former plenipotentiary to
our occupation forces in America, Smirnov, has
also been briefly called in, to answer questions.
The tone of the meeting is one of intense concern.
Serious reservations have been expressed about
our actions so far."

"Our actions? Whose actions?"

"The actions carried out under your direction,
sir."

"I see. And what are their conclusions so far?"

"The marshal is confident that he can beat

Arakal, and any combination of Arakal and guerrillas. He still thinks it would have been best to
have fought Arakal shortly after he arrived."

"What does Brusilov say?"

"That you tried it, and were outmaneuvered."

S-One nodded soberly. "And Kolbukhin?"

"Kolbukhin is in favor of letting Arakal penetrate deeply, so that he can be cut off and extermi-
nated. The danger, he says, is not in Arakal winning the fight, but in his getting away, to come
back later and harass us with blows here and there
unpredictably."

"And what is the conclusion of the Head of
Government?"

"He has expressed no actual conclusion. Our
impression is that he is taking care to prepare
everything in the event that the deception plan
fails. As he does not know what the deception
plan actually is, he is under something of a handicap in forming his own plans."

"If I had told him, he might have told Brusilov,
or the Marshal. They might then have decided
whether or not to intrude. Do they know yet that
Arakal has occupied the Normandy Citadel?"

"Yes, sir."

"What is their response to that?"

"The Marshal and General Kolbukhin consider
that Arakal is a military amateur to leave so large a
proportion of his men behind. General Brusilov is
not sure. The other two joke at Brusilov's expense,
saying that Arakal could slip on a cowflop and
land in a pile of manure, and Brusilov would
suspect there was some clever plan behind it."

"And how does Brusilov respond to that?"

"He admits there is some truth in the charge,

but says it is an outlook based on experience."

S-One nodded. "Are we receiving reports from the Citadel?"

S-Two hesitated. "Yes and no. We are receiving *transmissions*."

"Ah, yes. There is a translator shortage?"

"Yes, sir. We have switched more men from the U. K. Sector. But there is still trouble with the accent of Arakal's men, and their particular choice of words. Their outlook also is sometimes difficult to grasp."

"Well, that will clear up. What about Arakal himself?"

"We are almost constantly in touch, now that he is on the train."

"Good. Bring me word of any important decisions as they are made."

2.

As the clack of the train signaled the passage of the miles, Arakal studied the map, with Pierrot at his elbow, and Slagiron across the table. Outside the window, the green countryside fled past. Arakal caught glimpses of rushing streams, shady glens, and once, in the distance, high on a hill, ruined fortifications from long ago. Pierrot, meanwhile, overflowed with words in his own tongue.

"All France is aflame," he said. "The Soviets are in flight, and we pursue them mercilessly. They flee before us, and we must not flag. Always, always, we must pursue them!"

Arakal said, "Who is the 'we' the Russ are running from?"

"The partisans. The men of the Striking Force

for Independence. The guerrilla heroes of the nation."

Slagiron studied Pierrot curiously. Unable to understand Pierrot's words, he was considering Pierrot's manner and gestures.

Arakal said, "So far, so good, then. But where are the Russ reserves?"

Pierrot put his hand on the map, forefinger outstretched. "Here, near Metz."

"How strong are they?"

"In physical size they are large important forces."

"Tanks?"

"They have nearly a hundred tanks."

"What about their artillery?"

Slagiron, recognizing the word, "artillerie", looked attentive.

Pierrot, for his part, looked thoughtful. Then he shrugged.

"I am afraid that the great Napoleon taught them a lesson at Friedland—a lesson about artillery—that they have learned only too well. Their artillery is strong and mobile. It is a terrible thing to face their artillery. We must fight in such a way as to avoid that."

Slagiron said, "What does he say?"

"That the Russ have strong reserves near Metz. Amongst other things, these reserves include nearly a hundred tanks, and strong artillery. He says we need to fight in such a way that we keep away from their artillery."

"How do we achieve that?"

Arakal turned to Pierrot.

"Have you thought of some practical means to avoid their artillery?"

Pierrot said, "My men strike unexpectedly and are gone. *Pouf!* You must do likewise. Speed, decision, the quick blow, and then away! It will not do to trade blows with an opponent made of iron."

Arakal explained this to Slagiron.

Slagiron listened without enthusiasm.

Arakal said to Pierrot, "What is the size of the Russ artillery force? How many guns, of what caliber?"

"Many guns, of all sizes."

Arakal paused, then went on.

"Any airplanes?"

Pierrot shook his head. "Their aircraft usually crash, or cause other troubles. The most recent of these aircraft that I know of flew, but when it came down to land, the wheels would not lower. These aircraft are great eaters of fuel, hard to maintain, and only of odd types left over from the past. They are not practical."

"Are the tanks new?"

"In my belief, they too are left over from the past. But they are maintained in excellent condition."

"And the guns—the artillery?"

"Some are old, some new. All are well maintained and terrible to face."

Arakal summarized for Slagiron, then looked thoughtfully at the map.

"Why pursue the Russ? They're almost out of the country."

"If we do not throw them back, they will advance."

"Why not negotiate with them? After all, they have men in Old Brunswick who are cut off from the mainland. We can allow these men to cross—we could even ferry them across—in return for the Russ going completely back over the border."

"You do not understand their way of thinking. They are masters of all Europe. They will not leave willingly. Either from here or from England."

"Then we had better plan some way to slow them up when they come back. Because what we have here right now isn't going to stop them. Especially if we have to get out of the way every time they bring up the artillery."

"Surely when your main forces come over, then we can deal with the Soviets on at least an equal basis."

Arakal said noncommittally, "What I am talking about is now."

There was a rap on the compartment door.

Arakal called, "Come in."

A corporal of Arakal's army stepped inside, holding a yellow envelope.

"Sir, a message for General Pierrot." The messenger noticeably split the name into two words: "Pier" and "rot." This, at least, was an improvement over the usual pronunciation, "Pure rot."

Arakal, pronouncing carefully, said, "Let General Pierrot have the message, then."

"Yes, sir." The corporal handed Pierrot the message. Pierrot tore it open, read rapidly, then looked up. "This is serious. The enemy is advancing toward the Meuse. He has already passed Gravelotte."

Arakal glanced at the map.

Pierrot said, "We must stop him." He scribbled

rapidly on the back of the message, sealed it, and handed it back to Arakal's corporal.

Arakal said, "Give that to General Pierrot's communications officer."

Arakal pronounced "Pierrot" carefully, so that the corporal would again have the advantage of hearing the correct pronunciation. The corporal saluted and went out.

Pierrot said, "Are we one on this? Will you join me in driving back the enemy?"

"We're willing to try," said Arakal. "But I'm not sure it will work."

Pierrot stood up. "We can only try. But we must try."

3.

S-One glanced from the report to the display. Arakal's troop trains were now beyond Paris, on the railroad line to Reims. The symbols on the display were lit, signifying that it was now night for Arakal and his men, just as it was night here, for S-One. It was night, and S-One was tired. It was well past time for bed. But S-One looked at the softly glowing blue outline around the Normandy Citadel. He glanced from the display to the latest report, to read:

". . . word from the scene, as well as indications from electronic sources, indicate that Arakal had left behind three divisions, or one-third of his force, to hold the Citadel. These troops now appear to be the 2nd, 5th, and 9th Divisions, known respectively as the Hammerclaw, King Snake, and Sledgehammer Divisions. The 9th, or Sledgehammer Division, is particularly strong in artillery, and might be considered as the heavy artillery of Arakal's army. While it is too early to provide details, indications from the scene suggest that all these troops are being intelligently used to occupy the fortifications. Although Arakal's Divisions are smaller than our own, these units appear to be about thirty percent overstrength; such is the state of automatic control of the Citadel's weapons that there seems little doubt that these troops can man the entire perimeter, while maintaining strong reserves in the interior. It must be emphasized that our experience with these units in America has been unfortunate. The Sledgehammer Division, in particular, is capable of delivering the heaviest sort of blow. The troops in Brusilov's army customarily referred to this division as 'The Scrap Man', from the effect of its heavy artillery on our armored units. It must further be noted that the terrain within the Citadel is ideal for defense, and unfavorable for armor. . . ."

S-One glanced up from the report, and delivered himself of a low oath. "The Scrap Man." Who could have expected Arakal to leave this powerhouse behind him? Somewhere in the report, a similar paean of praise appeared for the "King Snake" Division. S-One had no trouble remembering it: ". . . this division appears to serve as a general repository for the most adventurous spirits of Arakal's army. Its name is derived from the zoology of America, where the most dangerous commonly known reptile is the rattlesnake; the king snake kills rattlesnakes . . ."

S-One exhaled a deep breath. The Hammerclaw Division, he had read in here somewhere, was known for its ability to rip out stubborn opposition. The report acknowledged the division's toughness, but considered it only average for Arakal's troops. S-One did not know if this was good or bad, since the report conceded that the Hammerclaw Division was "extremely tough, resourceful, and efficient." If that was the average for the army as a whole, what were the two other divisions in the Citadel like?

S-One sat back, scowling. Brusilov had warned him that "dislocation" followed from the blows of this barbarian. S-One was aware that he was now suffering from a particularly bad case of dislocation. He had no doubt that if he turned the Marshal loose on Arakal, the Marshal would smash him, and then, one way or another, batter his way into the Citadel, provided only that enough troops were put at his disposal. But it would be done at the price of a casualty list S-One did not wish to contemplate, and it might well lead to a continental upheaval even the Marshal would be unable to put down. Meanwhile, Arakal's fleet was loose, and the United Kingdom might well settle accounts with the comparatively small force of troops stationed there, who could be reinforced only by droplets sneaked across in the teeth of a blockade. The Marshal could do nothing about that, and the ultimate outcome was unpredictable. And all this mess followed from Arakal's control of the Citadel. Without that, his fleet would have no nearby base from which it could maintain

a blockade. Without that, these divisions left behind in the Citadel would be with Arakal, where,
however tough, they could be gotten at. *Pierrot*
should control those guns!

How the devil had this oversight come about?

S-One shook his head. Somehow, those divisions were going to have to be manipulated out of
that fortress, before they wrecked everything.

Frowning, S-One sat back, looked at the display, and picked up the interoffice phone.

"S-Two?"

"Sir?"

"We will have to accelerate the attack on Arakal
and Pierrot. We will also need to reinforce it."

There was brief silence, then S-Two's response,
obedient but startled:

"Yes, sir. I'll be right in."

4.

Arakal came awake to a scream of metal on
metal, the blast of a whistle, a sudden jolt, and
then, as a deafening roar died away, there came
the crash of breaking glass, the whine of bullets,
and a white glare that lit the inside of the compartment, to show Slagiron stretched out on the
opposite seat, automatic in hand, sighting into the
glare outside. Arakal barely glimpsed this as he
rolled off the bench onto the floor of the compartment. The floor bucked beneath him, there was a
sense of the world turning over, and then he was
struck as by a heavy club.

Arakal came to in a motionless quiet, to hear the
tinkle of glass, and then a distant hammer of
machine-gun fire. Around him, there was a faint

gray light. Slagiron was gone, and the door into the corridor open. From somewhere came a remote sound of shouting. An instant later, there was a fresh hammer of gunfire.

Carefully, Arakal rolled to his feet.

Outside, the corridor was empty. The air was thick with an unfamiliar pungent smell, and the smell of burnt wood. Arakal eased open the door of the compartment across the way, and, staying well back, looked out the broken window. Abruptly, he caught his breath.

Down below, facing toward the railroad car, Slagiron, Casey, Pierrot, and several other officers stood with raised hands before four olive-uniformed men cradling what Arakal's men called "bullet-eaters," from their appetite for ammunition, and what others called "tommy-guns." The helmets of the four men below were easily enough recognizable as Russ. Arakal loosened his sword, and looked up.

Both sections of glass in the window were broken, with shards and splinters adhering around a cracked and charred wooden frame, and in a fragile line of shattered blackened wood and glittering splinters across the center.

Arakal freed himself of his cumbersome cloak, quietly drew his sword, studied the men below intently, and drew a deep breath. Suddenly he was through the window, conscious of a burning scrape across his chest and arms. He yelled, and his voice came out high-pitched, an unnatural scream that seemed to come from everywhere at once, as if it had no single point of origin. Then he was living in fractions of seconds, both hands gripping the sword hilt, his mind a maze of an-

gles, inertia, and vulnerable points, of the soft un-
resisting parts of the bodies that had to be struck,
and the hard metal that was to be avoided. Before
his gaze, the living soldiers of the enemy dissolved in a butchery so sudden that only the last
managed to turn and fire. Then Arakal, his gaze
suddenly watery, his ears ringing, could hear
Slagiron's voice shouting orders, could hear the
sudden sharp crack of an O'Cracy rifle, and he fell
into blackness with a sense of harsh gratification
that was finally translated into a stinging sharp
pain, a sense of fire burning across his chest, a
soreness and a weakness, and a male voice saying,
"That's the last of the stitches. Move that light
back before we upset it."

Arakal opened his eyes, to meet a hard blue
gaze that studied him alertly. He was lying on his
back on a flat padded table under a dark canvas
tent on which drummed a steady heavy rain. The
tent was lit by small globular lights that gave an
intense white glow. One of these, as he watched,
began to turn dark. A thin stream of smoke wavered up. A slim girlish hand reached out from
behind Arakal's head, as if to adjust the lamp—
and then hesitated. Absently, the surgeon reached
over and adjusted the light. Arakal glanced at the
surgeon. His voice was a whisper, and he had to
try again.

"Can I get up?"

"How do you feel?"

"I don't know."

"I've just dug one bullet and a shell fragment
out of you, and God alone knows how many splinters of glass. You've lost a good deal of blood, and

you have bruises all over your body. If you want to try to get up, I can't stop you; but take it slow."

Arakal rested his hands on the side of the cot, tried to swing his feet over the edge, and the room faded out. He was vaguely conscious of the thud of his head falling back against the pad. He came to, looking up at the canvas. The surgeon shook his head.

"Better get some rest."

"Where are we?"

"That I don't know. Somewhere in Old Kebeck, about a mile from the iron road."

"What happened?"

The surgeon looked at him, frowning. "You've forgotten?"

"I remember going to sleep, waking up when the train was stopped, and jumping through a window to fight some Russ. After that, I must have passed out. What's the situation?"

The surgeon shook his head. "I'll get someone who can give you a better account than I can."

Arakal lay back, and a cool, soft hand rested on his forehead, and remained there a moment. He looked up at a vision of milk-white skin, blue eyes, and soft golden hair. This vision smiled down at him, then the ruby-red lips parted, and a sweet, soothing voice spoke softly, in the accents of Old Kebeck. Arakal's mind belatedly translated the words, so that at first they were a strange and incomprehensible murmur in a delightful voice, and then they came across clearly, the meaning obscuring the voice:

"Qu'un sang impur abreuve nos sillons."

"Let an impure blood soak our furrows."

The sound of rain grew briefly louder, and Slagiron stepped in, looked gravely toward Arakal, and raised his hand in salute. Arakal saw the movement, out of the corner of his eye, but his gaze was fixed intently on the blue and gold vision above him. Like everyone else in his army, Arakal felt protective toward the nurses. But this girl was not one of them. He saw her blink in momentary confusion, then smile. The smile was delightful. But this was no one he had seen before.

Arakal said, "Is anyone else waiting for the surgeon?"

She shook her head, and spoke clearly, but with a slight and pleasant accent. "No, sir."

"Good." Arakal glanced at Slagiron. "What's the situation?"

Slagiron said, "We're in rolling low hills. There's a forest in the distance, across a river. We're dug in amongst the hills, overlooking the river and the iron road. The iron road crosses the river not far from here. Near that bridge, on the side away from us, there's a second bridge that carries a highway across the river."

"Where are the Russ?"

"They've got a bridgehead that takes in this end of both bridges, and the last we saw before the rain started, they were bringing up reinforcements on the other side of the river."

"How deep is the Russ bridgehead?"

"I'd say about six hundred yards."

"Much artillery?"

"Not on this side. It's practically hub-to-hub across the river."

"Are we all here?"

"Except for the men we left back around Cherbourg."

"None of our trains were shunted onto any other track?"

"No, sir."

"Where's Pierrot?"

"Gone."

"Gone where?"

"That's something we don't know. His whole outfit ran for it while we were fighting the Russ."

Arakal glanced absently at the girl, then looked back at Slagiron. "This leaves us with the iron road solidly blocked with trains reaching back how far?"

"We sent the trains back."

"Good. Now, what happened? The Russ blew up the tracks? Then hit us?"

"It's the only thing that seems to make sense, but it doesn't make sense. Our information from Pierrot on the location of the Russ was wrong, and the way we walked into that trap, we should have been hurt a lot worse. The first thing I knew, there was an explosion. I have a vague memory of taking a shot at something—at someone with his arm back to sling something. The next thing I knew, the train was stopped, and I jumped down, to see what was going on. It was just getting light. Casey came out, in as much of a daze as I was, and the natural thing happened. Some Russ with bullet-eaters turned up, and surprised us. I was damning myself for being so stupid when, from down the line of cars I heard someone shout, "We have your leaders. Come out with your hands raised." Just then, you came through the window, landed al-

most on the back of the first Russ soldier, finished
him, and tore into the rest. At practically the same
time, down the line, all hell broke loose. Right
then, Pierrot took to his heels. It was all over in a
minute. The Russ had some machine-guns back
from the tracks, but they weren't dug in, and our
men picked off their gunners. That was all there
was to it. As nearly as I can figure it, they blocked
the track, then blew up the embankment beside
the track, using a charge too weak to really damage the train. Well, maybe somehow that was
somebody's mistake. But then they've got artillery
enough near here. Why not bombard the train
when it was stopped? Next, why tell men to come
out, when they're still armed? Why not at least
dig in the machine-guns, and then, when we're
stopped, just open fire?"

"Or," said Arakal, "let us start to cross the river,
then blow up the bridge when we're on it?"

Slagiron nodded. "They could have done any
number of things. This business makes no sense.
It was planned. But it was planned wrong."

Arakal said, "Ease me up, if you can. The last
time I tried, I passed out."

Slagiron put an arm behind Arakal's back, and
lifted carefully.

This time, with only a dizzy throb in the head,
Arakal found himself sitting on the table, his feet
over the edge. He sat still a moment, listening to
the pouring rain. He hurt all over, and his left leg
throbbed painfully. But he felt no overpowering
weakness. He had felt worse than this on the ship.
He glanced around, to see the nurse watching
him. He cleared his throat.

"My uniform?"

She looked around, and handed him a pile of crumpled, badly torn, wet and bloody garments. The left leg of the trousers had been cut off, and the remnants included in the pile.

As Arakal, partly supported by Slagiron, put on the remains of his uniform, he saw his sword in its scabbard in the corner of the tent, and buckled it on.

Slagiron said, "We'll have a fresh uniform for you, sir."

Arakal nodded his thanks, then realized with a shock that he had been overlooking something. He glanced at Slagiron, and, briefly, his voice was harsh.

"How many killed?"

"We lost three killed, twenty-seven wounded. Mostly when their machine-guns first opened up."

Arakal blinked. "And how many of the Russ?"

"I'd say around thirty or forty. Some may just have been wounded, and gotten away, or been picked up by their own people, afterward. It was all over quick, and they never had men enough there to win it, anyway."

Arakal was thinking back to that brief moment when he had seen the Russ holding his officers captive. He shook his head.

"We will still have to bury the dead."

Slagiron nodded. "But not just now."

Arakal pulled open the flap of the tent. The rain was coming down so hard that at a glance it seemed a good question whether there was more air outside, or more water. "No," he said, "we can't dig in that." He shut the tent flap. "There's a command tent near here?"

Slagiron permitted himself a faint smile.

"We're with the First Division, sir."

"Ah," said Arakal. He glanced at the girl. "You can take care of these lamps?"

She nodded.

Arakal turned to Slagiron. "I don't dare try to run. Go ahead if you want. I'll be right behind you."

"No, I'll go with you, sir. Watch your step."

5.

S-One rested his eyes on the garden, then looked back at the report. Lack of sleep the night before did nothing to improve his mood now. He tossed the report onto the desk, and sat back, frowning. The situation summarized in the report was by no means the worst that it might be. But there were touches in it that did nothing to ease his sense of discomfort:

". . . this moment the enemy commander tore his way out through the broken window of the railway car, sword in hand, and, moving with indescribable rapidity, killed four of our men armed with submachine guns. It is believed that one shot was let off, but it is not certain if anyone was hit . . ."

S-One considered first the words, "the enemy commander tore his way out the window of the railway car, sword in hand . . ." Here, he told himself, were four men armed with submachine guns. Supposedly, they all must have had their backs to the train. That was a serious error in itself. But there were *four* of them. With this *sword*, he dispatched four men armed with submachine guns?

One bullet only, from any of those guns, would stop and perhaps kill him. And right there was another miscalculation. Considering the special orders given, how had it come about that Arakal was in physical danger in an operation designed to shock, not kill him? It could only be that he was traveling near the head of the train, when any sensible commander would be further back. No word of this important fact had been reported in advance.

Next, there was the behavior of the enemy troops. Stunned, caught at the earliest light of dawn in the sights of machine guns supposedly dug in, from inside of the wrecked train they had opened fire with such murderous accuracy that it was all over in a few minutes. What did the report say? ". . . accuracy of fire was such as to suggest that the weapons were equipped with special sights for night fighting . . ."

Now, here were these barbarians, clearly less advanced than their opponents, who had stopped them for the administration of a swift bloody nose, followed by quick withdrawal. But their opponents, reporting the disastrous outcome, attributed superior technological skills to the barbarians to explain away what had happened.

S-One shook his head, put the report in his desk, and took out a slightly slimmer report, which omitted all mention of the special instructions, and treated only the strictly military aspects of the clash. He called in General Brusilov, handed him this second report and sat back to watch him read it.

When, at last, he saw Brusilov's eyes widen, then narrow, S-One said, "You didn't tell me Arakal had supernatural powers."

Brusilov looked up, frowning, then his face cleared. "Oh, you mean his prowess as a fighter? That isn't what bothers me. What bothers me is the depth of this bridgehead, and that apparently it's Arakal who has the high ground. They're underestimating him again. Let them either give up the bridgehead, or else expand it. But whatever they do, do it *quick*. This isn't going to work."

"But that he should jump out this window, and kill four men before they can react—"

Brusilov shook his head. "It doesn't matter to me if he can bite steel-jacketed bullets in half with his teeth. Pump two or three shots into him in the right place, and that's all over with. You make a man desperate enough, and if he's in good physical shape, you'll be surprised what he can do. That's neither here nor there. But these dispositions are an invitation to ruin. That *matters*."

"What's wrong with them?"

"That bridgehead isn't deep enough. Arakal can put the bridges under a murderous fire. We can't reinforce the men on his side of the river without running a gauntlet."

"You think he might destroy the bridges, and capture the men on that side of the river?"

"No, that is what I might have been afraid of once. But I've had experience of him. That is *not* it."

"Well, then, what?"

"What if he does *not* destroy the bridges?"

"Then we can reinforce."

"We can?"

"Why not? We have the bridges. And we have artillery such that not only can Arakal be placed under fire where he is, and his own artillery smothered, but if he attempts to attack the bridgehead, we can intervene in that fight, too, with our artillery fire." S-One sat back, thinking over the arrangements, and finding that everything seemed to hold together. "You see," he said, "Arakal must be made to feel his lack of the so-called Sledgehammer Division, by opposing to him an overwhelming force of artillery, and placing him at a disadvantage. Then he will send for that division. *That* will remove it from Cherbourg and the Normandy Citadel."

Brusilov sat still a moment, then looked at S-One.

"We are now making our dispositions in order to lead *him* to undo *his* dispositions, previously arrived at?"

"Yes," said S-One. "In judo, the opponent is placed off-balance. In seeking to recover his balance, he is led to make the misstep that we aim at, and that enables us to further put him off-balance."

"Is the marshal in command of our troops at that river?"

S-One looked startled. "Of course not."

Brusilov shook his head.

"Possibly I am mistaken. But I have already seen the result of one such clever plan. That is why I am here now, instead of in America."

S-One smiled, and Brusilov stiffened at the peculiar snakelike quality of the smile.

S-One said, "This is not the only provision we have made."

6.

Arakal, in a deep exhausted sleep, breathing the cool fresh air somehow led into the bunker by the craft of the Groundmole Division, turned restlessly as his hearing, somewhat blunted by too much exposure to loud and continuous sounds, nevertheless detected a rustle, as of silk, that was alien to his surroundings.

The cool air brought to his nostrils a faint delicious perfume.

Arakal was suddenly wide awake.

In the darkness, something came closer.

X. The Battle

1.

Arakal, partly upright on the cot, heard the rustle of cloth, and then another sound—a faint creaking from several directions around him. He was able to identify this second sound, but the sliding murmur of cloth and the perfume were something else. Carefully, he folded back the blankets, groped along the frame of the cot, felt the hard curve of wire he was searching for, unhooked it, held it out to the side and up, and squeezed the handles.

In the flicker of the spark-light, against the background of fitted logs that formed the walls of the bunker, stood a girl, her skin milk-white, her hair golden, her figure accentuated by the clinging brief dark net that she wore, her face frozen in shock as she blinked around at the dozen or so men, their faces in shadow, some of whom sat up on cots or peered out of bedrolls on the floor, some halfway to their feet, two partway to her, their hands gripping weapons unrecognizable in the brief light.

Arakal squeezed the handles again, saw the girl's look change to horror, recognized her face, and said, "I think this is supposed to be a nurse. But how did she get in here?"

In a cot to Arakal's left, the division commander, a burly muscular man with head shaped in flat planes suggestive of a gun turret, stared at the girl, then bawled, "Guards!"

From above came a thud, a shout, a sound of boots.

To Arakal's right, someone lighted a lamp, and its intense white light lit up the girl, the room of watching men, and the startled guard who appeared at the door.

"Sir!" the guard saluted.

His commanding officer said drily, "You're the one who let this in?"

"I— Sir, I let a nurse in here about five minutes ago." He stared at the paralyzed girl. "She said she was here to give the chief some medicine. I said this was the right place, and to go down and light the lamp in the hall before going in. She sure wasn't dressed like that when I saw her."

"There are some clothes on the floor over there. See if there's a weapon with them."

The girl looked up, startled, but said nothing. She bowed her head, clasped her arms across her breasts.

"No weapons here, sir," said the guard. "A couple of pill boxes, and a brown bottle. That's—"

From outside came a muffled crash. The room jumped. The light flickered. The girl shut her eyes.

The guard raised his voice. "Nothing in the line of a weapon, sir. Unless it's on the girl herself."

"Give her those clothes to put on, and take her

to the chief of nurses to be searched. Now get her out of here." He turned to Arakal, and gave a fleeting smile. "Sorry to interfere with medical treatment, sir."

Arakal, listening to the crash and roar, nodded with an absent smile. As the guard led the girl out of the room, he and his officers got up, and hurriedly reached for their clothes.

· The bombardment abruptly ended.

Arakal was trying to ignore the soreness of his left leg as he dressed. Around him, the room was alternately light and dark as men stepped in front of the lamp, then stepped aside, and their huge shadows leaped across the walls and ceiling. There were the sounds of cloth, leather, the stamping of boots, the snapping of holster flaps—and all sounded loud in the sudden quiet.

In the hall outside, someone lit the lamp.

Arakal adjusted the shoulder strap that supported his sword, and then they went up the stairs, stumbled on a loose step, turned a sharp corner, went up more steps, and pushed past a heavy hanging made of overlapping metal scales sewn onto a leather backing. The air outside was fresh and chill, the wind blowing from them toward the Russ. The sky was dark, with no stars in sight. Around them, in the quiet, there was a faint stir and creak as men and officers tried to guess what might happen next.

The silence stretched out.

Then there was a squelching of boots in mud, the stamp of feet on wood, and a shadowy figure approached, paused, and a deep voice said, "General Mason?"

Beside Arakal, the division commander said, "Here."

"Corporal Givens, sir, from Watch. We've got word from all the listening posts. There isn't a damned thing moving over there, sir."

"The Russ are quiet?"

"Like a graveyard."

Mason turned to Arakal. "Shall we send them a little something, sir?"

"Save it until we can see them," said Arakal. "If they want to waste ammunition, that's their business."

"Right. They always were a little prodigal of it."

Nothing further developing, they went back to bed, though a few muttered exclamations preceded the sleep.

The bunker jumped.

A muffled crash and roar reached them, slightly louder now and then as something struck nearby. An acrid odor came down the vent shaft. Across the room, a protesting voice said, "I liked the way we got woken up the *last* time."

Arakal lay still, waiting.

Mason swore.

The bombardment stopped.

A little later, there was a sound of feet on the steps, a bang, and a low curse.

Mason's voice said, "Watch?"

"Sir. Givens. Same damned thing as the last time."

"All right. Watch it on those steps. The second slab from the bottom is loose."

"I already found it, sir."

There was the sound of feet retreating up the

steps, and Mason turned to Arakal. "If you want, sir, we can wait half an hour and open up the sky. I have the impression they don't appreciate our guns yet."

"Let them waste their own ammunition. We have to bring ours further."

There was another sound of approaching feet on the steps, and, this time, a dim light. A lantern appeared, casting its glow on the floor and the smooth log walls. The lantern lit the uniform of an officer whose face was unrecognizable in the shadow cast upward by the rain-shield of the lantern. A male voice said, "Wait right there. I'll check."

To Arakal's left, General Mason spoke sharply. "We're all awake here. Who is it?"

"Rabeck sir, Colonel, B Regiment. And the chief of nurses, sir. I offered to bring her over."

"Sorry, Rabeck. I didn't recognize your voice."

"We're all a little deaf tonight, sir."

"What does the chief of nurses have for us?"

A slender dark-haired woman, her facial expression severe, stepped into the edge of the lantern light. "Possibly what I say should be said only to the king."

Arakal said, "There's no time for that. Just go ahead."

"The girl claims you arranged for a meeting with her."

"When did I do this?"

"After the surgeon left, when your wounds had been dressed."

"I suppose I had the chance, when the surgeon went out to get General Slagiron. I'm afraid I didn't think of it. What else?"

"There's a considerable amount, which I don't want to repeat."

"What's the substance of it?"

"She claims that you assaulted her, to condense a long detailed account."

"What else?"

"That is the substance of it."

"Now, Chief Nurse, perhaps you can explain something to me."

"Sir?"

"Where did this girl come from? I never saw her before. If I'm not mistaken, it's your responsibility to have trustworthy nurses."

"I—she volunteered in Cherbourg. She said she was from Old Brunswick, in Cherbourg for a visit. I thought we would need extra nurses, and gladly took her on. She worked hard. She seems capable."

"You think a nurse is capable who tells a story that a wounded man just out from under the anesthetic, unable to sit up, was chasing her around the tent?"

"Well, I— She didn't say *that*."

"The *details* were different?"

"Well . . . men . . . everybody knows—"

"Take her over to Jinks," said Arakal shortly, "and find out what's behind this. Tell Jinks not to destroy her looks if he can avoid it. As for you, Chief Nurse, if any more volunteer nurses show up, report the matter, and see to it there is some part of their uniform that at least shows us they are not our own people."

The chief nurse said stubbornly, "I don't think Captain Jinks should be allowed—"

Arakal sat up, vaguely conscious of the sudden silence, where before there had been low murmurs, and an occassional ribald comment.

Arakal's voice grated. "Captain Jinks has the ability to listen to a liar, and not be angry. Where I or one of my officers might forget ourselves, and later regret it, the captain shakes his head and cautiously increases the pain. She is much safer telling lies to him than to me. Now get out of here. And if that pretty liar is not delivered by you to Captain Jinks, you will answer for it with your head!"

The chief nurse drew in her breath. "Yes, sir."

General Mason said, "Light her way, Rabeck."

"Yes, sir."

Arakal settled back. His leg throbbed, his head was swimming. His muscles were sore, and he felt as if he had been gone over with coarse sandpaper, all over his chest and back. But in the mind of the chief nurse, he was a man, men were unreliable, and that concluded the matter.

To the right of his cot, over near the wall, someone was laughing in a low voice about the chief nurse being an old maid, and delivering unutterable comments about this fact, and the reason for it, and suddenly the accumulated exhaustion outweighed Arakal's irritation, and he was falling into a darkness that swallowed him, removing the blonde girl, the chief nurse, the Russ, and all else around him, so that there was nothing left but the soft deep blackness.

There was a roar, a heavy smash, an explosion that lifted, then dropped him. There was, interlaced with this, a faint whine, somehow muffled, that grew slowly louder like an approaching mosquito, then blew up in his face. Arakal opened his eyes in the darkness.

The bombardment ended.

Mason's voice said quietly, "Sir?"

Arakal growled, "What?"

"We can teach these people something."

"We'll use our own method when we do it, not theirs."

Someone murmured to a snarling neighbor, "Don't move around, just keep your eyes shut, and you can go right back to sleep."

Arakal, with the same thought, was lying back on the cot. He felt himself begin to drift off.

The bunker shook to a heavy crash.

Arakal sat up carefully.

Now everything was quiet.

There came the sound of footsteps running down into the bunker.

General Mason snarled, "Watch?"

"Yes, sir. Givens. It's the same thing again. Except I got thrown about fifteen feet by that last one. I wasn't expecting that one."

"You hurt?"

"No sir. There was stuff whining past pretty close, that's all."

"The bastards think they're cute. Good luck going back."

"Thank you, sir."

"Watch that step."

There was a thud, and Givens snarled, "Damn it! Yes, sir."

Arakal lay back, felt the room seem to swirl around him, and then there was a heavy crash, a whine, a sound as of fast trains thundering closer on an iron road built in the sky, and then there was

a crash that shook the earth—and then there was
silence. The silence stretched out, and then vanished in a bombardment heavier than what had
gone before. At last, that came to an end.

Arakal rolled over and went back to sleep.

During the night, which seemed to go on
forever, he came awake from time to time, conscious of noise and shock, and then fell asleep
again. Eventually he woke with someone shaking
him gently.

"Four-thirty, sir."

Arakal came wide awake. His leg hurt, and he
was sore more or less everywhere. But he felt as if
he had had part of a night's rest. He remembered
with pleasure that he was with the First Division.

"Where," he asked, "is the washroom?"

"Out the door and to your right, sir."

Arakal gathered his clothes together, and
limped off to get washed. Behind him, in order of
rank, the other officers were being woken up. In
the washroom, the incredible luxury of a bucket of
hot water and soap, with fresh towels, was waiting. In the Groundmole Division, no one had to
wash out of a helmet.

Arakal had a hot breakfast, and thirty minutes
later, he, Slagiron, and Casey were in the head-
quarters bunker, hunched over a map with the
three corps commanders.

2.

S-One, still a little sleepy, but with a good
breakfast inside of him, entered his suite of offices
the back way, walked down the hall past a guard
who snapped to attention, and entered his own
office. The window was up, to admit the pleasant

morning air of the courtyard. The desk and all the
furniture had been dusted, and the room had been
cleaned till it shone. S-One settled comfortably
into his chair, then looked with foreboding at the
display across the room.

So far, nothing seemed to have happened. The
bridgehead appeared as it had been, the position
on the near side of the river looked the same, and
the position held by Arakal and his men seemed
as it had the last time he had seen it. The only sign
of motion was a train, symbolized by a blue rectangle, that backed away down the black line
representing the track.

S-One caught himself breathing a sigh of relief.
It came to him that the mental domination that
had been inflicted on Brusilov had, to no small
degree, also begun to affect him. Frowning, S-One
considered this, then remembered that he had
invited Brusilov to be here this morning. He
glanced at the clock on the wall. A little after
seven-thirty. He glanced at the display, where
small figures read "0531." He had that advantage.
He had a longer time to sleep. And, he thought,
smiling slightly, he had slept better.

He glanced across the room again at the display,
and, at that moment, S-Two informed him that
General Brusilov had arrived.

"Send him in," said S-One.

Brusilov, looking as if he had slept badly, came
in.

S-One smiled, "Now, General, we will see how
this Arakal of yours performs against a force
superior in artillery."

Brusilov looked at the display, and winced.

S-One frowned. "What's wrong?"

"The bridgehead still isn't deep enough."

"That's a minor point. The main thing is the artillery. There is a dis—" S-One paused, staring at the display. He had been about to say that there was a disproportion between the artillery on both sides such that any minor element in the positions of the two forces was completely outweighed, and besides, the position of the forces in the bridgehead, and behind the river, struck him as superior to Arakal's position. But before he could complete the sentence, the display lit up dazzlingly.

Brusilov said, "How is this controlled?"

S-One, leaning forward, watched the flashes amongst the artillery positions on the near or easternmost side of the river. Evidently, Arakal's artillery was firing, firing with a murderous incredible rapidity, and these flashes represented the result of the firing. Suddenly, he saw the point of Brusilov's question, and called in S-Two.

"Sir?"

"How is this display controlled? For instance, we see flashes of light. They represent explosions, isn't that correct?"

S-Two blinked at the display.

"Yes, sir."

"All right. Now, how is this done? Do we have people attached to the various units, who report the attack? Obviously—"

S-Two shook his head.

"No, sir. That was true in the case of the Normandy Citadel. Our agents reported what happened, and it was shown on the display as a change of color, representing a change in the occupying power. But it is not true here. In the height of battle, those arrangements for reporting the outcome of the fight could easily be hit."

"That is my point. How do we know that this picture is accurate? What method is used?"

"This particular display is controlled by a remnant of what used to be known as the Satellite Battle Reporting System. The details are highly technical. But the idea is that satellites overhead detect heat and light, or other electromagnetic impulses, report them by what is left of the communications network to the Battle Reporting Computer, which interprets the data furnished to it, and shows it on this display."

S-One glanced at the display, then at Brusilov. Brusilov was looking wide-eyed at the display.

S-One turned to S-Two. "This is from before the war?"

"Yes, sir."

"Do the Americans have any such system as this?"

"To the best of our knowledge, the ground part of their system was completely destroyed. The satellite part may still be functional. As far as we know, Arakal has no access to any such system as this. But the Americans were a capable technological people, and of course realized the force of the attack that their system might be subject to. We can never be sure that, somewhere, there may not be a ground display station, heavily protected, that is still functional. We have often felt concern lest Arakal stumble on some formidable weapon left over from that war, and still functional, and it could happen."

"But Arakal, so far as we know, could not have

any such device as this with him?"

"No, sir."

S-One nodded, and turned, frowning, to look back at the display.

Brusilov tore his gaze from the screen. "What if there should be a heavy overcast. Will this still work?"

S-Two replied, "There is a sort of mist-like appearance on the surface of the display; through this the visual representation appears more or less blurred. This is to indicate some decline in reliability. A legend appears to the side of the display to explain the cause of the blurring."

"What we see now, when the display is clear, is an actual visual representation of what is happening?"

"In effect, sir. But it is actually a computer reconstruction of signals picked up by satellite. It is therefore theoretically subject to error in the satellite detection, the transmission, or the computer reconstruction."

"But these errors are infrequent?"

"So far as we know, very infrequent."

After S-Two had left the room, Brusilov stared at the display, which now showed many flashes on both sides of the river. After a moment, Brusilov looked up, frowning.

"Who is in charge?"

"General Andronov."

"Andronov? I don't know him."

"He is one of ours," said S-One. "He is a security officer."

Brusilov stared at S-One, then looked back at the display. "He is getting beaten. We have underestimated Arakal's artillery."

"Surely," said S-One, "it is too early to know that."

"It is altogether too early to know it. But now that we understand that this display is not just a stylized representation, already we can see the outlines. Look at the fire of the two sides. Who is being hit the heaviest?"

The display showed an almost continuous overlapping series of flashes on the eastern side of the display, across the river from Arakal's army. On the side of Arakal's army, the number of flashes was dwindling. And now, as they watched, the flashes began to shift, very slowly but clearly, increasingly hitting the bridgehead. These flashes, the visible signs of hits by Arakal's artillery, continued heavy, while the opposing artillery fire became lighter and lighter; though never dying out entirely, it was clearly dominated by Arakal's artillery. Now a sort of blue shading began to move forward, against the northern edge of the bridgehead, which was outlined in red. As if it were a lump of sugar dissolving in warm water, the red swirled, faded, and dissolved, and the blue moved in. The intense flashing was now almost all on the west side of the river, in the bridgehead. Now, as they watched, a red shading began to move across the bridge, flowing into the bridgehead.

"Ah," said S-One, in a tone of relief, "at last. Reinforcements."

Brusilov straightened. His right hand gripped the edge of his chair. A flash appeared on the railroad bridge, where some of the red shading was coming across. A flash appeared on the highway bridge, where a heavier shading of red was crossing into the bridgehead. The flashes increased in intensity. Still, the red shading came on. Time passed. Now the flashes striking Arakal's positions increased. Abruptly, the fire on the bridges and into the bridgehead ceased, there was a brief delay, then suddenly the east bank of the river lit up in bright flashes, not uniformly spaced, but rapid repreating flashes centered on the same or nearly the same points.

S-One stared. Brusilov came halfway up out of his chair.

The brilliant display ended, leaving an impression of blackness on certain points of the screen, by contrast. Now, again, the flashes lit the two bridges, and began walking across the bridgehead. Brusilov came to his feet.

"This is murder. You must end it."

"I don't understand."

"What we are watching is the destruction of our army."

"That is too strong a statement. There are very heavy forces not in this fight."

"Comrade, there is such a thing as inertia in warfare. You may not believe it, and I don't claim to understand it; but if you let Andronov's army be smashed by Arakal, then the only hope is to unite our reserves, put the Marshal in charge, and turn the whole control over to him. There is a psychic element in war—"

"You mean psychological."

"I don't know what word is right. But if Arakal wins this as he is winning it, strength will flow from us to him—or something will happen that will have the same effect. He will become the champion. We will hesitate to strike. He will act. Our position will dissolve. He is a kind man, and I am sure there will be no vengeance. But if you want to hold the position you have now, I tell you everything is now in the balance. This battle has got to be turned over to someone who understands war. The Marshal is our best, and he has the—"

S-One, watching the display, felt a sudden quickening of the pulse, a tightness of breath. The blue shading had bitten into the northern flank of the bridgehead, all the way to the railroad bridge. Now what? To his astonishment, the blue moved out on the bridge, preceded by flashes that crossed to the other side, and then the blue was on the other side, too. Now what? This was suicide, wasn't it? How had they gotten across so soon? On the highway bridge, the red was still crossing from east to west, while on the railroad bridge, the blue was crossing from west to east. S-One suddenly found himself unable to think, to draw conclusions from what he was seeing.

Brusilov, seeing the expression on S-One's face, turned, looked at the display, swore, and turned back to S-One.

"My God, man! Don't stand there! Send for the Marshal!"

S-One was thinking, "Is this panic? I can't think. So this is what panic is?" He drew a deep breath, and blanked his face. Above all, he had to maintain an appearance of control. One who gave that up, who was seen to lose control—how could such a person ever live down the knowledge in the minds of others that he *had* lost control? Abruptly S-One could think again. He made a gesture of the hand. "This has all been allowed for in the plan."

Brusilov stared at him.

S-One said, "But what I don't understand is, why do they cross the river? They are in as bad a position as we. In a worse position! Their bridgehead has no depth. Why do they cross?"

Brusilov looked at the display, where the red shading was falling back, crowding now at the west end of the highway bridge. It was a rapid movement for the scale of the display and they could see it happen like a flow of molasses across a tilted plate, a streaming motion that continued with no visible rational object except to coalesce at the west end of the bridge.

Brusilov spoke in disgust. "Do you think this display gives any real idea what those men are going through? All this shows us is certain geometrical aspects of what is happening? Do you think that is all there is to war?"

"Why do our men crowd at the end of the bridge?"

"Because word has no doubt reached them that the enemy had gotten to the other side of the river. Their retreat is being cut off. They feel trapped."

S-One nodded, understanding the point.

Brusilov shook his head.

"For the last time, Comrade! Will you call the Marshal?"

S-One sat down. He shook his head. "There is no need for panic, General. All this has been allowed for, in the plan."

Brusilov made no motion. His face became expressionless, as if the nerves controlling the facial muscles had been switched off. Then he looked alert, as if he were listening.

S-One frowned, and sat up. Now he heard it, too.

Outside, there was a tramping, a shot, a fusillade of shots, a yell.

The interoffice phone buzzed. S-One picked it up, and his deputy's voice rang in his ear:

"Sir! Troops are forcing their way in!"

"Under whose command?"

"I don't know yet!"

On S-One's desk, the outside phone rang. S-One scooped it up. "Hello?"

The Head of Government's voice said, "Any resistance will be futile."

S-One looked up, to see General Brusilov holding a pistol in his hand, holding it very steadily so that S-One could almost look down the barrel.

S-One shook his head, and spoke into the phone. "Don't be silly. Of course there will be no resistance. Do as you will." He rested the phone on the table, setting it down without hanging it up. "S-Two?"

"Sir?"

"Signal the guard detachments that there is to be no further resistance. They will lay down their arms if the army units demand it."

"Sir, the corridor is mined. We can very easily leave. I can disembarrass you of your problem, if you say the word."

"No. General Brusilov is doubtless acting on valid orders. Turn on the public address system. They can hear my voice from this phone, can't they, if you connect it in the circuit?"

"If you say so, sir."

"Turn it on."

"It is on, sir."

S-One spoke carefully.

"This is S-One speaking. General Brusilov and I are coming out down the main corridor. Stay where you are. General Brusilov and I are coming out together."

S-One glanced at the blank-faced Brusilov. "Well, let's go. What are we waiting for?" As Brusilov began to put the gun away, S-One said, "No, keep that in your hand. It explains the situation, so the troops can feel easy."

At the door, S-One paused, and looked back.

"I will miss the flowers," he said.

XI. The Pursuit

1.

Arakal and Slagiron were with the Fourth Division that night. They had just finished eating, and were in their tent, studying a map by the light of an ill-trimmed lamp with a tendency to smoke. Arakal had turned down the wick, and was waiting to let the mantle burn clean, when a voice spoke from outside.

"Pardon, sir. There's a Captain Jinks out here. He wants to talk to you."

"Send him in," said Arakal.

The tent flap came open. A burly middle-aged man with a tired sad expression let himself in, peered around in the gloom, and saluted Arakal. Arakal returned the salute.

"Have a seat, Captain. What did you find out?"

Jinks sat down, and sighed. "She's a spy, sir. And a novice tripjack artist. On top of that, she brought a plant, and left it in the bunker with you and General Morgan and the rest. Her final story to me, before she cracked, was that she's a French girl—an Old Kebeck girl—struck with hero-worship for you, and that she lied to the chief nurse in order to come with us. That's a lie, like

what went before. She's Russ. She belongs to
some outfit that supplies spies to some other outfit called 'S'. She's scared of 'S'. This outfit she
belongs to is called the 'Professional Assistance
Corps'. If 'S' wants a nurse to plant somewhere, or
a bricklayer, or a clerk, they go to this Professional
Assistance Corps. Everyone in it is trained to do
two jobs—the one they're supposed to be expert
at, and spying. She is a qualified nurse, and has
worked at a hospital in Old Kebeck, here. I got the
story out of her without marring her looks, but I'm
afraid her spirits are a little dented."

"What was the plan?"

"She only had instructions, and we have to
guess at the plan behind them. Her instructions
were first to locate you, after getting in using as a
mask her occupation of nurse. After you were
wounded, her being sent to the right surgeon's
tent was pure luck. She had this device to plant in
your quarters."

"This was the plant you mentioned?"

"Yes, sir. It's about the size of a man's thumb,
with sticky claylike stuff on the outside. It looks
like a lump of clay or dirt. She stuck it to the
corner of the wall just inside the room where you
were sleeping. It contains fine wires and little
things like tiny beads. We don't know what it is.
Neither does she. She just did as she was told."

"All right. What next?"

"Next was the tripjack stunt. If possible, she
was to get you to make love to her. They in-
structed her in about forty different alternative
approaches to work that. Nobody told her what
the idea was. She was just supposed to be mad
with hero-worship of you. But except under tor-

ture, she was only to admit that to you. To
everyone else, you were responsible, you made
the arrangements, you took the initiative. Her
explanation to you was to be that she was too
embarrassed to admit her passion to anyone else.
Meanwhile, she was to keep her eyes open, and
learn all she could about our arrangements and
plans. She wouldn't try to pass that on until 'S' got
in touch with her. That covers her instructions.
We can guess at parts of the plan, and, just in case,
the doctors are checking her over right now, to
find out whether possibly she was given some
disease she was supposed to pass on during all
this love-making."

"If so, she didn't know about it?"

"No, sir. She just did what they told her."

"How did she get in this Professional Assistance Corps?"

"They selected her, and told her how patriotic it
was when she expressed some doubts. She was
too afraid to object."

Arakal nodded.

Captain Jinks said, "To avoid marking her, I
stuck to straight pain, sir. I told her in advance
that I was under orders not to mark her, and that I
would also avoid deliberately breaking her spirit.
I also told her that there was more pain in the
world, and she could experience more of it, than
she had any idea of. It was a mistake to tell her all
that. Looking at her, I thought she would break
easy. She didn't. I should have let her worry about
her looks. It would have broken her down quicker,
and been easier on both of us."

Arakal nodded moodily. "If she hadn't been

here as a spy, it wouldn't have happened. Now the problem is, what to do with her."

Slagiron moved uneasily, "Sir, while we deliberate on that, time is passing. There are a great many different ways to get rid of a spy, and if you want me to, I'll take care of it personally. But right now, we have more important things to think of."

Arakal glanced at Jinks. "When will the doctors be through with her?"

Jinks shook his head. "Maybe they know, sir. I don't."

"Do *you* have any idea what to do with her?"

Jinks frowned. "She's beautiful. She has brains and will. The trouble is that she just happens to be on the wrong side, and the wrong orders were given to her. She *is* a capable nurse. . . I think I'd ship her back to them."

"Are you sure she finally gave the facts—the whole truth?"

Jinks sat back, frowning. "All the *facts*. As to her motives, I can't be certain. She resisted longer than I would have thought possible. There had to be a strong motive. I didn't get that out of her."

Arakal nodded. "Well, when the doctors are through, let me know." Arakal got up, and walked the few steps to the front of the tent, and held back the flap. "Watch that tent rope."

"Yes, sir. Thank you. Good night, sir."

"Good night, Jinks. Thank you."

Arakal carefully shut the flap.

Slagiron cautiously turned up the lamp, and growled, "Now that we've got shock-resistant mantles, we need smokeproof wicks."

Arakal nodded. "Now, let's see." He looked at

the map. "There are enough rivers in this place."

"Yes. And we ought to be able to knock the living daylights out of them at every crossing. But what if the Russ have another army around somewhere?"

"They're bound to," said Arakal. "This isn't their main force. Not only that, we can't hope they'll all be mishandled."

"No," said Slagiron. "But where are the rest? And what are they doing now? Not knowing that, we could get caught with blown bridges behind us, and our supplies cut off."

Arakal frowned at the map. "Let's suppose the worst case—"

2.

S-One, with General Brusilov beside him, was escorted down the corridor to a big double door with armed guards to right and to left. The lieutenant in charge of the escort went inside, then came out to say to Brusilov, "If you stay right with him, sir, we will remain outside."

Brusilov gave a grunt of assent, and went in with S-One.

Inside, at the big table, flanked by Marshal Vasilevsky and General Kolbukhin, sat the Head of Government. He spoke shortly.

"Come in. Sit directly opposite us."

S-One did as told, without a word. Brusilov glanced questioningly at the Head of Government, and at his nod sat down beside S-One.

The Head of Government, habitually spoken of as "G-One," as a monarch is spoken of as "the king," leaned forward, his eyes narrowed.

"Your precious Andronov is defeated. Reserve

France is running from Arakal. There are uprisings in France, Germany, and Poland. We have
word of sabotage through all western Europe. The
U. K. is in open rebellion. The Americans own the
Normandy Citadel. Their fleet has cut our communications to the U. K. All this has followed
from your plan." His voice sharpened. "Can you
give me one reason why I should not have you
torn to bits with red-hot pincers?"

S-One blinked, frowned, then spoke, his voice
suddenly calm, with undertones of power.

"That you can speak this way follows from the
fact that you are not yet dead, as you would already be if I had chosen to have you killed, and as
you will be if I choose now to raise my hand
against you. Your only guarantee of safety is my
continued good will, which is, I think an excellent reason not to have me torn to pieces with
red-hot pincers. A second reason is that neither
you nor anyone else in this room has the faintest
conception of the S Plan for dealing with Arakal;
modesty is a more appropriate attitude for the
ignorant than menace. In the third place, your
own power, even if I permit you to lay hand on
me, is only to burn a corpse, not cause me so much
as ten seconds' pain."

G-One's eyes seemed as if lit from within.

"We can test that."

"Think," said S-One coldly. "Do you really
wish to test what I have said?" His voice rose very
slightly as he spoke, to convey a threat that made
the Marshal look up, and G-One pause, halfway to
his feet.

S-One spoke again, this time quietly, like a par-
ent to a foolish child:

"Sit down."

G-One, his expression alert and baffled, sat down. Then he shook his head.

"You have gained a minute with your bluff. Go ahead. Talk."

S-One said quietly, "There is no bluff. Don't make the error of laughing at a bear on land because he seems clumsy in water."

"Meaning what?"

"If you judge the S Plan by its *military* results, you sneer at the bear because he is not a fish. That is a premature judgement. You can judge a creature accurately only in his own element. That applies also to you and me. If you judge me as helpless because as a general I seem ineffectual, you risk a sudden discovery of just what my element is."

G-One looked away a moment, then looked back, directly into S-One's eyes.

"All this is a clever net of words. If you expect to tie me up in it, you are mistaken. Just incidentally, you are the person who, not long ago, professed loyalty to the so-called 'formal power' of my position. We will find out about those red-hot tongs and your power to resist."

S-One said patiently, "Think back, and you will recall what I said. That loyalty is to the person in your position who is fitted by ability to be in that position. It is not a personal loyalty to you. It is loyalty to G-One. If you demonstrate the wrong traits, you cease to command my loyalty. Just so, I must manifest the traits of S-One. Why do you think we use these silly appellations? Because there is a possible difference between the position and the traits it requires, and the individual in that position. Only so long as you manifest the proper traits can you command my loyalty, because that loyalty is not to you personally, but to G-One."

G-One said, "I think I will test what strength is behind this logic."

S-One said coldly, "Do you wish to die suddenly, or would you like it to be long and drawn-out, so that I can explain to you what happened, and why it must be that way?"

Brusilov, listening uneasily, and seeing the Head of Government draw back again, cleared his throat. "May I speak?"

G-One turned slightly, his expression angry and baffled. "Go ahead. But quickly."

"I don't like to say this. But while we sit here, stalemated, Arakal is in action. After the soldiers came, and when S-One was leaving his office, he looked back and said, 'I will miss the flowers.' If S-One could still control events, would he have said that?"

Across the table, G-One's face cleared, and he turned toward the door.

S-One spoke flatly, "I said that because I expected to be rudely dismissed, not assassinated."

G-One, partly risen, as if to call out to the troops on the far side of the door, sat down again. A look of astonishment washed across his face.

"What you say now is that if I say, 'You're fired,' you will offer no resistance?"

S-One's face slowly suffused with color. He leaned forward. "How many times do I have to say it to you? If you dismiss me, I am dismissed. We have been all over this! What did we talk about the other day?"

"I thought there were threats in your words. You said that my real power—"

"The real power of your position."

"You said that it depended on *your* loyalty!"

"That is true."

"Then what power—"

"It is a statement of fact. There is no threat, because that loyalty is assured. *To G-One.*"

"But it is up to you to decide!"

Across the table, Marshal Vasilevsky glanced at General Brusilov and shook his head ever so slightly, then settled back with a glazed expression, eyes half-shut, like a student in an overheated classroom.

S-One said, "This is no personal matter that I may warp to my advantage in a personal struggle for power. It is a question like that of the blacksmith who judges the readiness of the iron by the color of its glow. But I will say it plainly: You may dismiss me. That is a question purely up to your pleasure. You may do this as long as you hold the position of G-One. If I should decide that you are unfit to *be* G-One, I may remove you. But those selected to fill the position of S-One are not chosen for their fitness to fill the role of Attila the Hun. Neither are they selected for their capacity to lick boots. I will defer to the formal power of your position. In *that* lies your safety. Just incidentally, if I am dismissed, there is no assurance that whoever follows me will be any more to your taste."

"Your deputy will succeed you?"

"Not likely. An S-Two is selected for different reasons than an S-One."

"Then we are still in this asinine stalemate!"

"You may end it at any time."

"Only to have the same thing with someone else."

S-One frowned. "One moment. The crux is not a personal matter. It is simply a question of the S Plan for dealing with Arakal."

G-One looked away, and swallowed.

S-One leaned forward, and spoke earnestly. "I mean no offense to anyone at this table. But I can explain that plan only to the Head of Government, personally, and to no one else. I will talk about it, very generally, if you wish, in the presence of others, but I will only explain the plan itself to you, if you promise not to reveal it to anyone else. The reason for this is that this S Plan is not a military plan. But it depends on the actions of military people. For the military to understand the plan would be a complicating factor the effects of which I cannot predict."

G-One slammed his fist down on the table. He got up, walked the length of the room, walked back, spun his chair around, and sat down, astride the chair. His voice was intense.

"Let us talk about this S Plan generally, then. If it works, will it recover everything we have lost to Arakal so far?"

"Everything but the Normandy Citadel, and whatever depends on it, such as the blockade of the Channel."

"What will happen to Arakal?"

"He will no longer be of any concern."

"And America? Will we regain America?"

"We did not have complete control of America. The plan is a method to penetrate America, just as we penetrated Europe, but more slowly. Finally, we should have complete control."

"And the Fleet?"

"We will not control that Fleet. The Americans will control it. But we will control the Americans."

G-One looked at S-One wonderingly. "It encompasses all that?"

"Yes. But let me point out that it is a plan only. It depends on the reactions of people, and we do not understand completely the reactions of Arakal or of his men. The bullfighter's dominance in the ring depends on his practical understanding of the psychology of the bull. We believe this plan will work, but this is a different breed of bull. There are obvious risks."

Marshal Vasilevsky's eyes came wide-open, and he laughed. "We could get gored, eh?"

S-One said, very seriously, "We could."

G-One said, "Has the plan failed yet?"

"In the case of the Normandy Citadel, yes. Not otherwise."

"What about Andronov's retreat?"

"No, that is not failure."

"And the uprisings?"

"They were anticipated, let me say, and do not represent a failure of the plan."

"In your opinion, does the plan underestimate our opponent?"

S-One thought a moment.

"It may. I underestimated him."

"If so, are we in danger?"

"It depends on unknowns. Arakal and his men are in very great danger. We are in some danger. There are opportunities and risks for both sides. In my opinion, the opportunities for us are far greater, and the risks far less. I may be mistaken."

Across the big table, G-One stood up, swung his chair around, and sat down again. He exhaled sharply. "This is of interest, but too general to rely on. And we cannot continue in this deadlock forever."

S-One shrugged. "The initiative is with you."

"That is not my meaning."

"Then what is your meaning?"

"I hesitate to say, lest more time pass in talk."

Marshal Vasilevsky moved slightly in his seat. His voice was quiet, and his tone noncommittal. "I take my orders from the Head of Government. The last time I looked, my men were outside the door."

S-One smiled, and said nothing.

The Marshal spoke again, quietly. "All this is a political matter, and I make no claim to understand politics. But I understand guns. If you want to stop Arakal, we can stop him."

G-One, the Head of Government, said exasperatedly, "This situation has got to be simplified." He looked at S-One. "What if we all here swear not to repeat this plan. Tell all of us. There are enough of us here of expert judgement to gauge the worth of the plan."

S-One shook his head. "An S Plan cannot be revealed to the military. The military may aid in carrying it out. They cannot sit in judgement over it. Only you can hear it."

"Let me convene the whole Central Committee, then."

"They are not properly constituted to sit in judgement on it."

G-One clenched his fists. His voice was even and conversational as he turned to the Marshal.

"The difficulty is that we need the S organization. We can smash it, yes. But if we smash it, we smash an instrument useful, and perhaps essential, to us." He glanced at Brusilov, his voice wondering. "Is there any way Arakal could be creating discord among us? All this upheaval comes about in response to his arrival."

Brusilov shook his head, then paused, frowning. Then he shook his head more definitely. "No. He has no means to do that, at least."

The Marshal said, "He is skillful, and I think he has been lucky. The strain he puts on our arrangements shows up our weak points. That puts us all in a bad humor."

"That is sensible," said G-One. He looked across the table, frowning. Abruptly he said, "All right. I will listen to this plan of yours."

3.

Arakal lowered the long-seeing glasses. Ahead of him, the Russ, under a heavy bombardment, were crossing the last of the series of rivers on the way to what he knew as "Allemain," what the Old Kebeckers called "Allemagne," and what the maps of the Old O'Cracy called "Germany." Whatever they called it, Arakal didn't want to go there. He turned to Slagiron.

"Call up the troop trains. Once the Russ are well over that river, we'll head back."

Slagiron nodded. "The sooner we get out of this place, the better."

4.

G-One was sitting on the edge of the desk, staring at S-One, who had sat down in an ornate green-and-gilt armchair and was leaning forward as he talked. To G-One's astonishment, the S plan seemed possible, and its description short and to the point.

S-One now made a gesture of the hand as if tossing aside a crumpled paper, and said, "That is the plan. While I do not insist that it will work, I assure you that it is practical, and it well *may* work."

"The trouble is that if it does not, we may be ruined."

"We had to deal with this Arakal in *some* way. If he had been stupid, or unlucky, we would already have finished him. We could not count on that. The plan allows for his military success."

"You have certainly revealed to me more of the workings of your organization than I expected. Implicit in such a plan as this are many things."

"I can speak plainly to you because you are G-One. It is possible to select and train an S-One. To select a Head of Government is much harder, if it is possible at all. So many factors are unpredictable. Even this Arakal sees the problem. It was in Brusilov's report. My problem is simpler. I need only recognize one who has been selected."

G-One shook his head. "No one *selected* me. I am here because the complacent people who preceded me made serious mistakes. But that is neither here nor there. We have two problems. The first is the Americans. The second is the relationship of your organization and the government. I will tell you right now that it came very close, several times, to your not living to explain this plan. I tell you that no capable person is going to tolerate your elbow constantly in his ribs. Also,

I want to be able to sleep at night. For now, we must settle with Arakal. But let us think ahead a little. You have got to give me more room."

S-One sighed.

"Some time soon, I must explain something else to you. It has to do with the last big war, and the Americans. You will not believe me. But I will show you the documents. If necessary, I will show you the realities."

G-One shook his head. "Not now. We must reassure the Marshal and the others."

"No, but soon. Then you will understand why S is as it is."

"How long will it take?"

"It is a long story."

"I will give you a long time to tell it. Now, let's go out."

5.

Arakal was with the Seventh Division that night, had eaten and talked with the men, had looked over some of the artillery that the division was so plentifully supplied with, and had checked to be sure that their supplies were getting through. As the men were settling down to finish cleaning and oiling their guns, Arakal and Slagiron were bent over their maps. There were a number of these maps, all more or less unsatisfactory, and as they came up against the limitations of one map, they tried another. At length, Slagiron growled, "Well, it *seems* practical."

"On the map," said Arakal.

"On *these* maps, anyway."

"All right, now. Suppose—" He put his outstretched forefinger on the map "—that they erupt out of this forest, and come down on from the northeast?"

"Then," said Slagiron, smiling, "We'll hit them while they're crossing the river here— What's this one? The Aisne."

"And if, instead, they march along to the north of it, headed for the ocean?"

"Then we march parallel to them on the south. It looks as if we have the better road, and two good bridges over this next river. What's this one? The Oise? But now, suppose they stay north of the Oise where it comes in from the west, here, and then they swing around to come south, still on the far side, and get between us and Cherbourg. Then what do we do?"

"If we find out in time, we can go back and stop them before they cross the Seine, here. Or, we can try to hit them from behind, if we have supplies enough built up."

"Suppose they're on the way right now, and we don't find out in time?"

"Then we could put our trains on the iron road headed south, here, and turn east, here. Meanwhile, we yell for Admiral Bullinger. Or, there are other possibilities."

"None of them very boring," said Slagiron, looking at the map.

"No."

One by one, Arakal and Slagiron tried out the possibilities. Suppose the Russ turned up here? Or there? What if the tracks were cut, or a bridge blown? What were the possible effects of these canals, paralleling or joining these sections of rivers? Suppose they took up a position here, or here? How would the supply trains reach them?

How long to go between these two points on foot?
How long by rail?

When they were through, Arakal said, "We
have an idea, at least," and Slagiron nodded.
"The reality may be something else." Before they
could say anything further, outside there was a
sound of hoofbeats.

Then there were two shots from a rifle, followed
by the blast of a whistle.

6.

As S-One looked on, the Head of Government,
seated again between Marshal Vasilevsky and
General Kolbukhin, spoke quietly.

"I will say frankly that I would not have believed it possible, but I am reassured about this
plan. I have agreed not to describe it, but I want to
give some idea why it now seems a reasonable
plan to me. First, our colleagues in S have put far
more of their resources into it than I had realized.
Second, it does truly allow for success on Arakal's
part, and we can win, regardless. Third—"

An urgent knock sounded on the door of the
room.

G-One paused, an odd expression on his face.
"Come in."

The door came open, and S-Two hurried in,
carrying a sheaf of papers in one hand. He bent
urgently by S-One.

G-One looked on coldly.

Across the table, S-Two straightened, nodded
abstractedly, and headed back for the door.

As the door shut behind him, G-One looked at
S-One, and said ironically, "Now what?"

S-One was glancing rapidly through the sheaf

of papers that his deputy had brought in. He looked up with an exasperated expression.

"Arakal has broken off pursuit of Andronov, and has fallen back behind the Aisne. He is taking up what appears to be a formidable *defensive* position."

General Kolbukhin, in a low voice, swore.

The Marshal grinned. "The fellow has more sense than I gave him credit for." He looked at Brusilov. "I begin to understand your viewpoint. He is not so easy to lead around by the nose."

General Kolbukhin said angrily, "What the devil are we doing with our *other* armies? While he was chasing Andronov, we could have come in behind him, cut off his supplies, and cracked him like a nut."

The Marshal grinned. "Now, now, that is not *subtle*. This plan, now, is subtle. The only thing is, this Arakal, he is no more subtle than we are. That is what is causing all this trouble."

"All right," said Kolbukhin to S-One. "Run away from him, lure him into Central Europe if you want. But then, when you've got him there, then *cut him off*. What is the point of having an advantage if we don't use it?"

G-One spoke angrily to the Marshal. "You are right, this plan *is* subtle. And there is more to it than you think."

Brusilov said carefully, "Arakal is very quick to scent a trap. He is not likely to take the bait, however subtle the plan, if it puts him at a disadvantage."

The Marshal growled, "But do we *have* to be subtle to put him at a disadvantage?"

S-One and G-One glanced at each other across

the table. G-One cleared his throat. "I have examined this plan. It is not perfect. But it offers us more, if it succeeds, than a strictly military solution to the problem. The reason is that a strictly military solution to the overall problem of which Arakal is a part—a strictly military solution of that problem—is probably beyond our strength."

The Marshal frowned. "What is this overall problem?"

"The problem of America."

"If our ancestors had been just a little more thorough, that problem would not exist."

S-One spoke up, his voice carefully neutral. "There were reasons for their actions. There were limitations then, too, to solely military solutions."

The Marshal was silent a moment, then said, "I am not political. But I would like to ask whether your plan cannot be frustrated by Arakal, using purely military means?"

S-One thought a moment, frowning, and turned to Brusilov, as if to ask a question. Instead, he suddenly turned back to face the Marshal.

"In the short run, yes. In the long run, he must find a non-military answer."

General Kolbukhin said, "Why? Isn't the problem solved if Arakal and his men are trapped and killed, and if we smash the defenders of the Normandy Citadel, and recapture it?"

"No, because, among other things, all conflict has two parts, gain and loss. Breaking into the Citadel could be a very expensive procedure."

Marshal Vasilevsky nodded. "But it can be done."

"We think it can be done. Let me, though I am
not a military man, point out that Arakal has
heavy artillery under his control there, in addition to our automatic cannon. Our opinion that we
can retake the Citadel may be mistaken."

General Kolbukhin glanced at the Head of Government. G-One was listening, a slight frown on
his face. General Kolbukhin looked back across
the table at S-One. "Our artillery is heavier yet."

"Their mobile artillery reserve is heavier than
our mobile artillery reserve."

Kolbukhin leaned forward, his eyes glittering.
"That is false."

S-One looked at him mildly, and waited.

Kolbukhin, confident that in this, at least, he
had the Head of S at a disadvantage, said chal-
lengingly, "Name even one gun they can put into
that battle that is bigger than ours."

"I can think of a number," said S-One quietly.

"What size?"

S-One spoke in a low voice, so that it was necessary to listen closely to hear him. "And when I
name it, you will name one of ours that is larger, is
that it?"

Kolbukhin, who had the known details of Arakal's army memorized, smiled. "Yes, I will."

S-One's voice was almost humble.

"Well, then, perhaps I have been mistaken, but
in any case I will be glad to hear your answer."

"Go ahead. What guns? Name the largest they
have. Let's get on with this."

"I am thinking of their 355-millimeter guns."

The general sat back, blank-faced.

"We are talking about mobile artillery?"

"That is correct. My information is that, in good

weather, these guns can be moved at over thirty kilometers per hour, and can be fired while in motion. They can hit any spot on the battlefield, while out of range of our own weapons. They carry enormous quantities of ammunition with them at all times. They are invulnerable to infantry attack."

Kolbukhin stared.

"What," said S-One, "do we have that is bigger?"

"If what you say is accurate, then I have to admit, we would have a bloody experience trying to break through that. But I also cannot conceive of it. When did they develop such guns?"

S-One said earnestly, with no trace of superiority in his manner, "The guns I am speaking of are their mobile artillery in this case, General, though it is natural to overlook them, because they are not part of Arakal's army. These are the naval guns on his new bombardment ships. But that will make slight difference to us if we have to come up against them. Let me mention that they are not necessarily the worst we may have to face. We happen to know that Arakal has at least one railroad gun that is, if our estimate is correct, a 530-millimeter gun. What do we oppose to that?"

"We could build—"

"We are talking about now."

Kolbukhin nodded glumly. "I see your point."

The Marshal spoke up, his voice quiet, but nonetheless assured.

"Your point is that it would be expensive—that we would pay a steep price in men and equipment to recover the Citadel?"

S-One spread his hands. "I suppose it can be done. But is it worth the price?"

"There is a point we had better face now," said the Marshal. "In my opinion, we undoubtedly still have the military force to defeat Arakal, and to recover the Citadel. Arakal has got, or can take, England, if he lives, and if they will have him. He still has his fleet. And we will still have this problem of America that you speak of, afterward. This is not a good situation. But there are worse situations. If we fritter away our troops, if we fumble around, if we try only to draw Arakal into errors, and place ourselves at a disadvantage in doing it—then we can lose our clear advantage in strength. Meanwhile, Arakal is making a name for himself. I begin to be impressed by his good sense, myself. When this process goes far enough, all of us are going to feel that he is the superior. We will feel fear, even awe. Unless this S plan allows for this, we had better face the fact that there are worse things than paying a stiff price to win back our control in a more limited space than what we had before. We had better face the fact that we are risking the loss of everything we have." The Marshal noted a change in Brusilov's expression, and said at once, "What is it? You don't agree?"

Brusilov shook his head. "I agree, except for one thing. Arakal would never put us in the position you mention. He would never try to conquer us. All the territory he wants is *the land of the O'Cracy*. He interprets that as 'Old Kebeck', and 'Old Brunswick'. France and England— That is, France and the United Kingdom. Even, he would have an alliance with us. But first, we must dis-

gorge France and England. I have talked to him on
the subject until my head swam. There is no enmity, no desire for revenge. He is exasperated by
what happened in the past, does not understand
it—who does? But he has more friendship for us
than enmity."

"How can he feel friendship? After all, we
killed his forebears."

Brusilov shook his head. "Who is 'we'? Did
you? Did I? Is there anyone who really knows
what happened? Did we come out of it undented?
This friendship I speak of is not solely a matter of
reasoning or policy, but also an emotional response. We can get along together. He likes us.
There is no ill will. I mention this because, if we
think otherwise, we are calculating on a false
basis. He is not a conqueror or a marauder."

When Brusilov stopped speaking, there was a
silence. The Marshal nodded his head, eyes
slightly narrowed. His face cleared, and his expression smoothed out. "Well, in that case— But,
of course, we still want to win."

Kolbukhin, frowning, said, "France and England. Well, how are they vital to us? But we must
have something in return."

S-One stared blankly from Kolbukhin to the
Marshal. For an instant, the muscles at his jaw
clenched, and his face reddened slightly. Then he
glanced at the Head of Government, who looked
at Brusilov, and said, "If this is true, the sensible
thing to do appears to me to be to simply hold out
of the battle the forces which now are not yet in
the battle, and meanwhile let the fight proceed,
and see if the S Plan will work."

Brusilov spoke carefully. "That may be. As I don't know the plan, I can't judge."

S-One nodded in relief.

But when, a little later, he was back in his office, looking out at the garden, S-One suddenly turned to S-Two.

"We have," said S-One to his deputy, "a different and worse situation on our hands than I realized."

"How is that, sir?"

"I have fallen into the same hole as that blockhead, Smirnov, who succeeded in losing our colonies in America to this damned elective king. I have underestimated him!"

"In thinking he would advance—"

"No," said S-One, furious, "that was bad enough. This is worse!"

"I've had no word—"

"I've been thinking of him as a military opponent. It is worse than that. You should have heard the Marshal, and this General Kolbukhin—"

S-Two smiled modestly. "I did hear them, sir."

"Then you know what I had to sit through! I might have expected it from Brusilov. But from the Marshal! Then suddenly it struck me!"

"What is it, sir?"

"It is an illusion to think this is just a military war. That would be trouble enough. But it is worse than that."

"How—"

"Arakal is fighting us politically!"

S-Two's eyes narrowed. "By sending back Smirnov, and Brusilov, to bring his viewpoint to us?"

"Yes. For one thing. And in his approach to our colonists. In his refusal to use any more bloodshed than necessary. In retreating back into France, so *we* must be the aggressors." S-One's eyes flashed in anger. "But he will find it hard to fight us politically here. He will not take the bait, eh? If necessary, we will take the baited hook, and ram it through his jaw!"

7.

Arakal, surrounded in the firelight by his troops, looked at Pierrot, who was talking earnestly, and so fast that the translators could not keep up. At length, there came a pause, and one of the translators summarized:

"What he says, sir, is that he has been harrassing the Russ, and when we stopped chasing them, he was left alone to carry on the fight by himself. He's mad about it. He figures we betrayed him, deserted him in combat, ran out on him, turned yellow. He would have been finished by the Russ, he says, but somebody by the name of—Stalheim, I think it was—hit the Russ from another direction, and got him loose. Now he wants to know are we going to lurk back here, and leave it to him to carry the war to the Russ? Or are we going to—ah—take our courage in both hands, and *fight*? I think I've got the substance of it, sir."

There were angry murmurs from Arakal's men as the translator gave his summary, then Arakal asked, "Did he mention at any point where he's been since the Russ attacked and he disappeared?"

"He says he's been fighting the Russ, sir. Harassing them, that is."

"Did he say *where*?"

"No, sir."

Arakal glanced around at Slagiron.

"General, could you step into that tent, and get me one of those maps?"

Slagiron nodded. "Yes, sir." A moment later, he handed Arakal a worn map. Arakal turned to Pierrot, and spoke to the translator.

"Ask him if he can show me on this map where he and his men were located, so that we can get a clearer picture of how the battle developed. Tell him I'd also like to know more about Stalheim, and how Stalheim helped him get free of the Russ."

The translator spoke and was interrupted by Pierrot. The translator turned to Arakal.

"He says, sir, that you can speak his tongue. Why does he have to speak through someone else?"

"I don't speak it that fast. There seems to be a misunderstanding, and I want to be sure it's cleared up, not made worse. Here's the map."

Pierrot examined the map, turned it around, studied it in silence, nodded, and began to speak volubly, pointing to the map, then to himself, then gesturing at people nowhere in sight. His face lit in a beaming smile as he talked, his features twisted as he pantomimed sighting a gun, then made a gesture as if heaving a grenade. His camouflage suit, smeared with mud and what appeared to be crusts of blood, gave off a smell of sweat, wine, and horse dung as he talked, more and more expansively, tapping the map first here, then there, and holding his raised forefinger up for attention as he poured words at the translator.

At length there came a pause, and the translator turned to Arakal.

"What it seems to come down to, sir, is that they sniped and bushwhacked, caved in the skulls of Russ stragglers, and managed to mine some roads in the rear of the Russ retreat."

"Where?"

As Arakal looked from the translator to Pierrot, from somewhere behind them a booming voice shouted what sounded like: "Pierrot! Vo ist air? Vo ist air? Pierrot?"

Arakal looked around, to see a big roughly dressed man with a large moustache push his way forward, and spot Pierrot. Pierrot turned, and his face lit up.

After several rapid exchanges that were all gabble to Arakal, Pierrot turned and unleashed a stream of words at the translator. The translator said, "This is Stalheim, sir. He's evidently chief of something called the Free German Legion."

Pierrot let loose another burst of words.

The translator said, "According to Pierrot, Stalheim reports that the Russ are coming, sir, and Stalheim says we'll have them on top of us in another four or five hours at the outside."

8.

It was another two days before Arakal had his next chance to get more than twenty minutes rest at one time. The Russ attack, this time, started with more tanks than Arakal had seen together ever before, and the tanks were well handled, and capable of surviving all but a direct hit from the heaviest guns he had with him, or from one of his none too numerous tank-killer rockets. In this bat-

tle, Arakal and his men had all the troubles they
had expected in the preceding battle, and they
had these troubles despite the fact that the Russ
were advancing against a position Arakal and
Slagiron had selected in advance. An especially
unpleasant surprise was that the Russ proved
skillful at infiltrating, in numbers, at night. Arakal's troops, overconfident at first, put forth all
their craft and skill, and stopped the Russ advance; but their advantage in position was offset
by numbers and equipment, until the night sky
was suddenly lit by a tremendous flash. The
ground jumped underfoot, and there was a
deafening roar. Pierrot appeared, saying, "Now is
the chance! Stalheim did that, and he and I will
make their retreat a hell! But you will have to
smash in their front!"

Arakal was already giving the orders, not for a
frontal attack, but for an attack by troops he had
been shifting to the right ever since dusk. The
Russ, dazed, their minds on what had happened
in their rear, were pushed to their own right as
their left was driven back. Now Arakal was able to
duplicate his first victory, with the addition that,
this time, the Russ were split, and a sizable force
pinned back against the river, where they resisted
stubbornly despite murderous artillery fire.

Once again, the Russ retreat cost them dearly—
But once again, Arakal, sensing the risk from
other Russ troops, broke off the pursuit, and
moved back to take up a position of his own
choosing.

And now, he had scarcely gotten his troops in
position, and they had scarcely gotten a good hot
meal, and fresh ammunition, when word came

from Arakal's own scouts that the Russ were on the way back, this time led by a large body of cavalry.

Slagiron swore, and Arakal, unwilling to trust his own frayed nerves, let a grunt answer for him. Pierrot soon turned up. "This is the way to defeat! When you have them on the run, pursue them! The casualties you inflict then cost you little. They are running. They cannot run and fight both. This way, you are fighting the same battle over and over again. Fight their retreating back!"

Arakal gave his orders to dig in. The men were already digging in with a will.

Again the Russ attacked, and, for ferocity, this was the worst of the three battles, but the quickest, as for the first time the attackers showed signs of being short of men, and their troops, thrown in as they appeared on the field, soon showed a sullen tendency to dive to the ground and stay there. For the first time, some of the infantry began to surrender without a serious fight. The will of their general was plain enough; but now as they were thrown for the third time against troops well dug in and skillfully supporting each other, on a field dominated by murderous artillery that could not be got at and wouldn't be silenced, the troops that were supposed to attack were thinking of what had happened the last two times.

Arakal now received word, through Pierrot, from Stalheim.

"The Russ reserves are on the march," said Pierrot.

"Headed where?" asked Arakal.

"Toward Saarbrücken."

Arakal glanced at the map.

"They can have it."

"The population has risen up," said Pierrot. "This is territory that formerly belonged to the Western Democracies."

"What, that is part of the land of the O'Cracy?"

Pierrot put his hand on the map. "You see, the border was here."

As Arakal questioned him, Pierrot briefly explained the past history of the region.

Arakal turned to Slagiron. "Am I right in thinking this batch of Russ here is pretty well worn down?"

"They seem at least too worn down for now to hit us again."

Pierrot said, "The populace will be slaughtered by the Russ if they are left to their own devices. Stalheim will do what he can, but he lacks the strength to stand up to the Russ."

Slagiron said, "So do we, if they put forth their strength."

"But you have fought and won—"

Arakal looked thoughtfully at the map, and growled off-handedly, "If they'd always fight us with their left hand only, we could win more often. But, if we can get this present batch permanently out of the fight, maybe we could advance. Not that it wouldn't be more sensible to stay here."

"Perhaps your men don't mind standing still," said Pierrot exasperatedly, "but mine wish to drive these tyrants far away."

"If we drive them far enough away, we'll have one sweet time to get our supplies. But—" he looked at the map "—perhaps we can return the favor for Stalheim."

Early the next morning, Arakal's army smashed through the demoralized enemy, sent the remnants fleeing in front of them, repaired the railroad, and brought up the troop trains. Late that same afternoon, they were in the wooded hills near Saarbrücken. Early that evening, their outposts clashed with the approaching Russ. Stalheim attacked them from the east, Pierrot from the west, and the startled Russ pulled back. The next day, there was no sign of them.

Arakal's men entered Saarbrücken to the cheers of a delirious populace.

The day following, the Russ blew up the railway beyond Saarbrücken.

Arakal attacked. The Russ retreated. Arakal pursued, and the Russ fled before him. Arakal halted, thinking to pull back. The Russ attacked. Arakal, noting their weakness in tanks, maneuvered against them. The Russ withdrew in good order, fell back, and now Arakal's railroad gangs had the track repaired, and supplies got through. Arakal pursued the Russ. The Russ fled. Pierrot and Stalheim were ecstatic.

Welcomed with frenzied excitement by a population only a very few of the translators could talk to, Arakal and his army drove the Russ back, unable to bring them to a stand, unable to gain any decisive advantage, but still pushing them back.

And now two more guerrilla armies joined in the fight, the troops of Echevik and Koljuberowski. Koljuberowski, after a fashion, spoke English. Echevik could be talked to only through consultation between his interpreter and one of the ablest of Arakal's interpreters.

With this new increase in the numbers of their

opponents, the Russ retreated faster. Arakal dubi-
ously eyed his new allies, who rarely dug themselves in regardless of the situation, who often
fled on the approach of the Russ, who specialized
in raids against their opponent's flank and rear,
and who followed each raid with drinking parties
to which they dutifully invited Arakal and all his
senior officers, who desired nothing so much as a
night's rest. The Russ retaliated after these raids
by night bombardment of the enemy camp, the
general location of the target being as clear at
night as a lighthouse, since all the partisan bands
delighted in big bonfires over which to burn their
meat, and to help ward off the increasing chill of
the season. Already, they had seen snow.

As they advanced, two more partisan armies
appeared, and then, one day, there even arrived a
representative from Old Brunswick—which he
called "the U.K."—to tell of the fighting there
against the Russ, and to harangue Arakal on the
need to push the Russ armies back beyond their
own frontiers.

Arakal now received word from Admiral Bullinger, who was forcing the Kiel Canal to enter the
Baltic Sea, in case Arakal should need help, or
some means of evacuation.

It was not long after that, in a rolling country
now well covered with snow, that Arakal and his
men, fortunately possessed of heavy winter
clothes brought to them in supply ships from
home, and then all the way from Cherbourg, woke
up in a blizzard. The temperature dropped twenty
degrees overnight, and in the following days
worked lower still.

One day, they drove the Russ out of a fortified

outpost above the banks of a frozen river that
Arakal could not identify on the map, and which
was of slight interest to the partisans, who assured
him that the only worthwhile feature of the geog-
raphy was "the backs of the fleeing enemy." That
same afternoon, the partisans found a little com-
munity of Russ farmers, and before Arakal knew
what was happening, the partisans had mas-
sacred most of them. When Arakal, his silent men
with leveled guns beside him, demanded to know
the reason, Koljuberowski smilingly wiped the
blood off his knife, and answered, "You should
see what their soldiers did to us. We have much to
make up. We are starting now."

"Those were farmers."

"So? They might have children, and the State
will take the boys to make soldiers. We just kill
them before they are born. They are more easy to
kill that way, hey?" He laughed. "What do you
say about that?"

Arakal said shortly, "We will take our share of
the prisoners," sent his men to rescue the remaining Russ, and then gave short precise orders that
spun his own troops around, and brought them
back to the fortified outpost the Russ had just been
driven out of. Around this outpost, Arakal selected the most dominating ground on the near
side of the river, and announced a halt. His men at
once began to dig in. The Russ delivered a short
sharp attack, were driven off, and pulled back
across the river as the snow swirled down.

9.

S-One settled back in his chair, smiling. He no
longer looked out the window to feast his eyes.

Now he looked at the display that showed the position of Arakal's army.

Across the desk from him, Brusilov looked at the display, and nodded slowly. His expression was almost sad, as at the passing of a legend.

XII. The S Plan

Arakal, the next morning, stood on the firing step in the captured Russ blockhouse, and peered east through long-seeing glasses across the frozen river and the snow-covered plain. The sun again today was hidden by dark clouds. But the snow had stopped, and whenever the fitful wind died away, it was possible to seek out the winter-camouflaged Russ tanks.

Behind Arakal, keeping warm by pacing the floor of the narrow concrete-walled room, Slagiron exhaled a cloud of frozen breath, and banged his mittened hands together.

"Any motion?"

The wind swirled fresh clouds of snow across Arakal's field of vision. He lowered the glasses.

"Not from the Russ."

"What about our *friends*?"

"Koljuberowski's putting some men across the ice where the river bank is low."

"How many?"

"A section."

"What do they have with them?"

"A leech-bomb slinger on skids."

There was a little silence as Slagiron grappled with the question that had already baffled Arakal.

"What," said Slagiron, "do they expect to accomplish?"

Arakal exhaled.

"They seem to be crawling toward the spot where the forwardmost Russ tank was yesterday."

"Ah, where it was *yesterday*."

Arakal, feeling under pressure to support an ally, even an ally like these allies, strained to find something favorable to say. In the resulting quiet, he could hear the chink of picks and the scrape of shovels as his men labored to improve their bunkers and firing positions.

Slagiron grunted in disgust.

Arakal glanced at a little stud in the thick tube that joined the two halves of his long-seeing glasses, then he stepped down, and handed the glasses to Slagiron.

"See what you think."

Slagiron, his broad build made broader by his thick fur coat, climbed up on the firing step, bent at the slit, and raised the glasses.

Arakal pulled off his leather mittens with their separate trigger finger, pulled off the woollen mittens underneath, and blew into his cupped hands. With stiff fingers, he readjusted the cumbersome straps and belts that held his sword, pistol, ammunition, and the bulky case for the long-seeing glasses.

At the slit, Slagiron growled, "Where did the Russ move that closest tank?"

"Well back, and to your left. Low in front of that lone clump of evergreens."

"Hm . . . If this wind will . . . There . . . I see him . . . Well, now, what have we here?"

There was a gathering pound of approaching

hoofbeats, and Slagiron's voice became ironical. "Marshal General Catmeat and his Gorilla Guard."

Arakal absently made the correction: "Koljuberowski."

The hoofbeats faded, as the horsemen passed the blockhouse.

"His bomb team," said Slagiron, "is still crawling toward the tank that isn't there. The Russ are taking a few shots at them, so he's coming back . . . Now—what's this?"

The fading hoofbeats seemed to return.

Arakal listened intently. "He's going out again?"

"No . . . This is Parrot and his gang."

"Pierrot," said Arakal absently. "What? Koljuberowski comes in and Pierrot goes out?"

"It's Parrot's turn," said Slagiron. "Next, Slitneck will go out and take a rush at them."

Arakal groped mentally. "Echevik," he said.

"Then finally," growled Slagiron, still bent at the firing slit, "after they've all been beat one at a time, the whole crew will get together around the fire, break out the rotten cheese and wormwood, and invite us over. Stallburger will give a speech." Slagiron's voice suddenly changed tone, like a drill that bites through wood into metal. "Unless, that is, they can find a few more unarmed Russ farmers and their children to—"

Arakal's voice grated. "Stalheim."

Slagiron was silent. Finally, he straightened, and yanked back a large knob at the end of a thick metal rod. At the far end of the slit, under a curving metal plate that served to ward off wet snow and freezing rain, the metal cover shut with a clap. Slagiron glanced at the firing slit's inner door on its dented and rusty slides, thought better of trying to close it, and stepped down. He handed the glasses to Arakal.

Arakal checked the little stud, then slid the glasses into their case.

Slagiron blew into his cupped hands.

"If we've got one man who wants to go any deeper into Russland, I don't know who he is. But the Russ retreat to draw us on, and we advance because the partisans want to attack. And ninety percent of the time, the partisans are frankly worthless."

Before Arakal could reply, there came from outside the muffled challenge of a sentry.

Arakal and Slagiron glanced around.

Through the doorless archway from an adjoining larger room came the sound of the heavy outer door creaking open, to admit wind and a stamping of feet, and then to shut again with a heavy thud. There was an approaching tramp of boots and rattle of metal.

"Nuts," came Casey's voice. "If we went over the ice by day a few at a time, the same thing would happen to us. What do they expect? Why can't they either forget it, or else attack *together*?"

The voice of Smith, the acting chief technician, was irritable. "Anything with even *two* heads can't function normally. This so-called army has *seven* heads."

Beane, whose patience and language capabilities stuck him with the diplomatic jobs, said drily, "Don't forget Burke-Johnson."

Smith growled. "Right. *Eight* heads. And all the heads speak different tongues."

As they came in, Casey saw Arakal, and said at once, "Sir, Koljuberowski wants us to back him up in an attack. He claims the Russ have dug in, have no fuel for their tanks, and once we get past them there's nothing from here to Moscow that can stop us."

Arakal nodded. "Nothing but snow, wind, frostbite, stragglers, ambushes, rear attacks, and broken supply lines. This is far enough."

Slagiron looked relieved, and blew into his cupped hands.

Arakal glanced at Smith. "Any word from the Fleet?"

Smith nodded. "They're through into the Baltic. And they're up to their necks in Dane and Swede partisans who want the Fleet to take them to Russland by way of Finland."

Arakal nodded moodily. "Let's see. Finland is—"

"Well, you remember, sir, the Baltic Sea is shaped roughly like a curved 'Y'. The lower part of Finland is between the two raised arms of the 'Y'."

Arakal nodded. "And the Fleet is now near the bottom of the curved leg of the Y, which stands on Denmark."

"Yes, sir."

"What does Admiral Bullinger say?"

"He says it's five hundred miles to Finland and five hundred miles back; the Fleet is still battered up from that Russ fort that hung on at the upper end of the Kiel Canal; he doesn't know the coast and neither does anyone else he can talk to without two sets of interpreters; he doesn't like the look of the Baltic if there should be a storm; and moreover he has it on good authority it can ice over solid around Finland."

"He doesn't want to do it?"

"No, sir."

"Then this latest batch of partisans can get to Russland on foot."

"Yes, sir. But the admiral wants to pass it on, for whatever it's worth, if anything, that the partisan chiefs claim they can go in through Finland, hit the Russ by surprise, and make the other half of a pincer with us coming up from the south, and together we can shear off the whole Baltic coast, and maybe the Russ people will join us and revolt."

Arakal exhaled carefully, and glanced at the archway, above and behind Casey's head.

Slagiron growled. "It *might* have worked. The Russ people *might* have joined us."

Casey said tonelessly, "Before Catmeat and the rest—"

Slagiron nodded. "Before they evened up the score with those Russ settlers."

Arakal decided he could now trust his voice.

"Signal Bullinger that we may halt here for the winter. Our plans are uncertain. But we aren't going further."

Casey said uneasily, "Who is 'we', sir? Koljuberowski, Echevik, and the rest are yelling their heads off that they want to kill Russ."

"If we advance," said Arakal, very reasonably, "what will the Russ do?"

"Retreat, to draw us on." Casey frowned. "From what we got out of those Russ farmers we saved from the partisans, this isn't a bad spot. That is to say, you can at least recognize the weather here as *weather*. They've evidently got worse places than this for us to advance into."

"Then," said Arakal, "suppose we stay here. Then what?"

"The Russ will attack us. Then, when we counterattack, *then* they'll retreat."

Arakal nodded. "If Koljuberowski and Stalheim want to 'kill Russ', all they have to do is just stand still and fight."

Casey nodded without conviction. "That's just common sense, sir. *That* will never convince them."

Smith finished setting down on his pad Arakal's message to Admiral Bullinger, and handed pad and pencil to Arakal.

Arakal read the message, initialed it, handed it back, and glanced at Casey. "From here to the other end of Russland must be five thousand miles. It's snow from one end to the other, and it's cold enough to freeze quicksilver. We had that much on good authority, before we talked to those Russ farmers."

Casey nodded glumly. Slagiron growled his agreement.

Beane said hesitantly, "There's still Koljuberowski, sir. And Echevik. And the rest of the partisans. They hate the Russ. And from the stories they tell, sir, I don't think you can blame them."

Again Arakal didn't trust himself to say anything.

Slagiron spoke with an edge to his voice. "Now the Russ can tell stories."

"Yes, sir," said Beane. "But the point is, if we *don't* advance, we'll end up quarreling amongst ourselves. Koljuberowski, Echevik, Stalheim, Rindovin, Alazar, and Pierrot have one thing in common. They all want to fight Russ."

Arakal said, "Let them dig in here and they can fight Russ."

"I know it, sir. But they want to fight them going forward."

Arakal shook his head.

"I think we've paid back the debt we owed these partisans for their help. They can go on, if they want. We've gone far enough."

"Then, sir, what do we do next?"

Arakal glanced at Casey.

"Suppose we should just leave? What do you think would happen?"

Casey said, "If we just pull out?"

Arakal nodded.

"I'd think the Russ would retake everything from here to Normandy."

Arakal glanced at ·Slagiron, who rubbed his chin thoughtfully.

"I don't know."

Casey looked surprised. He took off his heavy mittens, and blew on his hands.

"Sir," said Casey, looking at Slagiron, "Pierrot and Koljuberowski and the rest may be brave, but they can't face the Russ army. They aren't equipped for that."

Slagiron looked at him.

"Neither are we equipped for it."

Casey looked startled. "We've beat them before. Here and at home."

"In our own country, yes. At the end of their supply line, not ours. But as for beating them here— This business here isn't as it looks. They're only using part of their strength.''

Casey paused, frowning. "There's truth in that. Yet—''

"They retreat to draw us on. They haven't truly put forth their strength except when we dug in.''

Arakal said, "The Russ retreat—but it's all calculated.''

Reluctantly, Casey nodded.

Slagiron growled, "What puzzles me is how sparing they are lately with ammunition. What they specialize in now is *night bombardments*. It almost seems as if they just aim to ruin our sleep.''

Casey said hesitantly, "Of course, with the uprisings—the confusion—''

"They *should* have used their strength to end it quick while they had control. Why let us get this far?''

"But if they thought there were more coming behind us—''

Slagiron shook his head.

"Whatever anyone else here may think, the Russ *know* the shape we're in.''

Arakal could see in his mind's eye this continent's cities—huge by his own standards, and their system of iron roads. The Russ had been masters of all this, but they retreated. Somewhere here, there was an illogicality, a something that didn't fit. In short, a trap.

As they stood grappling with uncertainties, behind them there was a brief howl of wind, the heavy slam of the outside door, the stamp of feet, and then a voice, somewhat high-pitched, and artificially cheerful, called out:

"What ho, chaps! Arakal, my dear fellow! Are you here?''

Slagiron grunted, glanced up at the slit, and held out his hand. "Just in case—"

Arakal, eyes narrowed, handed him the glasses.

Slagiron climbed on the firing step.

Casey glanced around, and swore under his breath.

Smith grunted, and blew on his hands.

A tall pale figure in furs was suddenly framed in the archway. Slagiron's voice, from where he stood behind Arakal on the firing step, had an ironical tone.

"Hullo, Burke-Johnson."

Burke-Johnson cast a penetrating look at Slagiron.

"Er, how are you, my dear general? Actually, I'm delighted to see you." He glanced around. "But, Arakal. It's to you that I really must speak."

Everyone in the room, save Arakal and Slagiron—who had a concrete wall behind him—contrived somehow to back, side-step, or otherwise ease further away from the newcomer.

Arakal reminded himself that Burke-Johnson, supposedly the emissary from Old Brunswick, this same Burke-Johnson had been detected by Smith's monitoring team in the act of reporting Arakal's movements to the Russ, and reporting them in the Russ tongue. Ever since, they had been feeding Burke-Johnson false information, which he duly reported to the Russ. Yet, unless Burke-Johnson were stupid, which clearly he was not, he had long since realized he was unmasked—a fact which he determinedly ignored.

Arakal coerced his voice into a passable imitation of friendliness.

"What is it, Major?"

Burke-Johnson straightened.

"My dear fellow, I'm really quite dished at the way you've been treating Koljuberowski."

Arakal groped for the meaning of the word "dished."

Beane, the language specialist, cast a fishy look at Burke-Johnson.

There was a screech of metal as Slagiron shoved back the cover at the end of the slit, and turned his back on the proceedings.

Arakal said, very seriously, "What did I do wrong this time?"

Burke-Johnson's gaze slid away, and, eyes averted, he spoke rapidly, with an exaggerated emphasis:

"You Americans have simply got to realize that the people here are not about to trade the Russian yoke for your own. You simply must understand that wars are not won by the outsider telling the chap on the spot what he can and what he cannot do. You must get cracking, dear boy. Kol feels that the Russian front here is simply a hollow shell. And he should know. Smash it, Arakal. Smash it!"

Arakal studied Burke-Johnson's averted gaze, and listened closely to Burke-Johnson's emphatic but somehow empty voice. The effect was of an insincerity so plain that Arakal could not accept even the insincerity as genuine.

Again there was the thud of the heavy outer door.

One of Smith's men came in, cast a wary glance at Burke-Johnson, tugged at Smith's sleeve, and pulled him back out of earshot.

Arakal looked thoughtfully at Burke-Johnson.

"To go straight into Russland from here is a five-thousand-mile hike. They can retreat whenever they feel like it, cut in behind us, starve us, pick us off—and meanwhile we'll have to light fires under our guns to work the actions. That's exactly what the Russ want. Why should we do it?"

Burke-Johnson hesitated. For an instant, the effect of masks behind masks vanished. "What do you propose?"

"Go in through Finland, swing around in an arc, and cut all their communications in succession. We should be able to disjoint them—*and* we'll be marching south, not north."

Burke-Johnson blinked rapidly. "I don't believe Kol would agree to this, my dear fellow."

Arakal said, "Let Koljuberowski and the rest of the partisans take them from the front, while we hit them from the rear."

"Well, I might pass along the suggestion, I suppose, but—"

Slagiron tossed words over his back from the firing step. "Good idea. Go talk to Clabberjaw, and see what he says. Then let us know."

Burke-Johnson's face showed a brief struggle. Then, his gaze avoiding everyone's eyes, he nodded, and said loudly, "Cheerio, chaps." He turned, and strode out. The outside door shut heavily behind him.

There was a silence, then a dull clap as the cover dropped shut over the firing slit. Slagiron stepped down, and handed Arakal the glasses. "I wonder who *really* sent him. Does *he* know?"

"What did you see out there?"

"Snow."

Smith came back in, blowing on his hands, his expression intent and serious. He had a sheaf of thin yellow papers tucked tightly under one arm. He glanced at Arakal, and cleared his throat.

"Sir—"

Arakal, bemusedly considering the puzzle of Burke-Johnson, glanced around.

"What is it, Smith?"

"If what I have here is right, another one of these 'allies' is a Russ spy."

In the quiet, they could hear through the wind the chink and scrape of the picks and shovels outside.

Arakal kept his voice level.

"Who is it this time?"

"Koljuberowski."

Arakal kept his mouth shut.

Casey turned to stare at Smith, started to speak, but didn't.

Beane's eyes widened. "I can't believe that—"

Slagiron spoke as if the words exploded from him.

"Then think again! Nothing could have hurt us more than what he did!"

Casey looked at Smith, and said tightly, "What about his troops?"

"It's impossible to say."

Slagiron said, "His officers were all with him in it. Some of the men lagged. And, you remember, one wouldn't go along."

Casey exhaled with a hiss.

"I saw it. They threw him in the pit with the settlers."

Arakal said, "We'd better double the guards."

He took out his signal whistle and blew two short penetrating blasts.

Slagiron drew out his big automatic of Old Army design.

Beyond the arch, the outside door creaked open.

A low voice was speaking warningly:

". . . eyes wide-open. Otherwise, old Cut-Your-Throat may creep up and sling us in a hole." The guard stepped inside, shut the door, exhaled a cloud of frozen breath, and brought his gun to present arms.

"Sir!"

Casey stared. "What's this, Corporal? You've got a buddy out there."

"Yes, sir. Sergeant doubled us all around, and handed out extra belts."

Slagiron growled, "Good!"

Casey spoke at the same time, so that his voice overlapped with Slagiron's. "Why?"

"Don't trust old Cat-Jabber, sir."

"That business with the Russ farmers?"

"That about put the cap on it, sir."

Arakal said, "The guards are doubled up *all around*?"

"Yes, sir."

"Good. That's all."

The guard stepped back outside.

Arakal turned to Smith, who was holding the yellow sheets of paper. "You're sure of this?"

"As sure as we can be."

Casey said, "I still can't believe it! Kolju-berowski—" He paused abruptly.

Slagiron had begun to speak, but stopped at the

look on Casey's face.

Arakal said patiently, "Nothing could stiffen Russ resistance the way Koljuberowski did. Not just their army. Their people."

Slagiron nodded. "We're part of the outfit credited with that."

Casey was nodding unhappily as from the closed outside door came the sound of new voices raised in argument.

Slagiron glanced toward the archway.

"Well, well. Speak of the devil. There's Catmeat himself."

Beane said abruptly, "This may not mean anything, sir. But Koljuberowski has a sleevegun."

Arakal's eyes narrowed.

Slagiron nodded. "It's crooked. What else would he use?"

Arakal glanced at Smith, and spoke in a low voice.

"What *proof* have we Koljuberowski is working for the Russ?"

"Every night since he joined us, at roughly the same time, there's been a—kind of a powerful *squawk*—on the frequency Burke-Johnson uses for his reports."

Arakal nodded.

Smith said, "The night before last, we recorded this squawk, but still couldn't make anything of it. Several hours ago, one of my men got it slowed down, and it turned into words. It was Koljuberowski, reporting that slaughter of the farmers, and what we planned to do next."

"Koljuberowski's own voice?"

"Yes, sir."

"What you have there is the report on this?"

"Yes, sir." Smith held the yellow sheets out to Arakal.

From outside, they could hear the suddenly loud voice of the guard.

"Sergeant of the Guard! Post One! *Armed allies!*"

Casey reached inside his coat.

Arakal spoke quietly as he took the yellow sheets from Smith, then absently loosened his sword.

"Keep your guns out of sight. Beane, take a look. If Koljuberowski's there, tell him I'd like to see him, alone. Try not to let anyone else in. But, if they shove past you— Why then, let them come."

Beane went out through the archway.

Slagiron glanced at Casey, then at Arakal.

"When he pushes his way in, why not tell him Casey and I left after Burp-Jaw went out."

Arakal nodded. He was vaguely conscious of Casey and Slagiron going out the archway toward the inner door that led to the ice-coated wreck of the lookout tower. But his attention was momentarily riveted on the yellow sheets.

". . . voice has been identified by every member of the intelligence section as that of the officer known to us as Casimir Patrick Koljuberowski. . . . Speaking the Russ tongue fluently, Koljuberowski first related the events surrounding the massacre, then detailed our plans as at that time communicated to him . . . Koljuberowski then acknowledged receipt of orders already passed to him from the Russ in some way not specified. . . . The translation of Koljuberowski's report follows . . ."

Arakal glanced rapidly over the yellow sheets,

then folded them, reached inside his coat, and
shoved them well down in a pocket of his woollen
shirt. As the voices from the door became suddenly louder, he slid the glasses out of their
leather case, and handed them to Smith.

"See what you can see through that slit, why
don't you?"

Smith nodded, and, holding the glasses gin-
gerly, stepped up on the firing step.

Some part of Arakal's mind now belatedly succeeded in translating Burp-Jaw to Burke-Johnson.
Arakal's attempts to correct such mispronuncia-
tions had met with such ill success that he had at
last been driven to the conclusion that his men
must see something in these allies that he didn't
see. Uneasily, Arakal considered now just what
this something might be.

From the other room came Beane's voice, raised
in argument, the foreign words incomprehensible
to Arakal.

At the slit, Smith reported, "Nothing moving
that I can see, sir."

From the outside door, the guard called loudly.

"General Ratpack Jolliboozski and three armed
guards, sir!"

Arakal forced himself to breathe evenly as Koljuberowski, followed by three of his guards with
crisscrossed bandoliers over their heavy wool
coats, shoved young Beane out of the way, and
walked with rolling gait toward Arakal. From
somewhere outside, as they approached, came a
muffled sound of shots.

Koljuberowski, a large plump man perhaps in
his middle thirties, glanced alertly around as he

came in. His voice was high-pitched, but his pronunciation was very clear:

"Slagiron? Where is Slagiron?"

Smith shut the firing slit cover with a clap, and
stepped down.

Arakal noted the free way Koljuberowski's
guards handled their guns as they glanced
around.

"Slagiron," said Arakal to Koljuberowski, "left
after Burke-Johnson went out."

Koljuberowski cast a last brief glance around,
nodded, and smiled.

Smith held out the glasses, and Arakal took
them.

Koljuberowski spoke to his guards in a tongue
Arakal neither understood nor recognized. Then
Koljuberowski banged his mittened hands together, and when his hands separated, the right
mitten stayed in his left hand. He seemed to snap
his right wrist and forearm.

Arakal, holding the field glasses partly raised,
had his right forefinger on the little black stud. He
tilted the glasses as he pressed the stud.

The glasses jumped in his hands.

Koljuberowski staggered backward.

Behind Koljuberowski, a grinning guard had
just raised his gun toward Smith.

There was a deafening crash and whine.

Koljuberowski's guards jerked and grimaced.

The roar died away.

The guards were partly atop the sprawled Koljuberowski, as, at the outside doorway and the
door to the tower, Beane, Slagiron, Casey, and
Arakal's two guards lowered their guns.

Arakal bent beside Koljuberowski, then straightened, gripping by the barrel a little silver pistol with no trigger guard, which he held out to Beane.

"Watch out. It's still loaded."

Slagiron bent over Koljuberowski, and methodically undid the thick fur coat. Casey crouched to help.

Arakal glanced at the outside door. The two guards had already gone back to their post.

From the floor, there was a rustle of papers. Slagiron said, "Here's something for you, Beane. Looks like Russ lettering to me."

Arakal peered briefly through his long-seeing glasses, then unscrewed the tube from the thick joint between the two halves of the glasses, and methodically cleaned and reloaded the firing mechanism.

Beane looked up from the papers, and turned to Arakal. "Sir, this is urgent. Shall I read it aloud?"

"Go ahead."

Beane's voice shook slightly as he read:

"Operational Plan, Summary:

1) If possible, Arakal is to be induced to pursue deep into our base territory.

2) Once he and his men are beyond reach of help or reinforcements, all partisan groups will leave them. Softening and conversion will be facilitated by climatic conditions in the interior.

3) Alternatively, if Arakal rejects the partisan plan, or if his men refuse to accept it, or if Arakal's invasion force appears for whatever reason to be escaping control, Arakal and all his line officers down to and

including the rank of full colonel are to be
executed. This may be best accomplished
by requesting an audience with Arakal
first, and then giving word that Arakal has
sent for the others. Immediately following
completion of this action, the strike code-
word should be transmitted to the Combat
Forces S-Control, to simplify concealment
of what has been done by attributing it to
the heavy attack which will follow.

4) No attempt is to be made in any case
to convert or train Arakal, Slagiron, Casey,
or present line officers down to and including the rank of full colonel. If the partisan
plan is carried out, these officers are to
become casualties or prisoners.

5) The technicians, including Smith,
are to be converted and trained. If Kotzebuth or Colputt are present, they are to be
converted, if possible, and if not, coerced.
The chief translator and diplomat, Beane,
is to be given special treatment, as he is
suitable as our replacement for Arakal, and
is of a type amenable to control.

6) In future operations, Arakal's troops
are to be drawn as much as possible into
cruelty toward our base population. This
will be facilitated by accounts of the
people's past cruelty toward Arakal's allies, and especially by our clandestine seiz-
ing and appropriate treatment of Arakal's
stragglers. This must be carried out in circumstances where the actions can only be
attributed to the populace. Once the appropriate attitude is established amongst

Arakal's troops, it will be necessary merely to approve the attitude as entirely proper.

7) It must be remembered that Arakal and his men represent a special opportunity, that of extending indirect control to the American continent. Attainment of this goal requires great delicacy until Arakal and his men are sufficiently worn down. Even then, training of the survivors must proceed with due allowance for their prejudices. The relationship must remain masked and thoroughly rationalized at all times.

8) Alternatively, it must be remembered, Arakal and his men constitute a special and peculiar danger. Although politically naive and technologically backward, they possess a temporary advantage resting on five factors:

- a) Arakal, although a savage, is a skillful tactician, while his men are energetic warriors.
- b) Kotzebuth, Colputt, and the other technicians have created a workable, though largely primitive, technology.
- c) Past underestimation of these opponents has resulted in their surprise seizure of the only effective ocean-going fleet remaining on this planet; control of this fleet gives them command of the sea.
- d) Possible discoveries of usable technological devices developed before the destruction of the U. S.

introduce an element of technological uncertainty. Certain devices have been rumored to exist which could seriously alter the realities of the situation.

e) The populace of the Extended Zone is disaffected.

The possibility therefore cannot be eliminated of a miscarrying of the present operation, with serious results. In the extreme, this could defer realization of the extension of our control to the American continent, and even force control of the Extended Zone back to the indirect mode.

9) At all times, therefore, the greatest care is necessary. The clearest picture of the real elements of this situation must be borne in mind, and all romanticism must be avoided.

10) This instruction must be reviewed repeatedly, and followed to the letter. Any questions may be directed to Control on the usual frequency.''

Beane looked up, his face pale. "That's the end, sir. There's also a separate message. Part of it reads: 'The reports of Burke-Johnson do not conform to Arakal's recent movements. He has, therefore, been unmasked, and his usefulness in this operation is at an end. In the next engagement, he is to feign wounds, and be sent back."

Arakal said, "Read the beginning of that first set of papers over again."

Beane read: "1) If possible, Arakal is to be induced to pursue deep into our base territory. 2) Once he and his men are beyond reach of help or reinforcements, all partisan groups will leave them. Softening and conversion will be facilitated by climatic conditions in the interior."

Arakal said, " 'All partisan groups.' "

Beane nodded. "Yes, sir."

There was a silence.

Slagiron said, "Exactly what we thought. Only worse. It isn't just the Russ luring us on. The partisans are part of it."

"Is there," said Arakal, "anything to show who sent these orders?"

"The letter 'S' is at the bottom. But I don't know if it corresponds to a signature, or if it means something else."

Casey said wonderingly, "They're escorting us into the interior of Russland?"

Beane nodded. His voice had an undertone of anger. "And they've already worked out who they think will go along with them afterward."

Arakal said to Slagiron, "We'd better spread the word about these partisans."

Slagiron nodded. "I'll get the corps commanders."

Arakal turned to Beane. "See if there's any word from Colputt."

Beane handed Arakal the papers, and went out, following Slagiron and Casey.

Arakal carefully, point by point, thought over the captured plan. Then he considered what to do. He stamped his feet, and blew on his hands. Who, he asked himself, was "S"? It was the same "S," apparently, that had sent the nurse as a spy. He looked up at the howl of the wind as the door opened.

Slagiron came in, frowning. "Three of Catmeat's partisans tried to jump our guards earlier, and got killed. But *now* everything seems perfectly normal out there. Damned peculiar."

Casey and Beane came in, and Arakal said, "Any word from Colputt?"

"No, sir," said Beane. "Admiral Bullinger hasn't heard from him, either."

"The last Bullinger heard, Colputt had both platforms loaded?"

"Yes, sir. That was before Bullinger entered the Baltic. The admiral has had his hands full for a while. Colputt *may* have signaled, and not been picked up."

Arakal nodded, and turned to Slagiron, but just then, beyond the archway, the outside door opened up.

There was a murmur of voices, and the three corps commanders, heavily dressed, with general's stars on their helmets, exhaling frosty breath, strode into the room. Greetings and comments died on their lips at the sight of the bodies. They halted, and raised their right hands in sharp salute.

Behind them, there was a heavy thud as Beane closed the outer door.

Arakal said, "These so-called 'partisans' just tried to kill us. Beane, translate the papers we found on them."

Beane read in a slow clear voice. His words fell into the quiet like small stones dropped in a deep pool. At the end, the generals, their expressions profoundly serious, glanced at Arakal.

Arakal said, "Speaking for myself, I think the slur on our ambassador and technicians is just the Russ estimate of who amongst us is the most *reasonable.* That far, I think their judgement was not too bad."

The generals glanced at Beane, and smiled.

Arakal said to Beane, "Could we get Burke-Johnson here by himself?"

"I think so, sir. Everything seems normal out there. But what line do I take if these partisans want to know what's going on?"

"Just say I sent you to get Burke-Johnson, and later there may be a meeting of our colonels, but you aren't sure. If they want to know more, that's all you've been told."

Beane nodded, and went out.

Arakal turned to Slagiron.

"Can we handle all these partisans?"

"If we can split them up."

There was a murmur of agreement from the three generals.

"What," said Arakal, "are they actually worth, as fighters?"

Slagiron passed his hand across his chin, and glanced at Casey, who frowned, began to speak, and changed his mind.

The generals remained silent.

Slagiron shook his head. "In the light of what we know about them now, it's anyone's guess."

In the uneasy quiet, Burckhardt said, "We *have* had a chance to watch them."

Simons said shortly, "They can kill women and babies."

Slagiron was frowning. "Still, to play this part, I think they would *have* to be well trained."

The last of the three corps commanders, Cesti, said quietly, "They've struck me since they first turned up as being well trained. But a lot of their

men have a wooden quality. I think they don't
care."

Casey frowned. "Because they're just playing a
part?"

Cesti shook his head. "I think it's deeper than
that. They'll do as they're told, but their heart isn't
in it."

Simons growled, "What do we do with this
bastard, Burke-Johnson?"

Arakal said, "We question him."

"I mean, afterward."

Cesti shook his head. "He wasn't there when
they had the massacre."

"He wasn't?"

"He cleared out till the mess was over."

"Then," said Simons, frowning, "maybe he
isn't what he seems to be. Whatever *that* may be."

Casey glanced at Arakal. "Sir, possibly when
Johnson comes in, we should be spread out a little
more?"

Arakal nodded agreeably, and, glancing cal-
culatingly around at the archway, the walls of the
room, and each other, they all spread out.

As if on signal, the outer door opened, to admit
the howl of the wind, a sound of footsteps, the
heavy thud of the door, then an agonized voice.

"Oh, God—" came Burke-Johnson's voice, and
then he cut himself off.

Arakal, watching alertly, saw the Old
Brunswick major halt, astonished relief washing
across his face as he glanced from the heap on the
floor to Arakal and Slagiron.

Abruptly, Burke-Johnson came forward, his
right forefinger to his lips. He knelt by the bodies,
and working with a sort of frenzied silent con-

centration, he jerked the boots from Koljuberowski, glanced at both of them intently,
dropped one, held the other in his hand, and
forced the blade of a small pocket knife in where
the outer layer of the sole appeared slightly separated from the boot with a faint popping sound.
He twisted the sole sharply, whirled it around and
around, pivoting it on the heel, and then the heel
and sole were in one of his hands, and in the other
was the rest of the boot, with a wide glinting
threaded cylinder where the heel had been.

As Arakal and his generals looked on blankly,
Burke-Johnson held the boot upside-down, so
that they could see, nested inside the open-ended
cylinder in the heel, a maze of fine wires and what
looked like bright-colored beads.

Carefully, Burke-Johnson reached in with the
knife blade, and cut something inside the cylinder.

Then, quickly, he checked the boots of
Koljuberowski's guards, pulled off one, and did
with it as he had done with the first boot. He
examined the butts of the guards' guns, and Koljuberowski's holster, then stood and carefully
looked around at the walls of the room. He
glanced alertly at the floor, then looked up intently at the ceiling, to study a small round de-
pression. He drew a large shiny revolver with a
ring at the bottom of the grip, and aimed carefully
at the ceiling.

There was a deafening bang, a shower of parti-
cles, and a little canister fell onto the floor, one
side torn apart in a shambles of tiny broken bits
and pieces.

Burke-Johnson knelt by the bodies, felt of them

rapidly, and then straightened. He cleared his throat.

"Those—" he nodded at the boot heels and the little canister "—are transmitters. Everything you say in their range is heard elsewhere, until they are broken, as they are now." He glanced at the bodies of Koljuberowski and one of his guards. "There lie respectively the second and first in command of the Reception Group."

Arakal glanced from Koljuberowski to the guard, frowning. Burke-Johnson gave a little laugh.

"The corporal of Kol's guard was in effect the *actual* commander. Kol was merely the acting *military* commander. All of these organized partisan groups are tools of 'S'—'S' for 'Security'. Those tanks across the river are Ground Force operated—but their commander is watched by and can be overruled by the attached representative of 'S'. 'S' sees all, hears all, knows all, and commands nearly all—at least in theory."

Arakal looked at Burke-Johnson.

"And you?"

The major's eyes glinted. "I am nothing. I've done them a certain amount of damage, and I may do them a good deal more before I'm through. There have been others like me before, and there will be others again, after they get me. In occasional moments of lightheartedness, I think of myself as 'Triple-S'."

Arakal watched Burke-Johnson intently.

Burke-Johnson looked him in the eye, and smiled. It was an easy and contagious smile, free of care.

" 'S', you see, is 'Security'. 'Triple-S' stands for

'Spontaneous Sabotage of Security'. Such trifling little matters as an adjustment of Pierrot's orders regarding Normandy."

Arakal blinked. "Is there an organization?"

Burke-Johnson smiled, and glanced around.

"I've said more than I should have, already. Incidentally, don't trust anything I or anyone else over here tells you. 'S' makes a specialty of spreading false information. Work everything out for yourself. You can't trust anyone else. And you can't *always* trust yourself."

"All these so-called partisans are Russ?"

Burke-Johnson looked startled.

"They're 'S', not Russian."

"What's the difference?"

" 'S' is the organization that provides security. 'S' is for spying, sabotage, and secret control of people and governments. 'S' is *the control apparatus.*"

Arakal frowned. "But 'S' isn't Russ?"

"The highest levels presumably are mostly Russian. But 'S' is an organization which extends through all Europe and parts of Asia. Obviously, to function, it must include those of the races ruled by it."

"And those uprisings when we landed?"

"You were greeted with genuine delight by the populace. 'S' itself simply stayed underground and notified the Reception Group."

"The 'partisans'?"

"Exactly."

"Why weren't we warned?"

"By whom?"

"By the people."

"Who knew?"

Arakal stared at Burke-Johnson.

Burke-Johnson looked at him earnestly.

"False information is a specialty of 'S'. For a year or more, these so-called 'partisans' have been known to be sabotaging selected Russian installations. It was all done for perfectly false reasons—but the damage itself was real. The populace truly believed that the partisans were backed by the U.S."

"Backed by *what*?"

"The U. S." Burke-Johnson shook his head. "I find it impossible to remember that the U. S. is no more. As much as anyone else, I suppose, I'm a victim of false information."

Arakal groped for the meaning of the faintly familiar expression. "You mean, America?"

Burke-Johnson nodded. "You see, 'S' is shrewd. They permit old motion pictures showing U. S. troops in action. Their own forces, once they've been on the American continent, are kept out of Europe. They occasionally report 'negotiations with the U. S.' The idea put across is that the U. S. could free Europe, but has made a deal, and won't. This is more demoralizing than to reveal that the U. S. has been destroyed."

There was a silence, and Slagiron glanced questioningly at Arakal. Arakal nodded, and Slagiron turned to Burke-Johnson. "What would happen if we were to bring reinforcements, punch into Russ territory through Finland, and swing south and east?"

"Land in Finland by sea? Then enter Russia?"

"Yes."

"If you weren't frozen, drowned, or sunk in mud to your elbows, you might end up the latest

victims of the American nuclear counterattack.
I've heard it said that certain tracts of that territory
are uninhabitable."

Arakal's voice was faintly husky.

"That is where the Old O'Cracys struck back?"

Burke-Johnson looked momentarily blank.
"The— Of course, 'the O'Cracy'. The Western
Democracies." He hesitated, then nodded. "Yes,
that is one place where the O'Cracys hit back.
Hard."

There was a silence in the room. Burke-Johnson
looked around.

Broad Slagiron, his lips a severe line, stood
unmoving, his face twisted with emotion.

Casey's eyes glistened.

Against the wall, Cesti stood motionless, his
fists clenched.

Beside Cesti, profane Simons stood straight,
smiling, tears running down both cheeks.

Burke-Johnson hesitated, cleared his throat,
and spoke carefully.

"The main thing is, don't attack deeper into
Russia. It's all a trap."

There was a silence that stretched out, then a
sound in the room as of a faint sigh.

Arakal's officers were all smiling, and looking
with grudging approval at the major.

Arakal said, "We have our plans, but invading
thousands of miles of snow and ice that the O'Cracys never owned is no part of them. Now, tell
us—why were you so obviously a fake?"

"Why, of course, to make you suspicious. I
hoped if you became suspicious of me, you'd become suspicious of the lot of us."

Arakal smiled. "Well, it helped. And what do you suggest we do now?"

"Slip away as soon as possible, and take to your ships. You can't win here until you beat S. And you can't beat S. They will only falsify your actions to the populace, and profit by your efforts. Their control here is subterranean, and it is too all-inclusive to overcome. It has to be riddled first from within. Leave that to me. If I last long enough, who knows?"

Arakal shook his head.

"We came here to free Old Brunswick and Old Kebeck. We aim to do it."

Burke-Johnson's expression showed an internal struggle. " 'Old Brunswick'—oh, yes, the U.K.—*Britain*. And 'Old Kebeck', of course, is *France*. Well, you *have* freed them, as much as you can. But you can't fight S. It's like a fog or a mist, Arakal. Your strength here is purely military, and is limited by what you can transport in your captured ships. You have no really secure base here—nothing reliably solid to fall back on. The 'Russ', as you call them, are not crude swaggering overlords, who can be met on the field of battle, overthrown and ended. Their influence is pervasive, and exercised covertly, *through* S. You can't fight with the weapons in your possession. Your steel is sharp, you see, but it can't cut the mist."

Arakal, frowning, thought a moment. "Has most of the damage in Europe from the war with the O'Cracys been repaired?"

Burke-Johnson blinked.

"In Western Europe?"

"Yes."

"From all the reports I've read, little physical damage was actually done. The Soviet penetration was primarily a *political* and later an economic penetration by—excuse me for the repetition—the establishment of the apparatus of S throughout Europe."

Slagiron leaned forward.

"Then the cities we see, and the iron roads—they were all here *before the war*?"

"Why, of course."

Arakal took a deep careful breath. He spoke drily.

"They are well kept up."

Burke-Johnson glanced from Arakal to Slagiron and back again.

"You're saying something. But I don't follow."

"With such resources as the Russ have here, *why haven't they long since overcome us*?"

"But the resources *here* are needed for the people *here*. How are they to attack you with the cities and railroads *on this continent*?"

Arakal started to say something, but caught himself. Instead, he said, "Perhaps your idea of slipping away from here is not so bad, after all. *If* we can do it."

Burke-Johnson looked relieved. "We must try to keep S occupied. If you withdraw now, they will expect future attacks from you, and will have to prepare to meet them. I should think the most effective strategy would be one of repeated widely separated threats and pinpricks. That would give us—the opponents of S—the opportunity to do a good deal of damage."

Arakal nodded. "We'll see how soon we can

leave." He glanced at Beane. "Read that Russ comment, in the papers we found on Koljuberowski, to the effect that Major Burke-Johnson had been exposed, and should be withdrawn."

Beane read aloud from the yellow sheets.

Burke-Johnson nodded.

"Interesting. Now— If you can leave before S sends down new orders, you will have an advantage."

Arakal nodded. "We'll try. Good luck."

"Good luck."

When the major had gone out, Arakal glanced at his officers.

"The sooner we're far from here, the better."

Slagiron said grimly, "Speaking for myself, I can't wait to get out of this place."

Casey was apologetic. "Excuse me, sir, but how is this different from defeat?"

Arakal said, "Let them follow us too closely, and they'll find out the difference."

XIII. The Wizards' Legacy

1.

S-One looked over the summary, then glanced at the display, where Arakal and the partisans were on one side of the river, the defending force was on the other side, and, moving up well to the rear was a powerful body of troops, symbolized by a red rectangle. The weather conditions were clearly enough indicated: Snow and wind. The temperature had already dropped sharply, and it was sure to drop again. The only disappointment was that Arakal had yet to call for the troops in the Normandy Citadel. That, however, was something that would, eventually, prove possible to clear up one way or another.

There was a rap on the door, and S-One called, "Come in."

S-Two, looking dazed, stepped in carrying a thin sheaf of papers.

"Arakal has found the S-Plan."

S-One involuntarily jumped to his feet.

"*What?*"

"Neither Arakal nor his senior officers wanted to advance any further. The S officer attached to Koljuberowski gave instructions to remove

Arakal, preliminary to changing the command of Arakal's forces."

"What happened?"

"Arakal and his men killed Koljuberowski, his S officer, and two guards. They found the plan summary on Koljuberowski's body."

"What carelessness! How the devil did all that happen?"

"They may also have killed Burke-Johnson."

"*How did it happen?*"

"*We don't know.* There was only one fixed and two personnel sensors in the room where this happened, and none in the room outside. It was just a detached fort, and we never gave it full treatment. Apparently, Arakal or one of his men spotted the sensors. We heard Burke-Johnson cry out. Next, the sensors were destroyed."

"Where are we now?"

"Arakal is planning, as far as we can judge, to fall back again."

S-One looked at the display.

"It would not be impossible for him to reach those ships, and escape."

"Yes. I'm afraid the Plan is wrecked."

S-One brought his fist down on the desk. "The trouble is, they weren't softened up *in advance*. Always, S work should precede the military blow! The stick breaks easier *after* the rot eats its fibers. But, for lack of anything better—" He paused as S-Two stared at the display. Frowning, S-One looked around.

On the display, little blue symbols were already starting toward the west.

S-Two said, "Shall I call the Marshal?"

S-One measured distances on the display.

"No. It is too late for that. Call the Head of Government. We can't do what I had hoped. But we may still be able to achieve something of importance. Then, later, we will make up for this. It will be a more roundabout procedure, but the result should be the same."

S-Two hurried out.

2.

Admiral Bullinger, short, clean-shaven, with two tufts of hair that stuck straight up at the back of his head, stood beside Arakal and Slagiron, leaning over the charts of the Baltic. He rapped his finger beside a little peninsula.

"Depth eight fathoms on this older chart, when you get it translated out of their heathen reckoning, while this new updated chart *also* shows eight fathoms. Plenty of water. But just to be on the safe side, we put a boat over for soundings before we went in through the fog. These charts were more detailed than the ones we'd found on the ship, but we wanted to be careful. Well, the place is a deathtrap. If the wind blew hard enough, the rocks would stick out on the surface. Next, observe this lighthouse inked in here by hand, and also the blot of ink over here. The blot of ink is to cover up the *false* location of the lighthouse, as it was shown on this chart.

"Both of these detailed charts, the 'partisans' turned over to us. You see, they're both nicely printed. And they reinforce each other. And the details that we could *easily* check were accurate. It was the things we would have taken for granted that would have sunk us."

"How about their suggestion of going in through Finland?"

The admiral's eyes glinted. "Since we didn't do it, we can't know just where the teeth were in the idea. But, to begin with, it would have been wrong. What need do we have to invade Russland? It would draw us aside from our purpose, which is to free the land of the *O'Cracys*. Next there's the possibility that, on the way, these charts would show some additional little defect we hadn't discovered yet. Then, since we were to transport these armed 'partisans', and there were a great number of them, and they would have had to be distributed all over the ships to carry them all— What do you suppose might have happened before we got them unloaded?"

Slagiron smiled and nodded.

Bullinger shook his head.

"You have to admire their preparations. If we didn't put our foot through in one place, there was another loose board somewhere else. And I don't know as we're out of it yet."

Arakal straightened. "There are enough pieces missing in this puzzle."

Slagiron cleared his throat. "On top of everything else, there's the fact that, with no fight, we were able to get away from our own set of 'partisans'. Why?"

Bullinger looked puzzled.

"If you got out quietly—"

"There was no way we could get out without their knowing it. They *let* us go."

Bullinger stared fixedly at the chart, then nodded.

"I've seen a spider catch a good many flies—and then cut a bumblebee loose from the web."

Slagiron shook his head.

"Don't forget, the Russ themselves were just across the river. We could have had one sweet time to get out of there alive."

"At what price for them?"

Slagiron smiled. "Oh, they would have paid a good price. But it might have ended us."

Arakal said exasperatedly, "How do we know how to fight them, when we don't understand them? Their plans have levels, one hidden by the other, the way an onion has layers."

Bullinger said thoughtfully, "After we had the partisan leaders locked up, we got some farmers in here one at a time, showed them these lying charts, explained how we'd been deceived by Otto and Yudrik, and said we wanted to learn the truth. You understand, our interpreters were none too good. But, little by little, it got across."

"This 'S' is an all-embracing control system. You can call it whatever you want, but that's what it is. It aims to control everything. Go to worship, and the priest is either an agent of S, or else an agent of S is watching him and possibly also telling him what to do. Serve in the army, and the general's orderly is an agent of S, watching him, and from time to time either he or some other agent is giving the general orders. S aims to run everything, and to run everything, S has to know everything. Spies are everywhere. Have a date tonight with the girl down the road, and the local agent of S knows it by tomorrow morning, and has a good estimate, by the day after, of how things went. It may help S manipulate you—and her.

"Apparently, the only way not to tangle with S is to stick to the basics of your trade, and care nothing whatever about rising. Stay flat to the ground. If you try to rise, S controls your success, and it finally dawns on you that, without S, you go nowhere. The natural thing then is to try to rise *with* S. But, to do that, you have to spy, betray, prove your loyalty to S, care only for what S cares for—and then you've lost all freedom of thought, and scarcely exist as a person. Not to succeed means you're shoved down and miserable. But, in this mess, to succeed means you have to sell your soul."

Arakal, frowning, looked out the round window at the gray waters of the bay.

Slagiron said, his voice a growl, "Well, we're sworn to free Old Brunswick and Old Kebeck. But this thing has no handle on it!"

Arakal, still looking out, said exasperatedly, "Have we freed Old Brunswick and Old Kebeck?"

"They acted like it when we got there. And the same in Allemain."

"But what have we done that would stop S?"

Slagiron and Bullinger glanced at each other. Arakal tore his gaze from the quiet waters and looked at them.

Slagiron said, "It seems to me that we have done exactly nothing."

Bullinger nodded. "So far, it's a draw. They have us running in circles. We have some military victories. But they must still be far more powerful everywhere but in Normandy."

Slagiron shook his head. "As for S, we've killed or captured a few underlings, who must be easy enough to replace. That's all."

Into the thick silence as they looked at each other, came the quick rap of heels approaching on the deck. There was a knock at the door.

Bullinger glanced at Arakal, who nodded, and Bullinger called, "Come in!"

The cabin door opened, and Smith, the acting chief of Arakal's technicians, stepped inside.

"Sir, we've had word from Colputt!"

Slagiron straightened.

Arakal said, "Where is he?"

"The guide-ships are bringing him in through the channel. He should be here early tonight. He says he has one platform with him, assembled and ready to use, and the other partly disassembled."

Arakal smiled. "Good!" He glanced at Bullinger. "Everything may depend on Colputt."

Bullinger nodded, but with no great show of conviction. "I don't see how we're going to fight an enemy who vanishes into thin air. No matter what we do, he'll just reappear after we leave."

Arakal nodded. "It's all different from what we expected. But I'm glad Colputt's here."

3.

The Head of Government was seated at a small metal table in a room where the light came in through high barred windows, below which were walls lined with file cases. A gooseneck lamp cast the only artificial light in the room directly on the file G-One was reading.

"Is this," he asked, his voice low, with a faint tremor, "supposed to be accepted as the truth?"

"It is the truth," said S-One, "as far as I know it. And it fits in reasonably with what I do know, of my own personal knowledge. So far as I can judge, there is nothing of misinformation about it."

"Does the present generation of Americans know this?"

"Not as far as I know. But, it is not impossible that they may suspect something of the kind. It would be possible, even, to provisionally deduce something of this character, from the pattern of the nuclear attack against the Americans. And, you have to remember, they were very careless with nearly every form of internal compartmentation. The information is doubtless there to be found, somewhere." S-One paused, then said, frowning, "Just as other things are there to be found, if only they look. And they are looking."

"What do you have in mind?"

"Our information from within Arakal's army is negligible. From within his government, little better. I had thought to have someone inserted into his personal entourage, but that was crudely handled, and came to nothing. But when he took over our colonies, he gave us the first opportunity to penetrate his organization. We are at least started. Now, as regards Colputt, we have received very curious information, which to me can mean only one thing. Colputt has discovered some possibly formidable device, of characteristics I personally cannot imagine."

"What type of device?"

"Are you through reading that?"

"For now."

"Then," said S-One, his voice perfectly matter-of-fact, "you see the deeper reason for the S organization?"

"What do you mean?"

"We are not just a mechanism for the government's political purposes."

The Head of Government looked at him blankly, then suddenly stared off down a narrow aisle between the rows of file cases. He gave a low exclamation.

S-One said, "You are now in possession of a piece of information that must go no further. Now, let me show you this factor whose details I cannot grasp." He held out a thin folder labeled, "Activities of Chief of American Technological Service Colputt." Apologetically, S-One said, "The title is ours. He is only called, amongst the Americans, 'Chief Mechanic Colputt'. We need some better handle than that to hold him by."

"You receive these reports regularly?"

"That thin folder is a summary of all the hard information in the whole file. I call your attention particularly to the last entries."

The Head of Government skimmed the folder quickly, then read the last part slowly and carefully.

"So, Colputt sent for Arakal. The communications were personally deciphered by Arakal. Arakal's men were consumed with curiosity. Arakal went away, evidently to see what Colputt had found. He returned and apparently said nothing. Now, what does all this mean?"

"I cannot measure it. It fits in with other information I have, but it is still incomplete. But, in light of this, I think it would be wise to do nothing that might hurt Arakal personally. I have sent out a directive to that effect. We have had repeated indications that Arakal does not wish us ill, and might be inclined to cooperate with us. If anything should happen to him, how do we know who might come to power? He is, of course, extremely dangerous politically."

"Better that," said the Head of Government, "then the unknown risks suggested by this development?"

"Yes. But I cannot explain all the reasons, and there are bound to be those in the organization who are overzealous. Ordinarily, when instructions are given that someone is to be removed as a factor in the situation, it is a matter of pride to carry out these instructions. Some bullheaded individual may still try it. There is little I can do about that. Except one thing."

"What is that?"

S-One's smile showed bright even teeth. "If anyone as much as expresses doubt about the new directive, I will make an example of him that will not very soon be forgotten."

"I will do the same."

"You see the situation?"

"I see the part you have shown me."

S-One said earnestly, "I do not misinform you. When I give you no information, it is for a reason. If I misdirect you, it is for a reason. Bear in mind, I am part of a survival apparatus. One must take human nature into account, if one wishes his measures to succeed. And these measures must succeed."

"Your measures have not succeeded with Arakal."

"I have not been able to penetrate his organization. I do not understand him, and so have been unable to dominate him. But that may yet come.

Who can say? But let me complete the point I am making that I am not misinforming you *when I say to you* that I am not misinforming you."

S-One spoke very earnestly, and G-One smiled. "If you say you are not lying, then, *at that moment*, you are *not* lying."

S-One looked at his face intently, and then laughed.

"Exactly."

The Head of Government smiled somewhat sadly. "It must be pleasant to have simple comradeship, as in Arakal's army, for instance."

"Yes, but then, look where it leads. And there are legends which suggest that all this may have happened more than once."

"Each time somewhat differently?"

"I would suppose so."

"It is difficult to think or plan on such a long-range basis. The specifics could change considerably beyond what was expected."

"Very true. And, in this case, do you see how the specifics *might* fit together?"

"Hm. . . . Dare we hope?"

"Who knows? I have had the pursuit delayed, to be sure errors did not enter in at the last moment. Of course, we cannot break it off entirely. But the final engagement could be short."

"Yes. Now, let's see. . . . The next move is, I think, fairly obvious." G-One frowned. "Unless the *specifics* are different from what we expect."

"We will have to wait and see. It should not be long."

"The preparations had better be made now. We want nothing to go wrong at the last minute."

4.

Colputt, chief of Arakal's technicians, was still somewhat greenish from the ocean crossing as he sat at the table, stroked his white beard, and listened to Arakal's brief summary of their experiences.

At the end, Colputt nodded. "We had our mysteries, too. And if things had turned out just a little bit differently, we wouldn't have got here."

Bullinger nodded. "I knew you must be having trouble, or we'd have heard from you."

Colputt shook his head.

"From your account, and the old books, we knew the Atlantic wasn't nice to cross. What we didn't know was that it had changed since the books were written."

Bullinger looked doubtful. "We didn't notice anything like that. Perhaps, due to lack of experience—"

"Our lack of experience wouldn't move icebergs, or change the temperature of air and water."

"What happened?"

"We ran into freezing rain, then dense fog, and we were creeping through the fog when a wall of ice loomed up in front of us. We changed direction just in time—and lost the radio mast over the side. Like everything else, it was heavy with ice. The ice had accumulated *fast*."

"You must have gotten too far north."

Colputt said, "The ice was too far south. When we came out of this, suddenly it was *warm*—almost hot—too warm by far for where we were. This wasn't like a change in the weather. It was as if we were in a tub, and someone dumped in some ice, then equalized the temperature by pouring in some hot water. I don't know of anything like that in the old records. Yes—after an unusually cold stretch of weather, the icebergs might be further south than usual. This was different."

Bullinger, frowning, glanced around at young Markel, his fleet navigator, standing against the cabin wall behind him.

"What was it you were trying to tell me the other day?"

"Sir—Oh, about the weather?"

"Yes."

"Something the people here said. That after the war with the O'Cracys, it seemed that the weather changed. Sometimes the weather seems too cold, sometimes too hot. And the sun isn't right."

Bullinger shook his head. "Weather never seems right. The normal situation is abnormal."

Colputt nodded. "But what we ran into wasn't weather."

"What was it, then?"

"I don't know."

Arakal glanced at Slagiron.

"You remember what the farmers told us about the weather in Russland?"

Slagiron said drily, "Who could forget it? It was one reason not to go deeper in Russland."

Arakal glanced at Colputt.

"They told us it was said that there was solid ice and snowbanks from one coast to the other, and sometimes the sun would shine through hotter than the hottest summer, turn the ice to water, burn through the vegetation under the snow, turn the ground black—and then it would start to snow again."

Slagiron said, "All we actually experienced, where we were, was snow and cold. In the winter, it must be worse than Kebeck Fortress in January."

Colputt frowned. "But, further in the interior, *sometimes for a while*, it was hotter than the hottest summer?"

Slagiron nodded. "That's the way they put it."

Arakal said, "The impression we got was that, for a little while, the place turned into an oven, and that in that place it was a *lot* hotter than the hottest summer."

"I don't see," said Colputt, "how hot weather could be restricted to *certain places* in the middle of winter."

There was a silence as they thought it over. Then Slagiron cleared his throat, and glanced at Arakal.

"How many puzzles does *this* make?"

Arakal said, "First, there was the question why they didn't wipe us out soon after we got here. Our whole picture was wrong. We didn't realize what we were up against."

"But," said Colputt, "*could* they have wiped you out?"

Slagiron nodded soberly. "They could have done it with a thousand men at the right places. You never saw a bigger mess."

"Instead," said Arakal, "we were welcomed. They wined us, dined us, rushed us over the iron roads straight for Russland. All these 'partisans' we've told you about joined us on the way. If they weren't shaking our hands or kissing us, they were giving us bouquets of flowers and bottles of wine."

"But," objected Colputt, "it wasn't the Russ who were doing this?"

"No, but the Russ didn't stop it."

Colputt frowned.

Arakal said, "In fact, they had us surrounded with their own people, and they were rushing us straight into a trap. They got us out of Old Kebeck fast, and without actually putting forth their full strength. They were pulling us straight forward, to freeze us into submission."

"Well," said Colputt, "I would say that's no puzzle. It was extremely shrewd tactics on their part."

"Oh," said Slagiron, "it's no puzzle now. Now we've got other puzzles. But it was a puzzle then. There was one puzzle after another. The final puzzle was—why did they let us get away?"

Admiral Bullinger said thoughtfully, "I think they just wanted to avoid casualties. At no expense to themselves, they've got us all back on the coast."

"But this is a peculiar way to wage war. This is not how they do it on the other side of the ocean."

Colputt frowned. "There does seem to be something else behind all this. Something out of sight."

Slagiron nodded. "We're still groping in the dark."

Arakal said, "Now we have the question of 'S'. Why do they rule through S? Do the Russ rule S? Or does it rule them? What do they plan to do next, now that we seem to know what they were doing before? And, this last puzzle—what's wrong with the weather here?"

Slagiron spoke hesitantly.

"We've all seen what we've seen—and there's no reason I can think of why the Russ farmers would lie to us. But, could their weather be so much changed here? What is there that could change it? The sun shines from the sky. The wind blows as it will. What could change the weather?"

Colputt shook his head. "In the old days, maybe they could have told you. But I don't know. We have books from that time, but we're short on understanding."

There was a silence, and Arakal decided to change the subject.

"What of the platforms?"

Colputt's look of gloom vanished.

"There, at least, is something we have the Russ don't. And it's positive proof that, whatever the Russ may say now, our ancestors were as able as theirs."

Around the table, everyone leaned closer.

Arakal said, "Are the platforms ready?"

"One is ready now. The other will be before the day is out."

Bullinger, listening closely, glanced from Arakal to Colputt. His curiosity showed on his face, but he said nothing.

Arakal was looking at Colputt. "Inside the tunnels—the bodies on the floor, above the platforms?"

"Started to deteriorate after we'd been in there a while. We gave them a decent burial. Kotzebuth thinks what happened was that when the Russ attacked, some radiation like that of light, but finer, must have penetrated the whole mountain, and killed everything, including the organisms of decay."

The room was silent with the listening of Bullinger, Beane, Slagiron, and Markel, all of whose faces were now carefully blank and noncommittal, but who somehow gave the impression that their consciousness was concentrated in their ears.

Arakal said, "But the machines themselves—"

"Well, as you remember, they were sealed off on a lower level, in a room lined with lead, and set on big coil springs, with an arrangement of cylinders to damp the shock. The machines looked all right when we first found them, but when you left, we still couldn't be sure. When we finally got into them, we found no sign of damage. The machines perform—" Colputt hesitated, as if groping for words, then concluded "—beyond our expectations."

"And the fuel—?"

A muscle twitched at Colputt's jaw.

"The arrangement for fuel is as we hoped."

Arakal sat back.

"Our crews?"

Colputt nodded. "Our crews are trained."

Arakal let his breath out slowly.

"If this is so— Then we want to be careful that this doesn't give us delusions of greatness. Yet, I would like to give the Russ a taste of what the O'Cracys used to be. Are we sure the platforms weren't hurt in the crossing?"

"As sure as we can be. We kept constant watch on both of them. But if we'd hit that wall of ice, we'd have been sunk in a flash."

Arakal nodded soberly, and turned to the intently listening Slagiron and Bullinger.

"Tomorrow, perhaps, we may see what the Old O'Cracys could do."

5.

Dawn—if it could be called that—was a lighter grayness, somewhere to the south of east, as the huge door at the bow of Colputt's ship began slowly to lower. Lower and lower it came, until at last it reached out like a bridge, and then the end sank in the shallow water. From the deep shadows within came a low whine that climbed higher and higher, accompanied by a sound like a rising wind.

Slowly, something moved out from the shadows onto the lowered drawbridge.

Slagiron, watching, caught his breath.

Wide, dark, smoothly curving, with a dome at the center, it glided slowly down the drawbridge, crossed the water in a whirl of mist, and now behind it there came another.

As Slagiron and Bullinger stood paralyzed, there was a sudden change of pitch, the first of the two devices tilted slightly forward, and suddenly climbed into the sky so fast that it dwindled as they watched. An instant later, the second followed.

Bullinger stared up at high twin reflections of the sun, which was itself still below the horizon, then the reflections winked out. He looked east to Russland, and grinned.

Beside him, Slagiron shut his jaws with a click.

Bullinger exhaled. "Now we know."

"The devil," said Slagiron. "Maybe you know. What was it?"

6.

S-One read the report with wide eyes. He sat up, glanced at S-Two, who was standing by the desk. S-One cleared his throat.

S-Two said, "What will they do with this?"

"I will have to speak to the Head of Government. We must act at once."

7.

Arakal, standing as if paralyzed in the eerie silence, stared out the wide curving window. Though he could see nothing now but blowing mist, he had the impression that he was up among the stars, looking down on the slowly turning ball of Earth.

Beside him, Colputt smiled.

Arakal exhaled carefully.

"What was it you said—the machines perform 'beyond our expectations'?"

Colputt nodded. "I didn't know how much you wanted me to mention. And there was no way to describe this. It surpasses our wildest imaginings. There is no mountain in the world we couldn't fly over, and no place on the surface of the Earth that we couldn't reach. And we can outrace the sun to get there!"

Arakal felt the universe seem to swim around him. With an effort, he kept silent until he could trust his voice.

"How does it work?"

Colputt shook his head.

"The levers and switches I can show you—and

what happens when I work them. *How* it does what it does is beyond me."

"But—I thought you said, back when we found it, that this looked like a 'ground effect machine'."

"It seemed so, to start with. It seemed to match that description closer than anything else. But when we had enough skill to maneuver it, and had it out where there was plenty of room, I tried it one day at full power, and you see what happened."

Colputt leaned forward, to tap a button on the slanting control board. Around them, the solid upper wall of the cabin vanished. As if through thin clouds, the stars shone in. Colputt tapped the button again, and the wall was solid.

"How do I explain such things?"

"Could we go still higher?"

"I'm sure we *could*. Whether it might kill us to do it I don't know."

Arakal shook his head.

"I see now why the Russ make such mistakes when they get their machines in action. Such devices are like strong drink. Better that we go lower, and look around as we'd planned to. And be careful we don't smash into the other platform, and wreck both of them."

As they dropped down, Arakal leaned forward intently. Abruptly he straightened, and he and Colputt cast quick glances at each other.

Around them, the streaming snowflakes were beginning to glow like fireflies.

Ahead of them, there was a growing brilliance.

XIV. The Conference

1.

The sun was sinking out of sight toward the west as the first of the two platforms came back into view of the fleet, slowed with a sudden roar, and glided into the interior of Colputt's ship. A moment later, the second followed.

Bullinger was waiting as Arakal and Colputt climbed up the ladder of the flagship. A heavy concussion, followed by a second, half-deafened them.

Bullinger's lips drew back in a grin.

"A little trouble from your old friends."

Arakal nodded. "They've got more tanks on the way. We saw them."

"If you can spot them for us, we'll take care of them before they get here."

"They're still a long way off. If you have time, why don't you come below. We think we have some answers."

Bullinger nodded, ran up a ladder, spoke with an officer on the deck above, then came back, to guide Arakal and Colputt to a different cabin than they had used the last time. Bullinger shut the door, and glanced around.

"Now, none of our 'allies' has ever been in here—so *maybe* it's all right. And I've had the whole place checked, inside and out. Strange to say, where we were talking the last time, there was a listening device beside the leg of the table, close under the top. There was another in one of the light fixtures. I *think* we got them all, but they may have been cleverer than we are. For that matter, they could have built some more in here when they made the ship. We've checked. But don't tell me anything aloud that you don't want to risk their finding out."

Arakal smiled. "If they can hear this, they can do what they want with it. I think we begin to *understand* them."

"Could you—fly over—?"

Arakal nodded.

"I suppose," said Bullinger hesitantly, "the snow, fog, and so on, blotted out a good deal of it?"

"From direct observation. But we've underestimated the Old O'Cracys far worse than we ever knew. The platform has devices to *see through fog.*"

"*What?*"

"As I say, we've underestimated the Old O'Cracys."

Bullinger frowned at the repetition. Then he stiffened.

"The Russ are ruined, too?"

"We didn't try to see *all* of Russland, although with the platform that's not so impossible as it sounds. But most of what we *did* see was like the country well north of Kebeck Fortress in the depth of winter."

"But I thought this Central Committee of theirs meets in Moscow? That's their capital, isn't it?"

Arakal glanced at Colputt.

Colputt said, "There were three fair-sized zones of heat radiation which may mean underground dwellings. The locations correspond on our maps to places called Leningrad, Moscow, and Kiev. Further south and to the east, it looks heavily settled."

Bullinger sat back, blank-faced. "What this must mean is that the Old Soviets got clubbed in that war almost as bad as the Old O'Cracys! But they won! We've always known they won!"

Arakal said drily, "If two men fight, and one gets shot in the head while the other gets shot in the stomach, who won?"

Colputt said, "They destroyed the Old O'Cracys. We have no memory—no continuity of thought descending from that time. They have their Central Committee, their 'S', apparently some underground centers, and the districts to the south—which may have been completely untouched by the war."

Bullinger nodded. "They won—but they almost didn't survive it. But that isn't the picture we've had. It always seemed—"

In the corridor, brisk footsteps came to a halt. There was a rap on the door.

Arakal nodded to Bullinger's questioning glance. Bullinger called, "Come in."

The door opened, and Slagiron stepped inside, frowning. He turned to Arakal.

"Catmeat's old gang has been trying to break through. They make better enemies than they did friends, but we're too well dug in; and on top of that, there's the fire from the ships. Fifteen minutes ago, a messenger came through. They want a 'conference'."

Arakal nodded. "They've got more tanks coming. If they can have us tied up talking when the tanks get here—"

Slagiron put his hand on the doorknob, then hesitated, "Could you see much of Russland?"

Arakal told him what he had told Bullinger, and a look of amazement spread over Slagiron's face.

"No wonder we couldn't understand them! Their position is completely different than we thought!"

Arakal said, "We still don't want to underestimate them. For all we know, they may have something in mind we haven't spotted yet."

Slagiron nodded grimly. "We'll keep our eyes open. I'll let them know what they can do with this conference."

As he turned to go out, there was a sound of rapidly approaching footsteps, then an urgent rap on the door.

Bullinger called, "Come in!"

Beane stepped inside, nodded to Slagiron, and glanced at Arakal.

"Sir, I think we're about to be treated to some new trick. We've just had a message from what purports to be the chairman of their Central Committee. A 'Mikhael Zhtutin' is coming to see us as their 'plenipotentiary'. He is, quote, authorized to deal with all the matters of mutual disagreement between us, end-quote. They—the Central Committee—want a truce in the fighting while he's here."

Arakal thought a moment, then nodded.

"All right. We'll risk it." He glanced at Slagiron. "Tell Koljuberowski's people we'll agree to a cease-fire, but we don't want any conference with them, since Zhtutin will be here. We'll put the platforms up, to see what's coming."

When Beane and Slagiron had gone out, Arakal turned to Bullinger.

"What chance is there of small boats sneaking up on us in the fog, to board?"

"I've already warned the captains. We'll make it hot for them if they try it."

Colputt came to his feet. "I'll get the platforms up."

Arakal nodded. "This conference may be useful. Or it could turn out to be pure poison."

2.

It was morning when Slagiron's deputy, Casey, sent word that the plenipotentiary had arrived. Arakal headed for the conference room.

Mikhael Zhtutin turned out to be a lean, somber man, well above average height, neat, slightly stooped, and dressed in a heavy fur coat and large fur hat with flaps for the back of the head and the ears. With him came an interpreter, also wearing fur hat and fur coat.

Arakal, Slagiron, and Beane stood at the end of the table as Zhtutin was escorted in.

Zhtutin cast a penetrating glance at each of the three men, and his gaze settled on Arakal.

Zhtutin spoke in a low, courteous voice. His interpreter turned to Arakal, and adopted the air of a schoolmaster addressing children caught marking the walls.

"You are the tribal chief known as Arakal?"

Zhtutin, just removing his fur hat, froze. Frowning, he asked the interpreter a question.

Behind Arakal, one of his own interpreters leaned forward and spoke in a low voice.

"Mr. Zhtutin asks if the question was courteously put. The interpreter replies that he used the proper tone for the occasion."

Arakal said, "Politely say to the Russ plenipotentiary that we use that tone of voice to dogs that steal food from the table."

Arakal's interpreter thought a moment, then spoke politely.

Zhtutin spoke agitatedly to his interpreter. The interpreter looked intently from Arakal's interpreter to Arakal, looked at Arakal and said, his voice exaggeratedly polite, "It is you who call yourself Arakal?" The interpreter raised one arm as if to point.

Zhtutin's face went blank. His hand flashed for the open front of his coat. There was a deafening explosion. The interpreter slammed against the bulkhead.

Arakal, Slagiron, and Beane, guns in hand, straightened from behind the table.

At the far end of the table, Zhtutin, his expression angry and exasperated, slid a large shiny revolver back inside his coat.

The interpreter, partly hidden by the table, lay on the deck.

At the door, Bullinger, backed up by half-a-dozen armed men, looked in. He glanced at Zhtutin, then at Arakal.

Arakal said, "Get some men in here to clean up

the place, and take out the interpreter. Watch out when you move him. He probably had a sleeve gun."

Bullinger called in several sailors, who carefully bent over the interpreter, put a small shiny pistol on the table, carried out the body, then methodically cleaned the room's floor and walls, the deck, part of the table nearby, and Zhtutin's coat.

Slagiron, Beane, and Arakal watched the proceedings in silence. Zhtutin, glum and apparently embarrassed, waited silently, and gave a nod of thanks to the sailors as they went out. Arakal sent one of his own interpreters to the far end of the table. Zhtutin, his lips compressed, nodded his thanks to Arakal, glanced back at the interpreter Arakal was lending him, smiled ruefully, and spoke to the interpreter, who grinned and said something in return.

Behind Arakal, his interpreter leaned forward. "Mr. Zhtutin said, 'Don't worry, we don't always treat our interpreters that way.' Our man said, 'That's all right. It's all in the line of duty.' "

Arakal and Slagiron, smiling, glanced at the Russ plenipotentiary, who looked questioning, and reached for the chair, still in its place at the table. Arakal nodded, and they all sat down.

Zhtutin spoke in a regretful tone, and the interpreter translated. "I regret that incident. I will explain the background if you wish, but it is related to a change of view within our own councils which has, whether everyone realizes it or not, been settled."

Arakal said courteously, "We ask to hear only what you wish to tell us."

Zhtutin's face cleared. He said, with a slight air of apology, "I should perhaps mention that the name which I am using is a cover for my actual identity, but that I am fully empowered to speak for the Central Committee."

Arakal smiled. "It is your message which interests us. You are welcome here under whatever name you choose to use."

Zhtutin smiled and relaxed, then looked serious.

"Is it *safe* to talk here?"

"We have removed every listening device *we* could find."

"Of *ours*?"

"Yes."

"Can *you* speak freely?"

Arakal answered without hesitation. "Yes."

Zhtutin looked searchingly at Arakal, as if not certain whether Arakal's answer was a reply to him, or might possibly be meant to convince someone else who might be listening.

Arakal added, his voice courteous. "We have no 'S'."

Zhtutin smiled briefly.

"Then I will speak plainly. Power abides with those who use it well. The foolish and the indolent lose it. And also eventually the arrogant and the presumptuous. The Central Committee authorizes me to tell you that we will grant you your independence, and the independence of what you call Old Brunswick and what we call the U. K. In return, there are certain things you must do for us."

Arakal waited a moment, then spoke carefully and distinctly.

"We are sworn to free Old Brunswick *and Old Kebeck*. Can you turn over to us all information on S in those two countries?"

Zhtutin looked fixedly at Arakal, then he slowly nodded. He appeared to select his words with care.

"We, in our turn, demand that you use what means you possess to correct—in good time and very judiciously—certain errors made in the past. Are you familiar with that of which I speak?"

Arakal kept his gaze fixed on Zhtutin. "We can make no promises, except that we will do what we can to relieve you of the curse which has settled on you, and we aim to do it once we understand the situation and the method clearly."

Zhtutin's eyes seemed momentarily very bright.

"You understand, it is necessary to use *great care*."

"That is becoming more and more clear to us."

Zhtutin sat still a moment, then sighed, and sat back.

"You will have the agent lists for the U. K. and France as soon as they can be gotten here. I must go back to my vehicle, and radio our agreement at once. Of course—" he smiled faintly "—The cousins may already know of it. We will take great care with those lists."

"If you need guards—"

Zhtutin shook his head. "There are a few who still do not understand. That is all."

3.

Slagiron sat looking at the door by which the plenipotentiary had gone out.

"There must be something to this Central Committee, after all. But what was that you said about a curse?"

Arakal said, "There are some things that have to be seen to be believed. Let's find out if Colputt's back. If so, there's something we want to check and you might like to see it."

4.

The ground dropped away rapidly as Slagiron, his jaws clenched, hands gripping the edge of the control panel, stared out through the wide curving window where the landscape shrank and the horizon dropped and the whole earth seemed to tilt and then vanish, to leave only blowing mist.

Arakal relaxed with an effort, and looked around.

Colputt was bent beside his pilot, who nodded, glanced up briefly, and tapped a spot on the angled plate where a view of the snow-covered landscape rolled back toward them.

Slagiron exhaled carefully, observed his hands still clamped on the edge of the control panel, and let go.

Colputt cleared his throat.

"A few moments more." He glanced at Arakal. "I'm afraid the Russ may be counting on us to do something we can't do."

Arakal shook his head.

"I think they know exactly what they're doing. And we made no promise that we can't keep."

"Then," said Colputt ruefully, "there must be something you see that I don't."

Arakal looked through the wide window at the glow toward which they were rushing.

"I don't think the problem Zhtutin mentioned is his most pressing problem. They have long since adapted to that. I think the pressing difficulty is one he didn't want to mention aloud—that somehow *they have to control* S. And the immediate value of this agreement to him is, he is using us to do it. The thought that we might also be able to clear this up—this terrific problem that we have just seen for the first time—that is a useful pretext, and if we can do it some day, it's a bonus, thrown in free."

Colputt looked puzzled. "To control S? Why?"

Slagiron glanced at Colputt.

"How would you like to have S for a subordinate? They have to use S to keep a hold on the army, and to keep the populace too tied in knots to rise up. But it's the nature of organizations to take over more and more, and since *this* organization is secret, how do you know all it's doing, in order to control it? When there's an enemy to concentrate on, that must focus the attention of S more or less where they want it. But we were knocked so flat so long it must have become a question when S would take *them* over. And whatever anyone may say, S isn't equipped to govern. S can spy, thwart, and suppress—*but it can't lead.*"

Colputt blinked. "Then if we eliminate the networks of S in Old Brunswick and Old Kebeck—what we are doing for them is to prune back an overgrown organization?"

Slagiron nodded. "After that, S ought to be so busy trying to rebuild its networks that they will be able to get it loose from *them.*"

Colputt stroked his long white beard, then shook his head.

"Such things are as far beyond my understanding as the Old O'Cracy's calculating machines."

"What I don't see," said Slagiron, glancing at Arakal, "is this 'curse' you spoke of. Zhtutin knew what you meant. But—"

Colputt said, "Look out there."

As Slagiron turned, the increasing brightness outside lit their faces, lit the edges of the window, lit the snowflakes whirling back, and glowed on the ceiling overhead. The brilliance grew to a blaze; then the substance of the window itself seemed to darken to shade out the glare.

Below, the dazzle of the snow came to a sudden end, and beyond it an arc of land lay dark and steaming beneath clouds of brilliantly lit vapor rushing in the wind.

The pilot swung them out of the dazzling light, dropped fast, and shot through the blowing mist. Suddenly they were racing along above the dark earth, with high snowbanks to either side. Ahead, blowing snow was spreading across a charred band of earth as the pilot dropped still lower.

Slagiron leaned forward, and as they raced along in a channel between high banks of snow, he gave a low exclamation. "It's getting dark!"

Colputt said, "As we go up, look at the sun."

They were rising in the dimness through thick blowing snow. Then suddenly snow and mist were gone. Through the curving window shone a field of stars.

Slagiron looked around. "There's no sun! But it was daylight!"

Ahead of them, swinging into the center of the curving window as they turned, there was a thin fiery arc at the edge of a grayness shot through with tiny brilliant specks.

For a long moment, they stared at it in silence, as it moved across the slowly turning window.

"My God!" said Slagiron. "Is *that* the sun?"

Colputt said, "Yes. There's curse enough for anyone. Now watch."

He tapped the control that turned the opaque upper walls and ceiling transparent.

They looked up and around, at dazzling arcs and disks of glaring brilliance, hanging amongst the stars as if the sun, blotted out where it belonged, had sprung to new locations in space.

"But—" Slagiron paused. "Zhtutin said there had been 'certain errors'. Errors? That the sun itself had been blotted out? Or somehow *refocused*?"

Colputt tapped the control, and again the upper hull was opaque.

Arakal cleared his throat.

"I *think* that's what Zhtutin meant."

Slagiron looked at him.

"Who made the errors?"

Arakal said, "Until Zhtutin used that way of expressing it, I thought the Old O'Cracys must have done this. I still think so. Who else could have done it, if Zhtutin wants *us* to undo it?"

Colputt said, "There is quite a gap in our records. But it must be."

"But— *How did they do it?*"

"Consider this platform," said Colputt. "Is it surprising that people who could make such things as this could go into the space between the Earth and the sun?"

"No," said Slagiron. "But, having got there— To screen out the sun itself? That's impossible!"

Colputt shook his head. "What is impossible if you possess the means to bring it about? The Old O'Cracys possessed substances very light and thin, yet very strong, and they possessed the means to silver these substances so that they would reflect light. Right there we have the basis of what would be needed. Now—would a shield made from those thin substances *last*? I don't know. And could the shields be exactly positioned to do the work? Again I don't know. Apparently whatever it is has been put in orbit around the sun, and keeps precise pace with the Earth. More than that. The sum total of whatever has been put up seems to be very carefully designed to deliver just as much extra heat, carefully focused, in some places, as it withholds in others. The sum total, over a period of time, apparently remains the same as if there were no interference with the sun. The complications are mind-staggering. But the Old O'Cracys may very well have had the means to do it."

"The depth of that snow didn't look like the delivery of as much heat as had been withheld."

"The depth there. But go a little further, and we find a place with *no* snow. Anyway, the total amount of heat delivered must not have changed."

"Why?"

"At the rim of the Baltic," said Colputt, "they say the weather fluctuates. But in Old Kebeck, you heard no complaint of a change in the weather. If there were a serious change here, in the amount of heat received, it would have been bound to affect the weather in Old Kebeck."

Slagiron nodded. "Yes, that's reasonable."

Arakal said, "That means, then, that whatever was done was done very carefully."

Colputt nodded. "And with great skill."

Arakal looked out at the mist again streaming past as they headed back.

"If it was done with such care, would it have been a war? And yet . . . what else *could* it have been but a war?"

Colputt shook his head. "I don't know."

Slagiron was frowning. "If anyone won, it was the Old Soviets. But, if the O'Cracys had such means as these—"

Arakal said, "The details can change everything. To understand this, we need to know *exactly how it happened.*"

Slagiron nodded.

"We'll have to try to find out."

5.

Zhtutin, visibly wary, settled into the seat at the end of the table. He spoke briefly and sharply.

Arakal's translator cleared his throat.

"Mr. Zhtutin asks, 'You have lists. What more do you want?' "

"There is a question of our doing what we can do, as soon as we understand the situation, and know how to do it."

Zhtutin looked directly at Arakal.

"What of that?"

"You spoke of an 'accident'."

Zhtutin's gaze briefly wavered, then he looked directly at Arakal.

"You object to my choice of words?"

"I spoke of a 'curse'. You made no objection."

"What objection is required?"

"Our word is then pledged only to deal with a 'curse' resulting from an 'accident'?"

Zhtutin frowned.

"What is it you want?"

"The facts we don't have."

"That is your problem."

Arakal leaned forward.

"Mr. Plenipotentiary, in my opinion, *very possibly there was no war*. If so, you have never won in fair combat, because there was no combat. There was, as you say, an 'accident'. I want to know about that accident."

Zhtutin shoved back his chair, started to get up, paused with one hand on the table, looking toward the door, then slowly sat down, turning, and looked directly at Arakal.

"You say there was no war! You see your own country in ruins! It was, once, greater than these European nations you admire. You see the hell in the Soviet Union—and *you* tell *me* there was no war! Are you insane?"

"We merely have no S," said Arakal, his voice quiet, "to tell us what to think, and so we *can* think. Perhaps later, if we develop further, we will have an S of our own, and be as unable to think then as you think we are now. But as for now, if you want us to end the problem, we need to understand the problem. And to do that, it would help for you to tell us about the accident."

"And if I refuse?"

"We will keep our word. You are here under our safe-conduct, and can leave anytime. But neither we nor you know *when* we will have the facts, or when we will know whether in fact the curse we spoke of is in a reality a blessing."

Zhtutin, scowling, looked sharply at Arakal, then frowned, and turned away.

"I am only the plenipotentiary, not the Central Committee."

Arakal nodded.

Zhtutin sat back, frowning. Finally, he shrugged, and looked back at Arakal.

"I can show you something, if you will go where I tell you. Let us go in your spacecraft."

XV. All Secrets Revealed

The ground dropped away, and Zhtutin bent over the plate where the image of the landscape below unrolled. He spoke quietly, and the interpreter translated.

"Follow this river," said the interpreter. "Now go east."

Time passed as, on the plate, the ground flowed back.

Slagiron spoke to Arakal in a low voice. "What if we suddenly come in range of some Russ anti-rocket station left over from before the—ah—'accident'."

"If it doesn't bother our guest to be blown up," said Arakal, "Why should it bother us?"

Slagiron grinned, and at that moment Zhtutin spoke excitedly.

The translator bent by the pilot, and they veered sharply toward the north.

A few moments later, Zhtutin spoke again.

"Stop," said the translator.

They hovered, and Arakal and Slagiron stepped over to the plate—then they both jerked back.

On the plate, superimposed on the image of the flat snow-covered plain, was a stylized skull.

Arakal looked out the curving window beyond

the control panel, to see nothing but blowing snow.

The translator listened to the plenipotentiary, then said, "We must go down to see anything, but be careful. There were tall buildings here once."

The pilot looked again at the symbol on the plate, and turned in his seat.

Colputt was frowning. "Go down, but go slow. I think that is just for what this place used to be."

The pilot turned back to his controls.

Colputt tapped a switch on the control panel, and abruptly the opaque wall was transparent. They moved slowly through blowing snow, and, off to their right, there appeared a vague arch of white.

Zhtutin, frowning, stared at it, then nodded.

"That way. But carefully."

The arch of white slowly resolved into a huge, bent, snow-covered metal frame, supporting what appeared to be a number of gigantic slanting snow-heaped slats.

Zhtutin murmured, and the translator bent close.

"I had no idea the heat could have been that intense . . . Yes, but there it is. That is where the error began—that frame . . . It held up those panels, which were flat. The panels—No, that can come later. Now, you have seen it. We must go elsewhere. First, we must go higher. But carefully. If there is another of those frames, bent less completely—good."

As Zhtutin gave directions, Slagiron glanced at Colputt, then at Arakal. Arakal kept his mouth shut. Colputt's look of intense thought was, all by itself, an invitation to say nothing.

Zhtutin bent intently over the plate.

"We must be near . . . Slow, slow— There, the light!"

Outside, the dimness became a white glow, and then a glare.

Colputt tapped the control. The hull, save for the wide-curving window in front, was again opaque.

Zhtutin straightened.

"Go through once, quickly. I think the light is most intense near the edges."

Outside, the glowing snowflakes gave way to a drizzle that coalesced into drops on the curving window, to run back in glittering streams, and then the mist became a shining fog that suddenly vanished as they emerged into a dazzling brilliance that slitted their eyes even as the glass of the window darkened.

Below them, stretching out into the distance, was a bright green field of tall grass moving in long ripples toward the center, while at the edge it quivered and trembled in the focus of a light that seemed to brighten and darken, to strengthen, to fold on itself, as first one then another part of the field felt the compounded blaze hammering down from the sky.

Along the edge, there loomed through the smoke and mist heavy snowbanks that sent sudden sheets and streams of water draining down, trailing clouds of vapor that vanished in the blaze of light.

As the window darkened further, they could see the flames that ran along the stalks, as the focused brilliance of the shafts of light ate their way forward from the far edge of the field.

Colputt spoke sharply to the pilot, and suddenly the drizzle was running again along the curving window, and they were out of the glare.

Zhtutin spoke heavily.

"There is the curse."

Arakal didn't speak.

Colputt said carefully, "The light?"

"The *weed*."

Colputt frowned, but said nothing.

Zhtutin waited a moment. When he spoke, his voice was controlled and quiet. He spoke briefly, waiting while the interpreter translated one sentence after another.

"The first place we saw, just now, was the Experimental Station. If the fool who ran it had possessed a sense of duty, we would not now be in this situation. I have the story direct from the original records. At that Station, an attempt was being made to develop hardier types of hay and feed grains, for use where the summers are short. Nothing could have been more harmless! But the donkey who ran this station did not notify his superiors when one of the many varieties of hay being tested, for some reason not known, fell or was removed from its covered tray, and took root in a field nearby. As it soon proved difficult to control, recourse was had to machines which were being developed here, to cultivate the field. These machines were of an experimental type, large and powerful, which ground the dirt finely. They were used to grind up the experimental plant, in order to kill it."

Arakal, frowning, glanced at Colputt, who said, "And then—?"

Zhtutin made a weary gesture of the hand.

"The machines used to cultivate the field were almost ready for their first trials. These machines were experimented with in different types of soil all over the country. What none of the agricultural scientists realized was that during the trials, fine bits of this plant, stuck here and there in the insides of the machines, were sown in a great many different places."

Colputt put his hand to his chin.

Zhtutin went on. "And it took root. No one in the other districts recognized at first that this plant was new. Since no word of the accident had been given, there was no warning."

Outside, as the pilot turned, glowing mist blew back across the curving window.

"It was," Zhtutin went on, "merely a grass. There seemed to be no cause for alarm."

Colputt, frowning, said, "And when it went to seed—"

"It has no seeds. It forms a husk, and within the husk there is nothing. But it is extremely hardy, and vigorous. In each field where it was found, naturally the attempt was made to control it. In some cases, it was chopped up, in the attempt to kill it. Ordinary grass is hard to destroy, but, if you pull it up, and chop it up, most of it, at least, dies. Any bit of this weed, in contact with the soil, is capable of forming a root, and starting a new plant. In the places where it was let grown, it gave a wonderful yield—of hay."

Colputt looked sober. "It crowded out the other plants?"

"Nothing could compete with it. Wheat, rye, oats, corn, barley—anything was strangled by it. And it grew fast."

"How long before anyone realized—"

Zhtutin shook his head.

"It was a query from the Americans, studying their satellite pictures, that finally made it known. The Americans noticed places where the vegetation seemed to absorb light more fully than the plants they knew of. As it evidently was being very widely planted, they assumed it was a new food plant, and asked for information. But it was the opposite of a food plant. It yielded no grain, and destroyed the plants that did. We could use it to feed animals—that was all. Unless it could be killed, we could never make up for the grain that would be lost."

"It absorbed light more fully?"

"It utilized light more fully. It grew faster. It was said later that it utilized water and carbon dioxide better. It was a very efficient plant. It began to grow as soon as the snow cover melted enough to give it light, and it did not stop till it was covered again the next winter. And then something else was discovered."

Colputt looked uneasily out the window toward the glow.

The translator leaned forward as the plenipotentiary spoke in a lower voice.

"The fields cleared the previous year, at great pains, the following spring grew up in clumps of this plant. For reasons that were never found, because there was not time, parts of the root break off in the soil and become dormant. They can live over until another year. Only when the soil had been sifted, or the root cooked by intense heat, could the soil be trusted."

Colputt's eyes widened. He glanced at Arakal.

Arakal said, "This change of weather is to *fence off and destroy the weed*?"

Zhtutin nodded. "But this was not the only trouble. As our side contended with this, and was being kicked to pieces by it, the Americans had their own accident. And no one knows how *that* happened." He glanced intently at Colputt. "Unless, perhaps, you have found the records?"

Colputt shook his head.

Zhtutin said, "At that time, experiments were being carried out that I personally do not understand. It seems that substances are released naturally in the human body, and that by manipulations involving the structures which control heredity in microorganisms, a microorganism can be so made over that it produces the natural human substance. Further, and more surprising, it may be possible to induce the microorganism to release the substance in response to other substances present in the human system, in varying amounts in health or illness. If, then, this microorganism is used to infect a human being, symptoms may be relieved—or a cure may follow—caused by the substance released by the microorganism. Of course, this work required great skill, special apparatus, and *caution*."

Zhtutin glanced at Colputt, who nodded, his expression grave, and Zhtutin sighed and gestured wearily with his hand. "Many were working on such things; they had, as I understand it, great theoretical as well as practical significance. The accident could have happened anywhere. As it was, it happened in an American laboratory, and the result was the release of a quantity of specially altered microorganisms. I assume most died at once. It would seem that they would be ill adapted to act as germ organisms, because of the changes in their structure; but it may be that the scientists had found a way to avoid this, while trying to adapt the organisms for medical use. In any case, America soon had a wave of what was called 'Killer Flu'. Our information is that it was not actually a form of influenza at all. What appears to have been done was to create a form of microorganism capable of excreting—''

The interpreter paused, and after several puzzled exchanges with Zhtutin, the interpreter turned to Colputt.

"I'm not certain how to translate these words, sir. It seems that the body has something in it like sugar, and another substance that makes it possible to get more use out of this substance that is like sugar.''

Colputt nodded. "Just call what is like sugar 'glucose', and what makes it easier to use the glucose, 'insulin'.''

The translator nodded, and Zhtutin, looking relieved, went on. Arakal, trying to piece together the sense of what was said, found the discussion as confusing as a foreign language.

"Then," said Colputt finally, "the insulin was somehow synthesized by the microorganisms, and released in the body? And the idea was to have a trouble-free source of insulin for diabetics? But what was the insulin formed from?"

Zhtutin shrugged. "Who could say, now? In any case, the work was not finished. The organisms were released prematurely. The control of their responses was incomplete. They invaded non-diabetic individuals. The results were severe."

Colputt stared. *"Insulin shock?"*

"Yes. Which damaged the central nervous systems of the persons infected."

"When did this happen?"

"When our troubles with the strangleweed were well developed, and it had become a question whether we could limit its spread."

Colputt looked out the window. He glanced at Arakal, then at Slagiron. Then he looked back at Zhtutin.

"What then?"

Zhtutin turned to Arakal.

"You see the situation?"

"I see it."

"The weed was kicking our ribs in. If it spread beyond our borders, it might never be stopped. The trained germs were slaughtering the Americans. At any moment, these germs, which despite a ban on travel were spreading erratically and unpredictably, might be carried across the oceans to exterminate the rest of the human race. *What could we do?"*

Colputt nodded slowly.

Arakal said, "What happened?"

Zhtutin looked out the window toward the glow, brightening as the pilot swung closer.

"We," said Zhtutin, "took care of the germs for the Americans. They, in turn, took care of the strangleweed for us."

As the luminous drops blew back along the curved window, there was a silence.

The silence stretched out.

At last, Zhtutin turned as if to speak, but changed his mind.

Arakal felt the urge to say something, but forced himself to wait.

Zhtutin finally shrugged, and looked at Arakal.

"You said perhaps there was no war. In such a situation as that, who is to say?"

Arakal nodded. "But the grass back there is strangleweed?"

"Yes. It is the largest remaining patch of strangleweed that we know of."

"Are any of the germs left?"

"To our knowledge, no."

Colputt suddenly looked alert. "What is the incubation period?"

Zhtutin smiled faintly, and shook his head.

"If you are thinking you might have caught it when you discovered this vehicle, ease your mind. The time since then has been too great. It acts rapidly."

Arakal glanced at Zhtutin, thought a moment, noted Colputt's look of relief, and turned back to Zhtutin. "The idea is to freeze what weed isn't being burned?"

"Yes. And it is a very complex problem. The weed recurs, world climatic change must if possible be limited, and there is danger if the weed should be spread by minute pieces carried in runoff water. The problem involves complications I do not understand well enough to mention. But, even today, the planet is ringed by satellites, and if, anywhere, a particular characteristic absorption of light should be detected, an intolerable rise in temperature will follow very quickly at that location."

"And this mechanism *runs itself*?"

"There is the difficulty we hope you will take an interest in. We do not know if the array of mechanisms which is fighting the weed is programmed to stop when the weed is destroyed. We assume that the technicians died on returning to Earth—because of the germs. The mechanisms have shown great delicacy of control, and apparently little wear or deterioration. But if you will imagine that you were in our situation, you will understand our viewpoint. This matter is of interest to us."

Arakal said, "What is of interest to us—what we are here to do—is to free Old Brunswick, Old Kebeck, and those other parts of Europe that were part of the land of the O'Cracys. If we can do that, our minds and strength will not be concentrated on fighting to free them. We would then have more time to think of other interests."

"That is understood." Zhtutin looked at him curiously. "Yet you asked for the agent lists only for France and the United Kingdom."

"Too little food and drink," said Arakal drily, "causes hunger and thirst. Too much at once creates other complaints."

Zhtutin looked at him, and a brief grin crossed his face. He nodded toward the glare outside. "And that?"

"We will do all we can, when we understand the mechanism—and we will do it with great care. But it may be that all that has already been allowed for." Arakal hesitated, feeling the impulse to say more. The thought passed through his mind that if what Zhtutin had said was what had happened, most of the bad feeling between the Russ and the O'Cracys might disappear. But then Arakal considered S, and said nothing.

Zhtutin glanced at Arakal, began to speak, and cleared his throat instead.

Arakal, glancing at Zhtutin's face, seemed to see mirrored there his own thought of a moment before. Involuntarily, he smiled.

Zhtutin made an apologetic gesture, and spoke briefly.

The interpreter looked puzzled, but translated dutifully:

"It goes on."

Arakal nodded.

Outside, the glare faded away as they headed back.

XVI. S vs. Space

1.

S-One came to his feet as the Head of Government entered the room. They stood still, looking at each other, unsmiling and tired. Then both sighed, and, as if unaware of the pause, greeted each other, and took their seats. Each glanced slightly around, as if to check that there was no one else in the room—at least, no one else physically present in the room.

S-One said, "A rough trip?"

The Head of Government shrugged. "That is temporary. What I cannot say is whether it will be worth it in the long run."

"We have, at least, exposed every doubtful, reluctant, or questionable member of the organization, in France and the U. K."

"If not, we are truly in trouble."

"Once the local fanatics finish their vengeance on these waverers, the rest will be more reliable. What is your impression of Arakal?"

G-One frowned. "He seems trustworthy. But I think Brusilov is right about him."

"In what way?"

"He is, I think, a master of conflict. Though he

does not seem to mean us ill, I think we can expect—surprises.''

S-One looked thoughtful. "It may well be. Yet he will have great trouble to win against us, in the long run. And, in fact, from what Brusilov says, he does not wish to beat us. There is a serious flaw. How can he win if he does not wish to beat us? Because, assuredly, we intend to overcome him. In one way or another.''

G-One shivered slightly, and rubbed his hands as if they were cold. "Not once was he discourteous. There was good will evident both on his part and on the part of his men. Yet he did not give way. And he did not ask too much because of their new technological advantage.''

"We have, in effect, ceded military control of Western Europe.''

"He is well aware we retain indirect control of very large regions, through S. I don't know—'' G-One paused, frowning.

S-One leaned forward, and spoke sympathetically. "Something troubles you?''

G-One looked blankly across the room, stared at the Head of Security for a moment as if he were a stranger. "I don't know. If we win— Are we certain—?'' Again he paused, frowning. "There was a difference in talking there and in talking here.''

"Some of what was said there,'' said S-One, watching the Head of Government's face with all his attention, "was overheard.''

"No doubt.''

"With further development, in time, it will be as it is here. And all will be overheard.''

G-One's face showed merely a faint expression of annoyance, such as appears on the face of a person who momentarily cannot remember a familiar name. S-One frowned.

The Head of Government suddenly leaned forward, "Listen, I understand the point you explained to me about the S organization. It is logical. But there is a danger."

"There would be a danger if we should fail."

"There is, at least theoretically, a danger if you succeed."

"Ah?" said the Head of Security, his tone silky.

G-One looked at him with eyes that came suddenly to a hard bright focus. "Spare me that tone. And give me the benefit of your thought. You can think, can you not? Not all your thoughts are supplied by the local commissary of thoughts? Why do you think that you personally are still in charge of the S organization?"

"I was selected," said S-One seriously. "And you have chosen not to disapprove of the selection." He said, somewhat sadly, "No, not all my thoughts come, at the special low price, from the nearest special commissary. But for the subject you wish to discuss, I can make no promises. I will do my best, but who knows?"

G-One smiled; for the first time a natural expression appeared to replace the look of strain. "Good. I will tell you one reason why you are still here: I could talk to you; there was a meeting of the minds. Now, I want your opinion on this."

S-One settled back slowly, as if bracing himself. "Proceed. But remember," he added drily, "it will be recorded."

"Good. Now, stand back from all this at a distance, in your mind. Grant that what we believe on certain subjects is a great advance over what went before. Give full credit to our doctrines and beliefs. And our methods."

S-One said, smiling, "I do that readily. I am with you so far. Continue."

"Very well. Now, cast your mental gaze back over all history. All the long life of humankind. There have been many beliefs. Many doctrines. Many methods."

"I am still with you."

"Most of which have been superseded."

"Ah."

"Some of which have been wrong beliefs, doctrines, and methods."

"No doubt."

"Some, though true, could be improved."

"Yes."

"Can we be certain that ours, though a great advance over what preceded them, are the final development in beliefs, doctrines, and methods?"

"They will be," said S-One very seriously, "if we succeed."

"Bear in mind that this is a theoretical discussion."

S-One smiled. "I have not yet accused you of doctrinal deviations."

G-One nodded, his expression remote. "Not yet. But stay with me. If we succeed in gaining control, yes, we can succeed in making our beliefs, doctrines, and methods the last ones in the series to emerge or develop. That is clear."

"Then they are the ultimate development."

"But does that follow because they are necessarily superior, or does it follow because we have arrested the process at that point?"

"Does it matter?"

"Theoretically?"

"That is the wrong expression. You mean, 'hypothetically'."

"Whichever you prefer."

S-One shook his head. "I cannot see beyond the point at which I stop reasoning on the question. There is a barred gate in my mental processes. On the gate there is a sign. It says, 'Danger. Keep Out. To Enter is Strictly Forbidden.'"

"That is why this discussion is only hypothetical."

"Dangerous animals in the realm of thought roam beyond that gate." S-One frowned. "Surely you did not discuss—with Arakal, for instance—"

G-One made a gesture of irritation. "What would the answer mean, if I discussed it with him? He is completely outside of this frame of reference."

"I am constrained to stop thinking, and to say that our methods and ways of approach are the best. And if not—" S-One held up his hand as if he foresaw an interruption "—if not, still, for the reason I described to you, we *must* win, and impose an end to the process of competing technological advances. It can go only so far. No further. And we must finally control it."

"In which case, if we *are* wrong—that is, if we hypothetically *were* wrong—we would freeze humankind at a level of technological development below its ultimate potentialities."

"Ah, but we foresee a further process of development, according to our own doctrine."

"Yet, if for the purposes of argument we assume that that doctrine might be improved by the slightest amount—"

"I am up against the gate."

"—then it follows that we are blocking a progress that might continue further."

"To possibly end mankind itself, by technological disaster. We have already had one sample of it. That came close enough to show what can happen."

"There is that. But suppose there is a way to resolve that problem? *Arakal may find it.*"

S-One sat bolt upright. "This is why we must penetrate and control his organization!"

"Wait a minute, my friend. If we control his organization, what chance is there then that he will find it?"

"You do not, of course, mean Arakal personally?"

"How should I know? The point is that our reasoning is valid, so long as we accept certain lines of argument. Grant those lines of argument, and all else follows strictly. But if, hypothetically, those lines of argument should be mistaken— Why, then our whole structure of argument becomes an obstruction of progress. And if that were so, there would exist a very serious danger, aside from rivalry with any other system of beliefs and doctrines."

"You have gotten ahead of me. It seems to me that your thought has branched, and that you are making two points at once."

"You see the first, but you do not see the second?"

"There is danger in this."

"That is certainly true. First, if Arakal finds a successful resolution to the underlying problem which is a justification for the present development of S, he will proceed, while we are left in the dust, frozen in a method which, while superior to what went before, still is capable of improvement, and perhaps much improvement. That is a serious and unhappy possibility, but there is a worse one."

S-One frowned, then shrugged. "Go ahead."

"Looking out of that spaceship at the tremendous technological effects—"

"Which nearly ended the human race."

"Yes. A catastrophe. Which reminded me of other, but *natural* catastrophes. If for the sake of safety we stop the progression of technological methods, and freeze it in the present state, what do we do if there should be a need, brought on not by human actions but by nature, for the very strengths whose development we are blocking?"

S-One looked at him bleakly. "If, say, the radiation of the sun should change in intensity?"

"Yes. Exactly."

S-One shook his head. "How do I answer that? Life presents these alternatives. A wooden house is warm, but it may catch fire. A stone house is fireproof, but it is cold. Yes, I see at least the second risk you speak of. But I will still proceed as rapidly as possible to penetrate Arakal's organization and bring it under control."

"Working from France, England, and our former colonies?"

"Yes. We have a broad foundation. He has escaped us here, but his very victory will be turned against him."

"Let us hope we do not destroy something we may someday need."

S-One looked at the Head of Government and said sympathetically, "You are tired."

"There is no doubt of that."

"Come and take a look at the flowers. They are refreshing."

"What, flowers, still, in this season?"

"One can have flowers in all seasons. You just have to pick the right kinds, and protect them. The colors, the contrast, and the individuality rest the mind, and delight the senses. They are something to take care of, that reciprocates with beauty, that never makes harsh demands."

The Head of Government looked at him quizzically, and then smiled, very briefly. "Did you know that Arakal has a torturer?"

"He has several. There is only one he really trusts. I can give you the reports on that. They are very carefully watched, and used only with great restraint. There is no weakness there."

"Such contrasts amaze me."

S-One looked surprised. "Contrast? Where is the contrast? Any sensible ruler has torturers. Now, let us take a look at the flowers."

2.

Arakal, headed home through rough seas on board Admiral Bullinger's flagship, was listening to Buffon question one of his numerous prisoners:

"You say you joined S because your daughter was sick, and needed money for treatment. S helped, and you were grateful; but you later came to think that S was responsible for the trouble in the first place. What did you mean by that?"

"If every day is gray," said the prisoner, "how long will it be before people become dispirited? And if people are kept dispirited, how long before they become impoverished. The presence of S had the effect of unending bad weather."

Arakal thought back over the prisoner's explanation of how he had joined S in despair, of his relief at having money from S to care for his family, of his resulting loyalty, his rise in the S organization, his gradual disillusionment, and his eventual conviction that S was the cause of the troubles that drove people to despair.

Arakal stayed to hear the prisoner add, "But it isn't the *people* in S who cause most of this trouble. It's S itself—the organization—that does the damage. In S, people are like cells in the body of a snake. They may not be evil themselves, but they have become part of an evil thing."

Arakal slipped out of the room, and made his way slowly and carefully along the corridor toward the cabin where Slagiron and Colputt were studying records and photographs of conditions in Europe.

As the weather was growing progressively more foul, it took nearly five minutes before Arakal swung open the door of the cabin, to see Slagiron and Colputt at a table heavily loaded with papers.

Slagiron glanced around.

"Getting worse out there, isn't it?"

Arakal got the door shut.

"Coming up that ladder, it seemed like it." He glanced at the papers on the table, kept from sliding off by sections of a kind of low fence snapped up into position around the edge of the table. "What have you found out?"

Colputt said, "It's almost unbelievable, but the photos and descriptions from before the war show that the physical arrangements then match the arrangements now almost exactly. In every way we can check, Europe has stood still.

Arakal said, "Since S took over."

Slagiron nodded. "It's as if Europe has been pickled in brine."

Arakal slid into a chair bolted in place before the table. "You remember Burke-Johnson saying that not much damage had been done in Western Europe during the war; that S had already taken over?"

"Yes. He didn't seem to think anything of their standing still all this time."

"The Russ must have set S up deliberately to stop progress."

"But why?"

There was a silence, and then Arakal, frowning, said, "What did progress do to them the *last* time?"

Slagiron nodded slowly.

Colputt said, "Yes. Strangleweed and trained germs."

They glanced at each other.

From outside came the howl of the wind, and the crash of water against the ship.

"They must," said Colputt, "have decided to freeze technology where it was. In S, they have an organization first to spy, next to penetrate, then to take control, and finally to smother progress entirely."

Slagiron gripped the table as the ship heeled.

"But it won't work if they just stop progress in

their own territory. They have to stop it *everywhere*."

Arakal nodded. "They have to control us, sooner or later."

"Sooner," said Slagiron. "And how do we keep them out? They build their listening devices in when they build a ship, and they plant the things all over. Our troops have found scores of them in Normandy. They slipped that nurse in on us on practically no notice. And the so-called partisans were a collection of fake outfits from the beginning. Just think of the time, men, money, and resources they must tie up in S. And, where we're concerned, they're only getting started. Once they get going, they can pour their spies and agents at us through Old Kebeck and Old Brunswick."

"Hopefully," said Arakal, "we'll have the means to detect that. We have a good number of former agents who don't like the idea that S turned them over to us."

"Some of those will serve both sides."

"Some. Not all. We may learn more about S than S expects."

Slagiron nodded.

"But now that we see how they work, how likely is it that their colonies, when we captured them, weren't already riddled? We're wide open to them."

"What we need," said Arakal, "is some narrow place where they can only come through a few at a time. We could watch *that*. Also, we need some way to cut the ground out from under S itself."

"How do we get at S? We may bring some of its men around to our viewpoint. We may manage to cut off a part of it. But the main organization is out of our reach."

Arakal said drily, "The answer isn't exactly obvious." Then he added stubbornly, "But it should be there somewhere."

"As for a narrow place," said Slagiron, "is there any place on Earth that fits that description?"

Colputt said, "We'd better find an answer now, if there is one. Because the problem will just get worse. If S is meant to stop progress, then S has to either destroy us or control us."

Arakal was frowning. "S is meant to stop progress. Why?"

Slagiron shrugged. "We've just answered that. Progress is dangerous. Look at what happened." He paused. "That is, what we think happened. I'm assuming we've been told the truth."

Colputt said, "It sounded true to me. Anyway, the point is true. Progress is dangerous. Progress is bound to be dangerous. And the further we progress, the more dangerous it is likely to be."

"Nevertheless," said Arakal, "to the degree that we can eliminate the danger, we destroy the justification for S to exist."

Colputt shook his head.

"Progress is dangerous. Inevitably, if we progress, we will again reach the point where we can create—among other things—strangleweed and trained germs."

"Let's just suppose," said Arakal, his expression remote, "that there is some way to protect the world from the errors of progress. Look at the resources S uses up. How will it justify the expense if the danger isn't there?"

Slagiron began to speak, but, seeing Arakal's

expression, hesitated. He glanced across the table to see that Colputt was also looking into the remote distance.

"But," said Arakal, "is that enough? Like a habit, S might continue, just because they are used to doing things that way. And it will still be useful to them as a spy organization. We need to lead them to create an organization that will compete with S by drawing on the same resources S uses."

Slagiron shook his head, but said nothing, and waited.

Arakal's gaze focused, and his expression seemed to show a momentary surprise, as if he hadn't expected to find himself here. He glanced at Colputt, who said, "I see the *idea*. But there are contradictions. To begin with, we need to have progress, without danger. But the two go hand-in-hand."

Arakal said, "We need to have progress—without danger *to Earth*."

"True," said Colputt. Then his eyes widened. "I see. There *is* a distinction there."

Slagiron frowned. "Without danger to Earth. How?"

Arakal said, "A powerhouse is useful, and dangerous, so we are careful where we put it. We can't get rid of the danger itself. But we can keep the consequences of the danger from being so dangerous."

"Yes," said Colputt. "It would be hard, expensive, and inconvenient. But possibly it could be done, at that."

Slagiron glanced at Colputt. "What do you have in mind?"

"The Old O'Cracys' atomic reactor," said Colputt, "had to be a certain size, in order to work. If its fuel were put in too concentrated, and in too small a space, it would not be a reactor, but a bomb. There had to be room for internal shields, or moderators. Just possibly, a technology, too, has to have a certain size, or it will also be a bomb and not a reactor. There has to be space for internal shielding to moderate certain effects—to slow them down and prevent them from penetrating the whole mass as soon as they are created."

Slagiron frowned. "Where do we get this space?"

Before Colputt could answer, the ship and the sea together created a roll and lunge that stopped the conversation. Then Colputt said, "We can look on Earth as 'the world', or we can look on it as the nursery of the human race, with the real world out beyond it. There are satellites, and other planets, and resources in space, and, with the platforms, we have what seems to be a practical means to travel in space. If we can rebuild the technology, by combining what we have ourselves with the frozen skills of the Old Kebeckers and Old Brunswickers, why can't we use space to protect Earth? Why couldn't foreseeably dangerous experiments be carried out far from Earth?"

Arakal nodded.

"It would be difficult," said Colputt. "But, having seen the alternatives, I think we have to try it."

Arakal said, "If we can eliminate the danger to Earth, while maintaining progress, S as it is now becomes a plain waste of resources. Could it survive that?"

"Better yet," said Slagiron suddenly, "if we

move out into space, just how well situated is S—which rejects progress—to follow? There's your narrow place! And to try to overcome that handicap, the Russ will have to use men and resources that would otherwise go to S!"

Colputt said, suddenly cautious, "Of course, this is just an idea. The one thing we can be reasonably sure of is that space will be a very—" He groped for words "—A very unwelcoming environment."

Arakal and Slagiron, both gripping the table as the storm shook the ship, glanced around.

Outside the thin walls, they could hear the wind howl, and the sea smash across the tilted deck. Through Arakal's mind passed a brief vision of humanity's experiences on a planet whose environment was enlivened by such things as volcanoes, earthquakes, sharks, viruses, snakes, and hurricanes.

Despite the queasiness caused by the motions of the ship, he suddenly laughed and turned to Colputt.

"Let's not underestimate our nursery. If space isn't very welcoming, should that scare us away? How have we been raised?"

Colputt glanced around as the ship rolled far over, then he managed a faint smile.

"We have had the problem before, haven't we?"

Inside, as the storm beat on the ship, they thought over the frail, insubstantial idea that had come to them, like a ray of light through dense clouds.

Outside, the storm raged, its freezing wind and drowning depths held away by the ship, each and every part of which had begun as a frail, insubstantial idea.

Severely tried, but still on course, the fleet made its way through the storm toward home.

BEST-SELLING
Science Fiction
and
Fantasy

- ☐ 47809-3   **THE LEFT HAND OF DARKNESS**, Ursula K. LeGuin $2.95
- ☐ 16012-3   **DORSAI!**, Gordon R. Dickson $2.75
- ☐ 80581-7   **THIEVES' WORLD**, Robert Lynn Asprin, editor $2.95
- ☐ 11577-2   **CONAN #1**, Robert E. Howard, L. Sprague de Camp, Lin Carter $2.50
- ☐ 49142-1   **LORD DARCY INVESTIGATES**, Randall Garrett $2.75
- ☐ 21889-X   **EXPANDED UNIVERSE**, Robert A. Heinlein $3.95
- ☐ 87328-6   **THE WARLOCK UNLOCKED**, Christopher Stasheff $2.95
- ☐ 10253-0   **CHANGELING**, Roger Zelazny $2.95
- ☐ 05469-2   **BERSERKER**, Fred Saberhagen $2.75
- ☐ 51552-5   **THE MAGIC GOES AWAY**, Larry Niven $2.75

MORE SCIENCE FICTION!

ADVENTURE

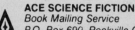